THE STORY OF ESTHER COSTELLO

By the same author

This is the Schoolroom

Three Corvettes

Depends What You Mean by Love

My Brother Denys

The Cruel Sea

'H.M.S. Marlborough Will Enter Harbour'

NICHOLAS MONSARRAT

THE STORY
of
ESTHER
COSTELLO

THE BOOK CLUB
121, CHARING CROSS ROAD
LONDON, W.C.2.

MADE AND PRINTED IN GREAT BRITAIN BY
CHARLES BIRCHALL AND SONS, LTD.,
LIVERPOOL AND LONDON

AUTHOR'S NOTE

The Story of Esther Costello is the story of a monstrous fraud in philanthropy. It is wholly fictional, and its characters portray no 'real life' persons, either alive or dead. In particular, it does not reflect in the slightest upon those many exemplary individuals and organizations rendering aid to the handicapped. If the book has any moral for the charitable, that moral is: "Give to those you know."

CONTENTS

PROLOGUE

In the late spring of 1916, after the bloody and abortive Easter Rising in Dublin, four men on the run from the police and the military reached the outskirts of a small village called Cloncraig, in the county of Wexford in southern Ireland. One of the men was an undoubted murderer; for the rest, that distinction was still to come. They were all members of Sinn Fein: they had had a fearful time getting out of Dublin after the fighting, with the police on their heels and few friends to trust: they all carried arms, and four hand-grenades apiece, and (between them) two hundred pounds of gunpowder stolen from a fireworks firm near Kingstown.

They had clung possessively to the explosive throughout a fortnight's hue-and-cry which had chased them farther and farther south; it was the tool of their trade, their cherished treasure, as a full wallet is to another man, or her fresh beauty to a young girl. It was never to be surrendered. But the weight of it was heavy and had hampered and nearly ruined them many times; now, after fourteen days' close pursuit, their weariness was desperate, and their pace a deadly mockery of their hopes.

Presently, as they stumbled down the road in the dusk, a figure rose beside them, melting out of the shadows like a ghost. The party of four stopped dead, their hands clutching their guns.

The stranger called softly: "Is it you?"

"Is it who?" said the leader, who was the murderer.

"Sinn Fein," said the stranger, as a man gives a password.

"Sinn Fein for ever."

"Up the rebels," said the stranger, and then: "You can't stop, boys. There's police all around."

"God damn them all!" said one of the party. "English hirelings, every one."

"You can't stop," repeated the stranger. "You'll have to break for the coast—and fast, too."

"We need rest," said the leader. In the darkness, he bent his aching legs to ease them. "We've been on the move for a fortnight."

"How was it in Dublin, then?"

"We killed four hundred of them—the murdering bastards. But they got James Connally. They've hung him already, for all I know."

"God bless Ireland," said the stranger.

"Where can we sleep?" asked one of the party.

"You can't stop," said the stranger again. "It's the coast for you."

"We'll sleep here tonight," said the leader, suddenly hard. "Where's the house?"

The stranger jerked his head. "Nearby," he said, unwillingly. "But it's likely to be watched."

"We've got guns," said the leader. "It'd better not be watched too close. We can use them again, if need be."

They set off up a side track, moving slowly with dragging feet: the heavy weight on the back of each man bore him down nearly to the ground. "Can you not go faster?" asked the stranger presently. "You'll have to move like hares tomorrow. . . . What's in the packs?"

"Something for you to take care of," said the leader.

"What's that?" asked one of his party, sharply.

"We'll be leaving it behind for a bit," said the leader. "It's making us too slow altogether."

"How do you mean, 'leave it behind'?" said another, a rebellious voice.

"Bury it, maybe." He turned to the figure at his side. "Have you got a cellar?"

"I have that. But——"

"We'll be leaving something with you," said the leader. "Something to take care of. We'll come back for it. Maybe not for a long time. But we'll come back." There was extraordinary menace in his voice. "Remember that."

"We've carried it a long way," said another of the party, whining against the decision. "It's cost a few lives by now. How do we know we can trust him?"

"*I* trust him," said the leader. He turned again. "Don't I?"

"I'll hold it safe for you. . . . What is it, then?"

"Something to take care of. Something to be kept dry. *Something that's never to be looked at*—not by you, not by your wife, not by the kids. It's to stay there till we come for it. And we'll come, too."

"Be easy," said the stranger. "It'll lie hid till doomsday —and beyond, if you like."

PART ONE

CHAPTER ONE

THE four children played in the ruined cottage just outside the village of Cloncraig—the cottage, long deserted, where the man and his wife and the children had all been killed, away back during the troubles. Its door hung askew, its windows gaped: grass grew between the turf walls and sprouted from the floor-boards. The Black-and-Tan place, their parents called it, and cursed the memory when the children were not by; but for the children—Esther Costello and her brother, Michael Fairlie with the limp, and young Denis Finane—for them it was just a fine place to play, and safely out of call of the grown-ups. Perhaps the cottage was haunted, perhaps the queer stains on the old walls were really blood; but it was full of good corners, and hiding-places, and secrets—a fine place to play indeed, and none better in Cloncraig.

It had become more exciting still since Esther discovered the cellar.

Esther Costello was ten, and the eldest of the four; the others followed her, though she was only a girl, because she knew the best games, and was daring always, and strong enough to punch their heads if need be. There was also (though they did not know this, and would have spat derisively if they had been told) an element of great beauty in her small, lively face. But to look at them otherwise, there was nothing much to choose between the four children: they were all ragged, barefoot, ill-nourished: the outdoor air had put a deceptive brown upon their faces, not really hiding the pallid skins below.

Their hair, which r▓▓▓▓▓
end to another, hung matt▓▓
and feet alike were filthy. The b▓▓▓▓▓▓▓▓▓▓
shorts, Esther a faded skirt and a ravelled woollen jers▓▓
The quartet, in fact, looked what they were—the products
of a poor Irish village, and of feckless parents who, lacking
the resources or the patience to train their families, thankfully
let them run wild.

The children were thus, as free young animals, singularly
happy for most of the time, and especially so on this May
morning, when Esther—newly-elected Captain of the Cellar
—was allowing them for the first time to see what she had
found below the flagged-stone floor.

The cellar itself was wonderful enough: a single dark space,
hollowed out beneath the living-room, and unsuspected by
the two generations of children who had always used the
deserted cottage as a playground. Its entrance was by a
trap-door beside the fireplace, masked by a stack of crumbling
peats and discovered by Esther when she was scavenging
for kindling. A ladder led down to it, and there, by candle-
light, she had come upon an empty room, stone-flagged,
swept clean, which must have lain hidden in musty darkness
for at least twenty years.

The cellar had become their headquarters for the most
secret meetings of all. But a few weeks later they had found
something else, something better still. Hidden treasure, no
less—or so it seemed likely to turn out.

It was, once more and inevitably, Esther who had chanced
to stamp on a hollow flagstone, and become curious, and, when
her brother and the others were gone, prised it up and discovered the strange hoard below. Four boxes they were,
wrapped tight in old newspapers, and round them all a big,
rotted mackintosh sheet.

And in the boxes?

"I'm not saying," said Esther, when she first reported the find to an awed audience.

"You've never looked," said Michael Fairlie.

That was not quite true. Esther had looked at one box, and been puzzled by what she saw, and put back the top staves again, without exploring farther.

"I've looked all right. Never you fear."

"Is it treasure?" asked Denis Finane, a small wizened caricature of a child who looked almost a decade older than his nine years. "Is it gold, then?"

"It's not gold," said Esther, tantalizing.

"Tell us, Esther," said her brother, Johnny Costello. "What's in the boxes?"

Michael Fairlie, limping round on his twisted leg, affected disdain. "There's nothing there," he said scornfully, over his shoulder. "It's empty boxes. Firewood."

"All right," said Esther, feminine and tough at the same time. "It's empty boxes."

"Don't listen to him," said Denis Finane, ready to weep with curiosity. "Tell us what's in them."

"Nothing," said Esther. "You heard him say."

And so her perverse mood had remained, until today, when at last she was going to show them what she had found.

What she had found did not readily identify itself to any of them. They went down the ladder by candle-light, one by one, and under Esther's direction the flagstone was prised up again, and the boxes levered out. Inside each of them was an old canvas pack, such as travelling tinkers carried but so rotten now that it tore when it was touched; and inside the pack two little kegs, like beer barrels, full of black powder—some of it wet, some of it dry still. Alongside each were three or four metal objects, like iron balls, but egg-shaped and fluted. Each had a small metal ring attached, hanging down from its middle.

Michael Fairlie dropped one of these strange things on the floor. It rang on the stone flag, setting up a small tinny echo. It did not bounce, like a ball; it did not break or crack: it did nothing. In the candlelight the children looked at each other, puzzled.

"Well," said Johnny Costello. "What is it, then? Some old game?"

" 'Tis powder," offered Denis Finane excitedly. " 'Tis powder, and these are cannon-balls."

"Balls is right," said Michael Fairlie, sniggering.

"There's a bad word, and well you know it!" said Esther sternly. "Your ma'll soap your mouth out, if I tell her. Behave yourself, then."

Johnny Costello was fiddling with the object which Michael Fairlie had dropped. "The ring's loose," he said presently. "You can pull it out."

He gave a jerk, and the ring came away, and with it a small pin. They waited, none the wiser, for some explanation, but nothing happened.

"Buried treasure!" said Michael disgustedly. " 'Tis nothing but a lot of old kitchen stuff."

Esther opened another of the kegs—the wooden staves were loose and rotted—and dipped her finger in the powder, and tasted it with the tip of her tongue. It looked like black sugar, but it was salty and bitter, different from anything she had ever tasted before. She stood in silence, disappointed that her 'treasure' should have turned out like this—nothing special, just dull and flat, with no sense in it.

Out of the corner of her eyes she saw her brother Johnny pick up another metal 'egg', and jerk out the pin, and then hold it momentarily to his ear, listening. She pushed the keg of powder she had opened back into the box again, and Johnny, following her, tossed the metal object on top of it.

Esther turned away into a corner, to snuff a guttering candle, and to think out what to say to them.

Behind her back there was a flash, and a monstrous explosion which delivered an intolerable blow at the nape of her neck. Above her head the whole cottage floor lifted, and daylight poured in upon them; but for Esther there was suddenly nothing but pain, and stifling darkness, and then oblivion.

CHAPTER TWO

THE grown-ups bore the wreckage home: the small corpses of the dead, and the bodies of the barely living. Young Michael Fairlie had gone limping straight to Heaven, and Johnny Costello with him: little Denis Finane lingered long enough to open surprised eyes to the ceiling before joining them. Only Esther Costello clung to life, and slowly made good her hold on it.

By some freak of the explosion—because she was a few feet farther off, or because her body was turned at some merciful angle—she was apparently unharmed: the pretty, young face was without blemish, the immature body unmarked and untwisted. The blood with which her clothes were drenched was, amazingly, none of hers. But the shock had been tremendous, driving deep into some hard secret core every trace of feeling, every normal faculty. She lay unconscious for many days and nights, while the doctor from nearby Wexford did what he could, which was little enough; she showed no sign of life, nor of death either. Thus she lay, while her small friends were buried, and the inquest was begun and then adjourned; and Cloncraig gossiped or speculated or kept its mouth prudently shut.

Her parents, mourning Johnny the only son, prayed long and fervently that Esther the only daughter might live. But when she did live, it might be that they wished within their hearts that they could recall those long prayers. For Esther Costello, on awakening, could neither see, hear, nor speak.

.   .   .   .

Cloncraig kept its mouth shut by old habit. It was a small village, of fifty thatched houses, two shops, and one 'hotel'—a rough public-house which did indeed boast a couple of rooms to shelter passing travellers. Hardly two hundred souls there were in Cloncraig, and all of them scratching a bare living from tenant-farming (with the landlord away in England), odd-jobbing, horse-dealing, and scrounging from each other. But like any other village of Ireland, north or south, during the present hard century, it had had its fill of 'incidents' and violence. It remembered the 'Trouble' of 1916, when many men on the run from Dublin had passed through, or had gone to earth there; and the worse 'Trouble' of 1921 and 1922, when the Black-and-Tans, of evil memory, had been quartered in Cloncraig for one terrible winter and one yet more terrible spring. Cloncraig, in fact, had had its full share of contemporary Irish politics, which had always consisted, in essence, of ringing the changes on Up-the-rebels and To-hell-with-the-British. Some of its inhabitants had played an active part, others had watched or held aloof; but all *knew* that below the surface of this drab, down-at-heel village, brave men and cowards, traitors and patriots, had moved and lived and written their own page of history.

But they did not want to turn such a page again, nor even to glance at it; and thus, concerning the explosion at the old Sullivan cottage, they kept a guarded, slightly satirical silence. For now, it seemed—even as late as 1943, with some of the lads away to the damned British war in spite of it all—even now, something had blown up again in Cloncraig; and there was danger in this renewal of the past, there were too many dark affinities, too many people involved. Cloncraig wanted no more trouble of any sort, and certainly not the gunpowder sort, the police sort, the eternal questioning and the prying from above.

Thus Authority—never very zealous in any case—met with a blank wall in its investigations: Cloncraig played dumb, and added a little to its public grief in order to shame private inquiry. Certainly there had been a fearful accident —three children killed, and a fourth driven out of her senses; but it was an accident in a vacuum, a terrible happening with no outer connections, and calling for no more investigation than would a typhoon or a cruel drought. It had just happened, that was all; and Cloncraig needed no coroner, asking awkward questions, to intrude either upon its past history or its present sorrow.

So much for the inquest, and for lame Authority, which soon gave up its researches. But in such places as the hotel —the Cloncraig Arms—gossip, looking over its shoulder from time to time, explored the truth about the explosion. There were many known facts to go upon; and nowhere was truth under more accurate appraisal than in one corner of the hotel's private bar, where the three bereaved parents —James Costello, Paddy Finane, and old Neil Fairlie— nightly assuaged their bereavement and were, by agreement, left alone to do so.

The landlord, Joe Lane, kept an eye on their needs, but for the rest he followed public sentiment in letting them be. The only one of the three who might give him cause for worry was James Costello—not because of the double bereavement he had suffered, but because Costello, an intermittent tippler already, might trade on that bereavement beyond what was seemly or tolerable. But there again, who was to judge him? At a time like this, a man needed a drink —many drinks, indeed—and should be reasonably free to take them, and find what comfort he could in the process.

There were many of these long sessions in the Cloncraig Arms, and some of them finished with tears, and some of them came near to ending in blows; for the liquor was never stinted—the three of them found plenty of friends in their sorrow, and many times the price of a drink was pushed across the counter towards Joe Lane, with a covert nod in their direction. It was on one such evening, but early on before they had taken over-much, that the trio reached its conclusions about the accident.

"I see it like this, then," said Neil Fairlie—and the others listened, for he was an older man, and known to have played a stalwart part in all the struggles of other days. "They tell us it was gunpowder that did it—and indeed I've seen some of the stuff that didn't go off, myself, and gunpowder it is. So here's old Sullivan's cottage, full of the stuff, and it's likely been there for twenty years and more, for the place has been empty that long, with no one near it except kids playing."

"And couples courting," put in Paddy Finane, who, though married ten years, was not past the courting urge himself. "Don't forget them."

"It's not gunpowder they'll be using to court with," said Neil Fairlie with a laugh. Then he went on: "It was there for twenty years, and it must have come from outside—Dublin, most like—and been left there for safety. I heard tell"—he looked down his nose—"of some men coming one night, and leaving a load of something for Sean Sullivan to take care of, and slipping off next morning, and never coming back to Cloncraig again."

"They were caught," said Paddy Finane. "God rest them—they've been hung or shot these twenty years. We know that."

"Well, then. . . ." Neil Fairlie blew noisily down his pipe. "The stuff lies there in the cellar: two years, three years, five years: Sean can keep his mouth shut all right, and there's no call to use gunpowder in Cloncraig. And then what happens to Sean himself? We know that, too."

"They killed him." James Costello, doubly bereaved, broke his silence to hiccup briefly but profoundly. He felt moved to recite the legendary story, which they all knew by heart. In their present mood, it palled no more than did the pattern of Mass on Sundays. "The Black-and-Tans got him, back in 1921, when the murdering bastards were quartered on us. They shot him and his wife and his kids, and all for a little bit of an ambush that didn't cost them more than a man or two. Who would want to live in the cottage after that?"

"There was a curse on it," put in Joe Lane the landlord, overhearing, as he came up with a fresh tray of drinks. "That's what killed the poor children. A curse, I say."

The others nodded, for form's sake; they did not agree, but it was not worth disagreement. Joe Lane was a newcomer, and from County Cork at that: let him think what he liked, and say it too. Landlords were the wrong side of the counter, anyway, and always would be.

"The only curse on it," said Neil Fairlie, half-contemptuously, when Lane had put down the fresh drinks and was gone again, "was that some of the stuff was still dry after so long. And somehow the kids must have touched it off."

"I heard there was bombs as well," said James Costello. "Little ones."

"Hand-grenades," corrected Neil Fairlie. "And mighty useful they were, in the old days. I shouldn't wonder"— he paused, and looked around him— "if there was a few more of them buried here and there in Cloncraig."

After a reflective pause, Paddy Finane said: "Aye. There could be."

"We don't want the police ripping the village apart entirely, just to find a few bits of hand-grenades."

"Let it rest, I say."

"It was hard on us," said Neil Fairlie heavily, "but it's

done now. They cannot bring the children back with an inquest, or with the police ferreting all round the place." He lowered his voice. "The less they know about what the children found, the better. Maybe it's just as well there's no one left to come out with the evidence."

Paddy Finane nodded. "Just as well. It might give them something to go to work on, else. . . ." He looked across at James Costello. "I heard tell that Esther was still fast in her bed."

"Yes, she is that."

"How is she, then?"

"The same," said Costello. "The same."

Esther Costello was indeed the same; and the word had, for her, a fearful connotation. She could not talk, though she could moan briefly when she wanted to attract attention: she could not see: she could not hear, however hard they roared at her. She was just a body, pretty enough to the eye, but seemingly abandoned and tenantless. . . . The doctor from Wexford, a country G.P. with a large, near-pauper practice, had tried his hardest, groping about in a territory he scarcely comprehended: before long he had brought in a friend, a big man from Dublin, to help find out what the trouble was. But nothing came of the visit and, after three months, Esther still lay as if drugged, mutely defying their care and skill.

"Maybe, with money to spend, we could do something more," the doctor said once to James Costello. "She could go to America for treatment. There's fine hospitals there, and new ideas about everything."

"Money," said James Costello, and shrugged. "I haven't the price of one drink on me, at this very moment."

"Better for you if you haven't," said the doctor shortly. He was a busy man, and a tired one, and he was near to

feeling that he was throwing away his time, caught in this
uncharted maze with these shiftless people.

Mrs. Costello looked up at him. She was a worn woman
of forty, a few years older than her husband: a woman of
no vitality and no looks, whom the bearing of two children
seemed to have emptied of all spirit, all life. Sometimes she
nagged, mostly she let things drift. The house was very
dirty, and she with it.

"What do we do, then?" she asked.

"Look after her well," the doctor answered, with little
confidence in his tone. He glanced around the filthy room,
and then down at the girl, who lay with her eyes closed and
her hands folded on her breast. "Keep her clean, too.
It'll all help. And wait and see what happens."

For a long time they let her lie on her bed, feeding her
at intervals, attending to her needs: it was easier to keep her
there than have her blundering round the house, knocking
into things and hurting herself. Now, three and four months
after the explosion, she was the same as when she was brought
in, except that she could move more readily, and seemed free
of pain. "A massive shock to the central nervous system,"
the doctor from Dublin had said; and the phrase was repeated
round the village with the wise head-shaking of baffled men
to accompany it. But 'massive' was a fine word, for sure. . . .
So Esther lay there, eating whatever was put in her mouth,
pointing when she wished to be set on the chamber-pot:
sometimes, with her parents out of the house, and no one by,
she would point and point for hours, and then, helpless,
relieve herself where she lay.

She came to recognize her mother's touch, and would
sometimes reach up and put her hand on the curve of Mrs.
Costello's chin, and nod, and even attempt a smile. But
the touch of anyone else—her father, or a compassionate

neighbour who came to sit with her—startled her pitifully; and by and by these others gave up trying to reach her in any way.

God alone knew what Esther was making of the lonely darkness and silence in which she lay: a lively girl of ten, suddenly plunged into a blank world, hideously null, with nothing in it save food coming into her mouth, and presently leaving her again, and her mother's chin as the only thing she could recognize without fear. For the most part she kept her eyes closed; but now and then, for no reason that she could communicate, her face would begin to work, and a tear would creep out from under her lid, and fall upon the pillow. If her parents saw it, they would wonder for a moment what was going on inside the pretty, blank head, and if she could be helped, and how. . . . But Mrs. Costello, dull and slatternly, was not equipped to deal with anything save the simple necessities; and her father—who had been a cobbler, and a good one, but had drunk away his skill and his trade for ten wasted years—her father took himself more and more frequently to the private bar of the Cloncraig Arms, and gave less and less thought to something which puzzled, angered, and defeated him.

The only person who tried to bring effective aid to Esther was Father Haggerty, the parish priest; and he was the last one who kept on trying.

"We must do something for her," said Father Haggerty, time and time again, prodding himself and his flock to a proper remembrance of their duty. "We must help her. She must get out and about." But he was an old man, long past his best; and though he and Esther had been friends in the past, and she could now recognize him from the feel of his straggling white beard, and the musty smell of his cassock, yet there was little enough he could do to help, and nothing to cure.

With all the will and love and prayers in the world, he could not reach her mind. Nor could anyone else. Sometimes he would take her for a short walk in the village, from the cottage garden to the nearest street-corner: he guided her, supported her, met stares and head-shakings with stern frowns. For a time they were a familiar sight in Cloncraig: the old black-clad priest and the stumbling, trembling child who only knew she was out-of-doors because of the thin sun upon her thin body. Now and again he would beckon the open-mouthed village children to come closer to them, the children whom Esther used to know, whom once she had gaily led.

"It's young Mickey Howard," Father Haggerty would say, forgetting that Esther could not hear. "You'll be remembering him. . . . Shake hands now. . . ."

The child—whoever it was—would put out an uncertain hand, and at its touch Esther would start and turn aside; then some mother, grim-faced or scared, would detach herself from the gaping crowd and lead her child away, with both of them whispering hotly; and Father Haggerty, frowning and shaking his head, would say: "There, now," and, with a hand under her arm, start their slow walk back again, their crippled progress, while the tears left Esther's eyes and ran down her puzzled, working face.

The village folk lost interest before long. Soon, indeed, they scarcely bothered to raise their heads as she passed.

Then gradually the familiar sight, of the old man near the grave and the young child who was struggling to rise from it, grew less familiar. Father Haggerty would have persevered, since he was waiting for a miracle; but the outings did not seem to give Esther any pleasure, nor indeed any feeling at all; and no miracle came, despite his love, despite his prayers. Presently he himself lost heart, because he could not reach her in the least degree, and there was nothing more to be done, and he was an old man and she a half-dead child, and God seemed to have turned His back on both of them.

Before long the priest, like the doctor, stopped coming to see her.   There was no way in which either of them could help.

Last of all, the parents themselves retreated.   Within a year, the Costellos had moved Esther from the house and down to a small shack at the bottom of the garden, where she was out of harm's way, and could find her path to the nearby privy herself.   Sometimes she crawled there on her hands and knees, sometimes, more daring, she walked upright; but after losing her way one rainy morning and catching her head a cruel blow on an overhanging bough, she mostly crawled.

When it was sunny she would sit at the shack door, motionless: when it rained she lay inside: when it was cold she burrowed deep under her blankets, and lay there like an animal enlaired.   This was a world she knew and trusted. Once, when she had diarrhoea, and had soiled herself, her mother struck her: Esther turned straightway and crawled under the protective blankets, and lay there a full day and night.

As the months passed she grew thin, and pale as a slug: only the useless eyes seemed to grow larger and, indeed, lovelier, burning coldly in the centre of a pinched grey face.

They fed her three times a day, and they tied a rope from the door of the shack to the privy, to guide her on her one essential journey.   Life reduced itself to this deadly cycle: the food in the mouth, the bucket underneath her, and all in silent darkness.

So, for two years, lived Esther Costello.

CHAPTER THREE

THE large black Cadillac, with chromium bumpers and white sidewall tyres, which entered by the dusty Wexford road, and pulled up outside the Cloncraig Arms, created an enormous stir in the village. Not only was it the first car from 'outside' which had visited them since the war's end, it was the first car of such opulence ever to arrive in Cloncraig. It was a sight to see—and the same might well be said of its single occupant, the woman who presently stepped from the driving-seat and began to look about her.

She was a woman of forty-one or two, tall, impressively built, fashionably dressed: a handsome woman, a woman of assurance, a woman (clearly) of the world. She was in black, with furs: her stockings were of fine mesh, her heels (by Irish village standards) wonderfully high. She looked "for all the world like a French whore", said Paddy Finane, who had never seen a whore of any nationality. But it was a fact that the stranger had a certain distinction, a certain urban elegance new to Cloncraig, and therefore dubious; and when she disappeared into the Cloncraig Arms, a large number of people waited about at the door in the hope that she might reappear, and were disappointed when she did not, and when her luggage followed her inside.

"Gone to bed," explained the landlord, Joe Lane, later, when the bar was at its most crowded. "A plate of cold mutton and pickles, a cut off the cheese, and two whisky-and-sodas. And just now a hot water bottle."

"That's what I'd like to be," said Paddy Finane,

snickering. "A hot water bottle to a big, handsome woman like that."

Encouraged by the laughter, he went on to suggest other offices he might perform, given goodwill on both sides.

"You!" interrupted James Costello, who was drunk already. "What's a little fellow like you going to do, in that line? You'd be hopping about like a flea on a bitch, asking the right way home."

The laughter, turning against Paddy, discomforted him. "There's good small ones as well as good big ones," he said belligerently. "I've never had a complaint yet."

"You've never had a —— yet, more likely," said Costello. "I'll bet that woman upstairs could teach you a thing or two."

"What's she doing in Cloncraig, anyway?" asked a voice at the back.

"Looking for a husband," said another.

The rough laughter brought Joe Lane to the front of the bar again.

"She's from America," he said importantly. "She's touring round in that car—seeing the country. Her name's Mrs. Bannister. She's just down from Dublin." He kept his major item till the last. "She says she was born here in Cloncraig."

"What was her name, then?" asked several voices.

"Maclean," said Joe Lane. "But there's none of that name here now. Must have been before my time."

Most people in the bar turned to old Neil Fairlie for confirmation.

He nodded. "There *was* a family of that name, that went away to America, near forty years ago. They lived down by the bridge. Neil Maclean—I mind him because he had the same name as me. There was two or three children, too. Aye, it might be the same."

B

"She's grown up a bit since then," said Paddy Finane, pursuing obliquely the thoughts which never seemed to leave him. "And married as well. Someone's a lucky man."

"Mrs. Bannister," said Neil Fairlie musingly. "That's a good Irish name, too. I wonder what old Neil Maclean came to, in America. He was a stone-mason when he left. Must have made money, by the look of *her*."

They discussed Mrs. Bannister for a long time—her looks, her gait, her clothes, the purpose of her visit. Presently the serving-girl, who had taken up the hot water bottle, put her head round the corner of the bar to report that the visitor wore a lace nightgown "you could see half a mile through", and had a special travelling-case with nothing but paint and powder and scent in it.

"What did I tell you?" said Paddy Finane triumphantly. "She's a real madam, that one."

It was years since Cloncraig had seen such a person; and not within living memory had the Cloncraig Arms housed a woman staying by herself, let alone one like this. The knowledge that just above their heads slept a woman of this special, exotic quality—married, but travelling alone without her husband—in silk and lace, with boxes of paint and powder close to hand—the knowledge that such a woman shared the Cloncraig Arms with them took hold of the men in the bar, pricking them strangely. She might have been there beside them: they could not keep away from her, they could not escape her effect. They could almost smell that perfume, touch that nightgown, see those soft reclining limbs. . . . It gave them all a continuing itch of masculinity. The talk that night was very bawdy.

On the floor above them, in the comfortable, creaking warmth of Joe Lane's best bedroom, the object of all their thoughts, Mrs. Bannister, was reading herself to sleep.

In bed, in the lace nightgown which had so scandalized the servant-girl, Belle Bannister was to some extent softened and feminized; but she still looked, and was, a self-sufficient woman with the combined elegance and toughness of metropolitan America. Good-looking she certainly was, with dark colouring and a fine, fresh skin, but the 'French whore' stricture of Paddy Finane could not have been wider of the mark. In Cloncraig, she shone with suspect brilliance: in her own *milieu*, she looked what she was—a handsome, tailored, slightly masculine woman well able to take care of herself, having lived her own life for twenty years and regretting very little of it.

Up from the bar below came the tinkle of breaking glass, followed by a bellow of laughter. Mrs. Bannister smiled indulgently. Those hill-billies down there were certainly enjoying themselves. And so was she, come to that.

The trip to Britain and the continent had been a spur-of-the-moment project—because she was free, and glad the war was over, and felt the need to travel after being cooped up for five years, and felt also that it was better to travel at forty than at fifty. But the journey to Cloncraig had been no accidental affair; it was a sentimental pilgrimage, planted in her heart by her father some years before he died. "If you get the chance, Belle, go back to the old country," he had said. "Go to Cloncraig, and see where you came from. You'll not be sorry." Now he was dead, and in spite of set-backs she could still afford to travel, and the old man had been right—she was not sorry she had come.

Of course, she could not remember the village at all: the Cloncraig of thirty-five years ago, when she was six, might be the same now or it might have changed, but she could recall nothing of it, either way. The Maclean family had emigrated shortly before the First World War: time had carried away all details of the event, save that the journey

was long and uncomfortable, and that for many years after
it they had been desperately poor. But her father, pro-
gressing from stone-mason to speculative builder, had made
his pile, and now, after his death, she had her share of it:
she herself had married, and that was over too; and so,
being free, she had come back to Cloncraig, as her father
had told her to, to have a look at the place where she was
born.

She hadn't meant to startle them in the village—she
was aware now of the effect of the Cadillac and of her own
get-up—but she simply hadn't realized what Cloncraig
would be like, and just how simple, how grounded in the
narrow past, an Irish village could be. It had made her feel,
for a moment, very much the American tourist of modern
legend.

"What a dump," she phrased it to herself aloud; and
then: "No—what a poor, left-behind place."

She would do better for them tomorrow, anyway: she
had some old tweeds in one of the trunks. . . .

A fresh burst of laughter came from below. Seemingly
they could enjoy themselves here, whether they had been
left behind or not. But that did not alter what she had seen
as she drove slowly through on her arrival, and what the
'hotel' itself told her—the shabbiness and the bitter poverty
that possessed the whole village, the village where she was
born.

It would be nice to do something for Cloncraig.

Despite the 'old tweeds' (a Glen Urquhart check which
had first seen the occidental light of day on Fifth Avenue),
Mrs. Bannister continued to cause a major stir in Cloncraig.
The children hung in swarms round her car, leaving small
and filthy fingermarks on the paintwork; good-naturedly,
she would sometimes select a dozen of them and, packing

them in like freshly netted sardines, take them on a tour of their village. The shrieks, the waving, the open-mouthed spectators, gave to such excursions a touch of royalty which would have affected a woman of far lesser vanity. . . . She explored the village, and bought from the general store a number of articles, such as nail varnish and egg-shampoo, which, laid in stock many years before when the proprietor had succumbed to the blandishments of a golden-tongued commercial traveller from Dublin, had defied all later efforts to dispose of them. She also paid a formal call on the place of her birth, a mean cottage at the lower end of the village now occupied by Cloncraig's blacksmith.

This visit was a qualified success, since Mrs. Bannister made heavy weather of the blacksmith's brogue, and the blacksmith could not make head or tail of an American accent ("She talked like a damned buzz-saw," he told inquirers later); but there was a good deal of dumb-show cordiality throughout, and the pound note which changed hands at the end was an effective sweetener. . . . It was a charm which worked on other occasions, too: when, for instance, she came down to the bar of the Cloncraig Arms and stood two rounds of pints and double-whiskies, there were many ready to swear that America must be a hell of a fine place, and its womenfolk its best ambassadors.

The wives of Cloncraig, generally, did not like her: she was far too disturbing, far too much of a woman, and the majority of them were fully conscious that their own feminine lures had long since languished of familiarity. The men, of course, looked sideways at her, and kept on looking: she was undoubtedly a grand figure of a woman, and the gossip about the transparent nightdress, and other items of her wardrobe duly reported by the hotel servants, had lost nothing in the telling. In this respect, she had made a friend for life of Paddy Finane, simply by strolling down to the river's edge with him one evening when dusk was coming on; the excursion had, of course, been totally innocent, but many knowing eyes had followed them, and Paddy was not the man to tell his story in concise words when a wink and a leer would serve far better.

With old Neil Fairlie, too, she scored a notable hit when she recalled her father to him.

"He often used to talk about you," she said, stretching a point for politeness' sake. "I remember your name very well."

"Is that so?" said Neil, flattered. "He was a good friend of mine in the old days. I expect," he went on, glancing delicately at the Cadillac, "he did well for himself in America?"

"He had a good business," agreed Mrs. Bannister. "Building houses and shops and factories."

"And will you be going back there soon?"

"Before very long." She smiled. "It's been nice here, but holidays can't last for ever."

"It's been very nice having you, ma'am," said old Neil gallantly. "We'll remember the visit, here in Cloncraig."

She was in the village for a full week before she met Father Haggerty.

Father Haggerty, of course, had heard of her, as he heard of everyone and everything in Cloncraig, one way and another; but their paths had not crossed, and village gossip about the rich woman from America had not encouraged him to seek her acquaintance. He was a priest, and an old man: she, it seemed, was a woman full of vanities who had left her religion long since. . . . But they met presently, one morning outside the village store, and exchanged courtesies: he found her pleasant-spoken, and oddly respectful—as backsliding Catholics often were when they encountered a priest. They met again, by arrangement, and talked for an hour; something was stirring in his old forgetful mind, something that concerned the people in his care, something to do with such women as this, who had the gift of charity and the power of riches. . . . Even as he talked to her, God seemed to be chiding him with some reclaimable error of omission.

He was the first person to tell her about Esther Costello. This silence of Cloncraig was no conspiracy: they really had forgotten the girl, so horribly stricken, who had lain out of sight and mind for more than two years, whom no eye ever saw. She did not come up in any conversation, because her very name had fallen out of currency: and James Costello, the only person in the village who might have mentioned her, was now a befuddled wreck who rarely managed a coherent sentence, and had addressed none of any sort to the visitor.

Mrs. Bannister was very shocked. "But what's been done about her?" she asked, as soon as Father Haggerty gave her the facts. "Hasn't she been hospitalized?"

"What's that?" asked Father Haggerty, puzzled.

"Have the doctors seen her? What have they tried?"

"There was the doctor from Wexford, and another from Dublin," explained Father Haggerty. "But they couldn't do anything for her at all, they said. That's nearly three years ago now."

"What's been happening since, then?"

"Nothing," said Father Haggerty. He looked at Mrs. Bannister almost humbly. "What could we do? It's a poor village—there's no money for big doctors, and hospitals, and such."

"But it's so appalling. . . . You mean she just stays in the house all the time?"

"In a little shed," said Father Haggerty. One of those

strange, chiding thoughts tapped gently at his brain. He
glanced once more, covertly, at Mrs. Bannister, at her rings
and her pearl necklace. "Would you like to see her, then?"

"I certainly would," said Mrs. Bannister. "Fix it for me,
will you, Father?"

Going down the overgrown garden path, with Mrs. Costello
fluttering ahead of them, and James Costello regarding
them owlishly from the kitchen door, Mrs. Bannister was
aware of a strange feeling. It was as if she were stepping
consciously into the future, doing something which would
involve her, irrevocably, in a new aspect of life. This crazy
cavalcade—the dirty, sallow woman, the old priest, and
herself—seemed to be moving into a queer country which,
within a few moments, might capture her entirely and remake
her mind and body. . . . Mrs. Costello, leading the way,
stopped in front of a lean-to shed, and pushed open its door.
A shaft of wan sunlight fell upon the floor as Mrs. Bannister
peered within.

"Jesus God!" said Mrs. Bannister.

Esther Costello, lying on her blanket bed, was indeed a
horrifying sight. She lay with her eyes open and her arms
crossed—the eyes like dead pools, the arms like yellow sticks:
she lay in frightful impassivity, as some mangy animal, used
to freedom, which loses in captivity the wish to seem alive
or to care for itself in any way. Her fair hair, cropped
close, was filthy and unkempt: there were livid sores round
her mouth: the pinched face above the scrawny neck was
like a shrunken skull. The bed had a tumble of disgusting,
threadbare blankets on it: there were bits of stale bread
on the floor of the shed, gnawed bones, hen-droppings.
The place smelt acridly and vilely, and the girl herself was
the noisome centre of it.

Even as they stared at her—the priest with shame, Mrs.

Bannister with horror—she moved. She levered herself up, threw aside the blankets, and felt her way along the edge of the bed towards the door. The three of them fell back, as before a leper or a loose animal, while she fumbled for the edge of the door and the beginning of the rope. Outside in the sunlight, she seemed to become, in some final degree, a blasphemy of the human shape.

She was dressed, they now saw, in a single garment, a kind of smock or shift, torn, stained brown, reaching halfway down her thighs: below it, her shanks were wizened like an old man's, and her spindly legs moved jerkily, as she felt her way along the frayed rope that reached to the privy. She turned her head this way and that, as if feeling for the sun: the blind eyes still roved about her hopefully, the head was cocked as if still expecting some faint sound from the world. The small developing breasts under the shift were a last cruel flourish of mockery; for by their evidence, their shy promise, she was, in all her horror, in all her degradation, a girl of thirteen on the bright edge of womanhood.

"She knows when she wants to go," said Mrs. Costello.

The priest and Mrs. Bannister prayed, the one for forgiveness, the other that she might not vomit.

They watched Esther return after a time, stumbling and groping along in the same way, and then burrowing under the blankets again in search of warmth. When the door was shut on her:

"For Heaven's sake, why don't you look after her properly?" asked Mrs. Bannister in a sudden fury. "That's the wickedest thing I've ever seen."

"We do the best we can," said Mrs. Costello forlornly. "Money's hard to come by, these days."

"It doesn't cost money to keep her clean. . . . She should be in an institution, anyway, with proper care."

"We do the best we can."

"God forgive us all," said Father Haggerty.

"Or better still, the doctors should look her over again, and see if anything's changed."

"Doctors cost money," whined Mrs. Costello.

"Father," said Mrs. Bannister, turning to the old man, "we *must* do something."

The priest nodded, hopeful and fearful at the same time, wondering what was in her mind, and whether it could be the miracle that long ago he had prayed for. "What can we do?" he asked, trembling with age and fear and hope. "What can we do?"

The Cadillac fetched the doctor from Wexford and then the doctor from Dublin; but neither could add anything to what they had said already—the 'massive shock' still persisted, and showed no signs of abating. Mrs. Bannister cast about her for the next step. The girl was now, at least, clean and properly dressed and fed—that much, Mrs. Bannister had insisted on, and had driven the insistence home with money, and a threat of prosecution for good measure; but these basic improvements were nothing like enough. She had been profoundly moved by Esther Costello—by the cruel mischance which had laid her low, by the shock of her appearance, by those childish breasts so bravely sprouting into a barbaric world. She wanted to do more, much more; and since there was little to be done on the spot, it must be done in some other place, somewhere where these things enlisted effective aid as a matter of course.

Thus her thoughts began to move, and thus also, anticipating her, did Cloncraig's; for Cloncraig, prompted and prodded by Mrs. Bannister's disclosures and by the freedom of her tongue, was rediscovering its conscience, and felt the need to assuage it, for comfort's sake.

"The girl ought to go to America," said Paddy Finane, to the bar at large, finalizing their discussions. "There's doctors there can work bloody miracles. They use electric machines. They can raise the dead themselves."

"Cost a lot of money," said Joe Lane, the landlord, judiciously.

"Mrs. Bannister could do it. She's got the money all right. She only needs telling."

"*You* tell her." said a voice. "You know her well enough, so you say."

"We could get up a petition," said another voice.

"What's that, then?"

"Write her a letter, and all sign it."

"Why do that, when she's upstairs ready to be spoken to?"

"Aye. . . . Better send up Paddy Finane. He can use his *petition*, and see what he gets with it."

"Now then," said Joe Lane, who was none too sure of the sound-proof qualities of the bar's ceiling. "Order please!"

Paddy turned to James Costello. "What do you say, then? Will you speak to her yourself?"

"What's that?" mumbled Costello, vague and fuddled. "Speak? What's that?"

"The girl. Esther."

"Oh—aye." He nodded. But he said no more.

"We'll all speak," said old Neil Fairlie suddenly. "Bit by bit. A hint here and a hint there. We'll put in a word, whenever we see her."

Paddy Finane considered the project. "Father Haggerty could say a word, too."

"Him, and anyone else who cares. We should do something to help the girl. If Mrs. Bannister could just take her to America, she might be cured straight away."

Now many voices joined in, eager to prove their goodwill, to show that they had not really forgotten the girl—it

was just that she had slipped their memory a little. The bar
became a glowing centre of generosity and resolution.
Tomorrow they would do this, the next day they would say
that. And the day after, all their wishes would come true,
and Cloncraig would be an entirely happy place again, with
no stain on its character and nothing to prick its conscience
from out of the blue.

The whole village turned out to see them leave. This was,
after all, Cloncraig's own invention, practically its own
doing. . . .

The car stood outside the Cloncraig Arms while Mrs.
Bannister was paying her bill there: as it waited, the crowd
thickened round it, staring at Esther, who sat in the back
supported and cherished by a cocoon of cushions and blankets.
Care and proper food (she had for months and years been
living on potatoes and soup-bones) had made a certain
difference to her already; she looked a little better than when
Mrs. Bannister had first seen her, three weeks before,
though she still had that sunken look, that desperate pallor,
that air of zoo-captivity hopelessly borne. . . . The crowd
round her was hushed by her appearance; but in their
silence there was something more than compassion, something
that peeped out here and there in a half-smile or a lift of
the head. They wore an ambiguous air; it was as if they
could not quite make up their minds what sort of an occasion
this was to be.

Mrs. Bannister realized the truth, as soon as she came
out of the front door. In Cloncraig, they were already
preparing to be pleased with themselves.

Maybe, from one particular angle, they had a right to
be, she thought as she began to say goodbye to those nearest
to her: the girl, shamefully treated, had been recalled to their
conscience, and now they were going to be quit of her, and

the relief was largely of their own making. Mrs. Bannister
knew very well how they had all gone to work on her: how
nearly everyone in the village, one way or another, had
chipped in, from Father Haggerty praying for guidance and
talking about miracles wrought by faith, to old Neil Fairlie
asking, was it true they had machines in America for putting
new eyes into people. . . . Paddy Finane, one evening, had
even become sentimental, saying she must be sorry to leave
Cloncraig, and *wouldn't she like to take a little bit of it with her*?
She had had to think twice about that one. . . .

Oh yes, they had given her the full treatment all right,
flattering her as the new-style magician, the American wonder-
worker, the only one able to wave the wand and produce
the pumpkin. But she had not disliked the process, because
she had half made up her mind already.

A voice in the crowd called: "God bless you, ma'am,"
and others took it up.

Not God, thought Mrs. Bannister, pulling on her driving-
gloves: this didn't need God or good luck—it needed pity,
and then plain American drive and common sense. . . . From
the very beginning, everything about Esther's case had shocked
her, impelling her to action there and then: it was not only
the girl's appalling appearance, it was the whole set-up—the
fecklessness, the defeated parents, the indolent cloud that
had settled on all concerned, the blind eye of Cloncraig.
If this was Ireland, then by God it needed the smartest kick
in the pants!

That sort of feebleness and futility wouldn't do for America;
and she was now an American, and must demonstrate the
new standard in her own person. The fact that she was
herself, by birth, a daughter of this very village of Cloncraig,
made it doubly necessary to prove that the local do-nothing
disease was no one's fault but their own. *Anyone* could take
a good sharp tug, and start setting themselves and the world

to rights. . . . In her own case, nothing stood in the way:
she had money, she was free of all ties, she had no children
to worry about: why then shouldn't she do what she could to
help, why shouldn't she take the girl to America and see if the
doctors or the clinics could do something for her? It would
be a nuisance, and a very big responsibility, and it might not
work; but she had nothing better to do, anyway.

The mixed motives seemed to rise up about her, prompting
and supporting her as she stood on the threshold. She saw
them as separate sentences, a frieze of reasons clicking into
place again as they had done many times during the past
three weeks. They were like the bedroom texts of her
childhood—reassuring, admonitory, half-trusted, half-despised.

It was flattering, in many ways, to be able to wave that
particular wand, and to have the ability taken for granted.

The poor kid, like Cloncraig, was due for a break.

The papers wouldn't be likely to miss it.

It certainly wouldn't do her any harm with her friends.

Already, people—strangers—were showing that they ad-
mired her for what she was doing.

There was the faint, unacknowledged pull of the child she
had never borne herself.

She had always said, from the beginning, that "it would
be nice to do something for Cloncraig."

But she was nobody's fool, and least of all her own; and
she wasn't deceiving herself, as she stood there, smiling at the
leave-takers and well-wishers. She knew perfectly well that
the motives were mixed, that the tapestry of her goodwill
varied tremendously, some of it pure gold, some of it shoddy.
But did it matter much, if in the end the kid came out the
better for it?

Mrs. Bannister got into the car and turned round to look
at Esther Costello. The girl was pitiful as ever, of course;
but she seemed comfortable, and at ease.

They were ready to go.

Father Haggerty, at her elbow, spoke another text: "God will bless you for this," and Mrs. Bannister, with a wave, drove off towards the New World.

CHAPTER FOUR

THEIR journey to America had, necessarily, a dog's-leg track: from Cloncraig to Dublin, from Dublin to Liverpool, from Liverpool to New York. Mrs. Bannister would have infinitely preferred to make the trip in one straight line, but there were too many things standing in the way. There were complications over the Cadillac, a possession so valuable, so tender, and so suspect that at times it seemed as though she would have to have it inoculated; and over her ticket, which made no allowance for a more direct route; and especially over Esther Costello, who (it seemed) could not become part of her personal baggage without surmounting a long series of official hurdles.

Mrs. Bannister grudged continually the wasted time, because she was eager to get home—home to America, the only place which could handle this challenging affair. She also disliked the idea of spending any more time than was necessary in England. She had a particular feeling about England. She had married an Englishman.

The crossing from Dublin to Liverpool was comparatively simple. Mrs. Bannister, by appeals of various kinds, managed to secure a stateroom to herself; the Irish Sea was dead calm, and Esther seemed to find nothing out of the ordinary in the few short walks she was called upon to make. Mrs. Bannister fed her, with the help of a motherly stewardess (whose first remark had been: "Poor thing—born like it, I suppose", and whose second was: "Syphilis, eh? I was reading about it only the other day . . ."); and together they saw that she was comfortable in her bunk. Only once had she shown

48

surprise or fear, and that was when they first reached the quayside, and Esther suddenly lifted her head, and sniffed the air. The strange, pungent smell seemed to frighten her, and she clung to Mrs. Bannister and tried to slow her steps, all the time cocking her nose upwards like an animal lifting its muzzle to a dark, unknown night.

What she had discovered was the smell of the sea, the sea she had never seen, and perhaps barely heard about.

It was on the small ship crossing to Liverpool that Mrs. Bannister and Esther achieved their first communication, their first direct signal. It seemed to Mrs. Bannister that Esther should be able to indicate when she wanted to go to the toilet, and that it should be by some kind of sound, rather than by the crude pointing gesture she had been taught to make. When next Esther pointed, Mrs. Bannister led her to the toilet, as usual, but once there she brought Esther's hands together in a single clapping motion, and then dropped them. After she had done this on two or three occasions, the girl understood that there was henceforward to be a connection between her needs and the clapping of her two hands. . . . Next morning, when she clapped her hands of her own accord, and Mrs. Bannister led her straightway into the toilet, there formed upon her face so enchanting a smile, so contented a look, that Mrs. Bannister could only stare at it in wonder.

It must be, she realized, the very first time that Esther had been able to ask for something, and find that it was immediately given to her.

She pressed the girl's hands in her own, moved and made happy by this thread that stretched between them already.

England was less satisfactory—as Mrs. Bannister, drawing on caustic memories, had known it would be. They had a suite in the Adelphi Hotel at Liverpool, and there they stayed for nearly three weeks, while Mrs. Bannister battled

for her two impedimenta—her Cadillac, and her ward.
As regards the former, there had developed some sort of
crisis over the customs: the travel agents in New York seemed
to have neglected some vital piece of paper when the car
was shipped to England, and the result was suspicion and
official horror when the time came to ship it out again.
The British customs authorities, bogged in tradition as usual,
could not see their way clear in any direction: Mrs. Bannister
begged, cajoled, banged her money on the table, called for
Consular help—all to no avail. She even went so far as to
hint at bribery—a gross error which, warned by a pair of
frosty eyes on the other side of the desk, she retrieved just in
time. Apparently they had a tradition about that as well.

But then, just when all seemed hopeless, the piece of paper
was discovered and forwarded, and officialdom lowered its
guard. The car could leave after all. But before that
happened, there was still Esther Costello—and she was
something else again.

What was she, in fact? What was to be her classification,
this helpless child, if and when she was cast upon the shores
of America? Was she an immigrant? Was she a visitor?
A holidaymaker? A displaced person? There were many
other questions, probing the past and the future. How long
would she stay? Who would be responsible for her, if Mrs.
Bannister died or went mad? Would she become a charge
on the public funds? Had her parents given their full consent
to the journey? Who was to be her legal guardian? What
was her health like? Was she literate? Would she seek
gainful employment? Would she try to overthrow the
Constitution? Had she had mumps? Measles? Yellow
fever? Might she not, behind that blind façade, perhaps be
a lunatic?

"It's a fine thing you're trying to do, Mrs. Bannister,"
said the young-old man at the American Consulate, fingering

a paper-knife, smiling at her in the particularly open way that people of authority use when they are preparing to turn down their thumbs. "But it gives us certain problems that aren't going to be easy to solve."

He restated some of them, while Mrs. Bannister turned her mind inwards. This was the Cadillac over again, she thought: there's just a piece of paper missing—only this time it affects a blind girl instead of a chunk of metal. But as the Cadillac had come right, so must Esther Costello: the plan, starting as a vague impulse of generosity in Cloncraig, had begun to grow and take definite shape, aided by half-a-dozen things—the compliments of people who learned the facts, the way the whole project made her 'feel good', the brilliant smile she had been able to bring to Esther's face already. She could not change her mind, and retrace her steps now; anything that stood in the way must be melted down or climbed over. And here, in this shabby, smoky Liverpool office, she must start melting and climbing.

She turned back to the man behind the desk.

"I know it's difficult," she said agreeably. "But I *do* want to do it, if it can possibly be fixed. . . . Can't I give an over-all guarantee that I'll always be responsible for her?"

"It could be arranged," answered the Vice-Consul. "But do you really want to do that?"

"How do you mean?"

"I'll be frank with you, Mrs. Bannister," he said, as if thus far he had only been playing the fool with truth. "The fact is, I can see this girl becoming a nuisance to you. Suppose the doctors can do nothing for her? Will you keep her on in the States indefinitely?"

"I hadn't thought about it," said Mrs. Bannister frankly. "But I'm sure they *will* be able to do something for her."

"And if not? Would you take her back to Ireland again?" The Vice-Consul's eyes met hers suddenly. "Wouldn't it be kinder not to start this thing—just to leave her where she was?"

Where she was. . . . Mrs. Bannister had a sudden vision of the shed at the end of the garden, the filthy girl on the filthy bed, the parents muttering their bedraggled chorus, the worn rope that led to the privy. She could almost smell that neglected inmate, that animal den. . . . That was 'where she was', and no one who had seen it, unless they were as unfeeling as clods of earth, could ever condemn her to it again.

"I want to get her out of it, and I don't want her ever to go back," she said, with sudden energy. "It was the most terrible place you ever saw. . . . If there's a guarantee to be signed, I'll sign it. Whatever you want, I'll put my name to it."

"You'll undertake to support her indefinitely?"

"Yes." A new idea struck her, though she passed it on as if it were an old one. "I'll probably adopt her, legally. Wouldn't that square it all up?"

"If the parents approve, of course."

"They'll approve."

The Vice-Consul, giving ground (or had she only imagined his lack of enthusiasm?) summed up for her.

"That's for the future, anyway. Let's say, *now*, that this girl is visiting America on a temporary permit, and that you'll be responsible for her support, in every respect. O.K.?"

Mrs. Bannister nodded.

"We'll have to send a cable, of course, and explain all the circumstances. When do you plan to leave?"

Mrs. Bannister smiled, giving him a brief glimpse of an attractive woman trying something on. "Tomorrow," she said.

He smiled in answer. "Or the day after. . . . I'll see what I can do. Maybe it'll take two or three weeks. It'll just round out your holiday nicely. Have you been in Liverpool before?"

"No," answered Mrs. Bannister, without enthusiasm. "It's not exactly Long Island, is it?"

"It's an interesting town," said the Vice-Consul, correctly. "The cathedral is new."

"I'm glad," said Mrs. Bannister. She rose. "Do what you can to hurry this up, will you? I want to get home."

While she waited—and there were many more snags and queries to be overcome, before the signal fell—while she waited in the big, solid suite in the Adelphi Hotel, Mrs. Bannister studied Esther, and wondered about her. She had done this many times before, but now, in this pause before action, she seemed to come face to face with the odds that ruled the future.

When she watched Esther, sitting passive in one of the deep arm-chairs, she felt that she was watching the biggest questionmark of her life. Superficially, the girl was much improved. She had put on weight, the facial sores were healing, she was clean and neat, she looked as many normal girls of thirteen look; she was pale, slightly awkward, and encumbered with legs too long and shoulders too thin, but there was promise of beauty in the unformed face, and the slight body held the likelihood of grace. Esther had gained confidence in her movements, too: she seemed to have established in her mind the exact shape of the suite—which she never left—as well as the placing of its furniture, and she would sometimes go on a tour of inspection. She could now move from chair to chair and table to table, without coming to any harm; she could walk straight from her bed to the bathroom, and, at exactly the right moment, put up her hand to reach for the doorknob.

Sometimes she would spend an hour on one circuit of the sitting-room, touching, feeling, stroking. Some things obviously puzzled her: to the telephone, for instance, she returned again and again, cupping in her hands this unknown object, frowning all the time. . . . But there were other things which she accepted instantly: and when food was set before her, and a fork put into her hand, she ate with perfect confidence, and her fingers closed round her glass without hesitation.

In fact, she looked better, ate better, moved better, and *was* better. But what, Mrs. Bannister wondered, was going to be the full scope of that improvement?

What was the actual material like? What was this girl's true nature? If she had been normal, what sort of person would she have been? Was she dull, was she clever, was she impudent or coarse? What had she been like when her darkness fell? How much had she known, and how much had she deteriorated in the dead, lost years? Her parents had claimed that she could read and write—but that was nearly three years ago. The priest had said that she was 'lively'— but she wasn't lively now. What was this village child's real quality: was it something that could be worked on, or was it beyond improvement in any case?

Suppose, for example (and here Mrs. Bannister's thoughts strayed uneasily), suppose the doctors could do nothing, by way of a cure: could anything *else* be done for Esther Costello? Could her mind somehow be reached—could she be taught the deaf-and-dumb language? A handful of other people had succeeded in this, but it had always seemed an outright miracle. How did you initiate such a miracle, not knowing what material you were working on? *And how much was she, Mrs. Bannister, going to concern herself in the effort?*

The many questions nagged her, as she waited for the

American Consulate to move; and there was no one to help
her to answer any of them. She would sit opposite Esther
in the silent room, and stare at her for long minutes at a time:
speculating, hoping, wondering about the future. If one half-
closed one's eyes, the girl was comfortingly normal—a pale,
long-legged child, in a short blue dress and white socks: a
schoolgirl, in fact, on the verge of growing up. (Oh God!
thought Mrs. Bannister suddenly: how did one explain *that*?
It was bound to happen soon. . . .) But one could not
really close one's eyes to anything about her: she was *not*
normal, she was hopelessly handicapped; she remained a
terrible responsibility and, if the doctors failed, a terrible
problem.

Once, in urgent need of reassurance, Mrs. Bannister
experimented. She did so hesitantly, unable to rid herself
of the feeling that she was indulging some questionable
impulse, that her act was indecorous, that this was what the
newspapers meant by 'interference'. . . . But the outcome
was so heart-warming that she soon forgot her earlier
reluctance.

Struck by a sudden doubt, she had wanted to find out if
Esther still remembered simple words, if such a thing as a
door or a chair was still known as a door or a chair, within
the appropriate corner of her head. The girl might have
forgotten everything, she might have twisted everything
back to front. Inside that derelict brain, the word for 'door'
might now be 'floor' or 'whore'. . . . Mrs. Bannister wanted
to know, once more, what the material was like.

When at last she resolved to put it to the test, the two of
them were sitting in their suite before dinner: the girl relaxed
in her usual arm-chair, with Mrs. Bannister opposite her.
Here, in the evening dusk, it was warm and peaceful: the
sound of traffic, and the newsboys shouting the *Liverpool Echo*,
reached them faintly from seven floors below.

While, earlier, she had been revolving the problem in
her mind, something she had once read, or a photograph
she had seen, had occurred to Mrs. Bannister. It had concerned lip-reading—but lip-reading by touch and by the
vibration of sound. She must have read it or seen it a very
long time ago, but now it had returned to her, pricking her
imagination. If the two of them experimented on the same
lines, it would mean that Esther would put her hand over
Mrs. Bannister's mouth, to try to *feel* what she was saying.

Mrs. Bannister had thought a lot about it, and now she
was going to try it.

There was no harm in the idea, she told herself, quelling
—not for the first time—some faint distaste or reluctance
within her. It was simply a hand touching a face, the face
of another woman. Why should Esther mind that? It was
not forcing her, it was not—anything out of the ordinary.

Mrs. Bannister glanced round the room. They wanted a
word, she thought. A simple word, a word the girl was sure
to have known in the past. They wanted one word only,
and then she could put Esther on trial with it.

Between them was the electric fire, glowing softly in the
twilight of the room. On an impulse, Mrs. Bannister crossed
to Esther, and, putting a hand under her arm, raised her, as
she always did when she wished to indicate that it was time
to move or to walk. Esther rose obediently, and stood
waiting. Mrs. Bannister led her the two steps to the electric
fire, took Esther's hands in her own, and held them out to the
warmth.

She watched the small hands uncurling as they felt the
glow of the fire-bar. Then she raised Esther's right hand,
and put it over her own mouth. She felt, with secret pleasure,
the young fingers gripping her trustfully about the lips and
chin. She spoke into the hand, enunciating with slow
care:

"Fire." And again: "Fire."

She repeated the whole manoeuvre, holding Esther's hand to the warmth, and then clasping it to her own mouth, and saying "Fire", slowly and with special emphasis. At the third time, Esther's face suddenly brightened, and she nodded. Mrs. Bannister repeated: "Fire", and felt the small fingers gripping and curling round her mouth, as if the girl feared to lose this linking word, which had suddenly reached her through lips she had never seen and never touched before: as if she clung desperately to the promise of speech. Tears came to Mrs. Bannister's eyes as she felt the fingers continuing to grope and to welcome. . . . She repeated, yet once again: "Fire", for sheer pleasure in this warm communion. The hand on her mouth, like a baby's clutch, was a sensual blessing.

At the repetition, Esther nodded once more. And then she did something else, something Mrs. Bannister had not bargained for. She opened her own mouth, and stood tense for a moment, her lips trembling, her throat working under the smooth childish skin. Then a sound came from between her lips.

It was not the sort of sound Mrs. Bannister had ever heard before. It was something between a groan and a cheep, ill-pitched and shapeless, though produced with mortal effort. But it *was* a sound, a single sound: to an eager mind, it was a word; and, with great love and faith, it was the word: 'Fire'.

By contrast with this moving moment, which seemed to put a seal of hope upon the future, the Atlantic crossing to New York was a frightful ordeal.

There were head-seas all the way over, and it was rough —far too rough for a medium-sized ship trying to keep to a seven-day schedule. The 7,000-ton liner was thrown about with great violence and spite, and so were her passengers;

and so, in an A-deck outer cabin, was Esther Costello who, pitifully sea-sick, terrified all the time, weeping with doubt and fear, lost much human ground during the nine days at sea.

There was nothing that Mrs. Bannister or the stewardess could do for her, save watch her all the time, and try to prevent her hurting herself. There was no conceivable way of explaining, to a blind and deaf child who had seen nothing bigger than a village pond, that here was the sea, and this was what it did to ships and to the people in them. There was no way of explaining that it was not the earth which was heaving and lurching with such drunken fury, but something else which, though wickedly active, was still permissible within nature. They simply had to make her endure, chancing the fact that she would feel herself betrayed by the senseless change from comfort to violence, and might lose faith and heart, and that all the benefits stored up in the previous weeks might ebb away again.

"If this was happening to me," said Mrs. Bannister to the stewardess, as together they watched Esther clinging to her bunk in terror, while the ship, poised giddily on the crest of a huge wave, swayed downwards towards its yawning trough: "if this was happening to me, and I didn't know what it was, I'd think people were punishing me on purpose. . . ."

She did what she could, by her presence and her warm touch, to convey to Esther that she was not in disgrace, that care and love were still wrapped round her, that they were all undergoing this crude torment together. But many times, when the girl cried out to feel the world beneath her rocking, it seemed as though the young heart, newly cherished, was being given too sudden and too brutal a test.

Mrs. Bannister spent virtually the whole voyage in the cabin, leaving it now and then for a brief walk round the heaving, deserted deck, and then going below to shelter

again. She took all her meals with Esther. Only on the last
day, when the westerly gale died, and the shelter of the
American coast-line steadied the ship again, did she emerge
from the self-contained, painful world below.

But she emerged, oddly, to find herself something of a
heroine.

Perhaps the stewardess had been talking, or possibly the
ship's doctor, whom she had called in one evening to give
Esther a sedative, and to whom she had told her whole history.
But whatever the source, the ship seemed to know all about
Esther and herself, and when she appeared in the ornate,
crowded bar for a drink before lunch, she found herself fêted
by a number of total strangers who seemed as eager to hear
the story from her own lips, as they were to pay for that
drink, and the next, and the next. They were headed by a
bushy-haired old man who, by his heavy-weight charm and
bland, booming self-assurance, was almost certainly a United
States senator.

"It's a fine thing you're doing, ma'am," was his initial
approach—backed by a fluent series of dry Martinis—and
the phrase (which echoed the Vice-Consul in Liverpool)
was the keynote of all comment. Mrs. Bannister was established as the centre of a widening circle of people, all intent
on showing their interest and goodwill, and all seemingly
overjoyed that on the last day of the voyage the relenting
weather had made this possible. An Englishman said it was
a dashed sporting effort; a famous actress proclaimed that it
was pure Hollywood. An unknown man, already drunk,
with a mulberry complexion, offered even money against
a complete cure. An Episcopalian bishop, ill at ease in this
sodality, promised his prayers. An old lady wanted to see
Esther, a young one wanted her autograph. The Captain
himself, toasting her at lunch, was complimentary and
solicitous. The ship's doctor winked at her. (So it was he

who had spread the word.) A Brazilian of olive aspect pinched her knee, and appeared scandalized when she did not scream. A child in a cowboy suit, with food round its mouth, stared at her, and said: "Gee. . . ."

It might have been a familiar ship-board routine to film stars and politicians, but to Mrs. Bannister it was all novel, and all wonderful. After the long days spent cooped up in the cabin, with a stolid stewardess and a sick, terrified girl for company, there was immense exhilaration in thus emerging as a public figure, in spreading butterfly wings and finding that they had the world's recognition and the world's acclaim. It was the first time that anything of this sort had happened to her: and the fact that at its core was hidden so strange an object, the blind girl in the womb of the ship, seemed to give the whole happy session a secondary aspect, one of dedication. When, at intervals, Mrs. Bannister withdrew below to look at Esther, it was like the High Priestess of the oracle leaving the pilgrims in order to visit the *arcana* within.

"Must be getting a little high," she told herself caustically, when this last thought struck her. She had looked in on Esther after dinner, and was standing in the door of the cabin. The girl lay passive now: the shaded lamp at the bunk-side showed her face pale and exhausted, but free of the look of wild strain it had worn during the past few days.

Mrs. Bannister crossed the cabin floor, and laid her hand gently on Esther's forehead. The girl started, as she always did when she was touched suddenly, and then her brow relaxed and she smiled, and put up her own hand to cover the visiting one.

"Only one more night, honey," said Mrs. Bannister. "Then we'll get you right, for sure."

Every mile the ship made westwards, every turn of the screw, seemed to be bringing them nearer to sanity and hope.

There was one more item in the voyage, and it was added the same night, when Mrs. Bannister left Esther and returned to the saloon.   There, the last ship's concert was just getting under way; and after it, at the suggestion of the old senator (who made a speech in which the words 'little lady' occurred eleven times), a collection was taken for Esther Costello.   It was, in the senator's phrase, "to help the little lady in her sore trouble".

The takings were handed to Mrs. Bannister, by the purser, when she was squaring her bar-account next morning.

They totalled seventeen hundred dollars.

CHAPTER FIVE

THE New York papers picked up the scent very quickly. Mrs. Bannister had hardly reached the hotel overlooking Central Park, ordered coffee, and put Esther to bed, before two reporters and a photographer were hammering at the door, in search of the story they were later to headline as 'STRICKEN COLLEEN SEEKS SIGHT, HEARING, SPEECH'. Mrs. Bannister, whose home for thirty years had been Boston, had never cared for New York until this moment. But so ready was its welcome, and so flattering its notice, that she found herself warming to it immediately.

She was lucky in the moment of her arrival, since a dearth of news had left a margin of public interest to spare. But the story itself was so good, and Esther Costello, in the first photograph ever taken of her, looked the part so completely—young, pretty, and forlorn—that there was a swift and impressive follow-up. In particular, large numbers of women reporters, eager to jerk their quota of tears from the promising facts, climbed in with a will. Their variants on the theme—one of which achieved brief notoriety, being couched in the form of an advertisement under the flaring headline 'YOUNG GIRL WANTS TWO OF EVERYTHING'—ensured that within a few days most people in New York knew the story, and speculated on its next development.

Of this, Mrs. Bannister was not sure. She had visualized a couple of days in New York, and then the journey home—home to Boston, where there were friends to welcome her, and doctors to take Esther in hand. In the end, she stayed a fortnight. She did not put Esther under treatment, since this might have prolonged their stay indefinitely; instead, the time was passed agreeably in shopping and in newspaper interviews. Telegrams from two friends in Boston indicated that the news had been picked up there, and that the same sort of welcome awaited her in her home town. But it gave her, besides the first feeling of satisfaction, a small twinge of doubt. This part of the adventure was fine. But what if there were an anti-climax, what if Esther proved to be beyond medical aid? How would the papers play that one?

It was this uncertainty that made her, within a few hours, pack up and put herself and Esther on the train for Boston. Her common sense, of which she had plenty, told her that she must now stop fooling around, and get to work properly.

Three friends met her at the station, as she had hoped they would; they were Mrs. Forbes, Mrs. Tempest, and Paul Marchant. The two ladies were of her own age, though sunk far deeper in the cushion of matrimony than she had ever been. Mrs. Forbes was large, and married to a cotton-broker; Mrs. Tempest was small, and widowed by a bank-manager. Paul Marchant, a dapper man of forty-five who dealt in hardware (though on a very large scale), was known to their circle as the man who wanted to marry Belle Bannister. The fact that he had worn this label for upwards of ten years, without action on either side, had never seemed to affect its validity. These three were her best friends in Boston; and the fact that they were there to welcome her made it a true homecoming.

As the train drew to a standstill she saw them all waiting in an expectant group, and she waved vigorously. They moved forward to greet her. After four months, nothing was changed. Mrs. Forbes had a new hat, Mrs. Tempest an old one; Paul Marchant carried a bunch of American Beauty roses. Mrs. Bannister was drawn down into their circle, with kisses and cries all round. It was like stepping, gratefully, into a warm bath.

"We read about you," said Mrs. Forbes, after the first greetings were over. "Quite famous, darling." She was good-natured enough to sound genuinely pleased.

"Where's the girl?" asked Mrs. Tempest. "Is she really blind?"

"Have you gone crazy, Belle?" said Paul Marchant.

Mrs. Bannister laughed. "She's inside. I'll bring her out in a minute." And to Paul Marchant: "Just a little bit, darling. I did it on the spur of the moment. You'll all have to help me."

Beyond them, three men, two with cameras, were moving up like skirmishers, intent on invading the party.

"The *Star-Telegram* called me up," said Mrs. Forbes in explanation. "I had to say when you were getting in."

"That's O.K.," said Mrs. Bannister.

At her elbow the train-conductor, who had been a useful ally during the past few hours, said, "Shall we help her down, ma'am?"

"Yes, do that. . . ." Mrs. Bannister turned, and there was Esther, poised at the top of the coach steps, with another man in uniform at her elbow. A flash gun went off, and then a second. Mrs. Bannister reached up to take Esther's hand: a voice said "Hold it!" and there was a third flash as she paused, automatically, and waited for release.

Mrs. Forbes said: "It's just like the movies."

Paul Marchant said: "Don't let them bother you."

"That's O.K.," said Mrs. Bannister again. "We're used to it."

Esther, having been helped down to the platform, stood, as usual, in patient composure. The others looked at her, momentarily without comment, since what they were looking at was less remarkable than they had been expecting. They saw a fair-haired schoolgirl in a short blue dress, pale, un-smiling, and still. She had an inward look about the eyes, but that was all that marked her out from the world.

"She's pretty," said Mrs. Tempest after a pause. She started forward, a small woman ready to do the right thing, hand outstretched. "Do we——"

"Don't touch her," said Mrs. Bannister proprietorially. "It frightens her."

"But can't the girl say *anything*?" asked Paul Marchant, struck by this particular aspect of femininity.

Mrs. Bannister shook her head. "She hasn't seen or heard or spoken a word for over three years."

"Poor kid," said Mrs. Forbes. "I hope the doctors can do something for her."

They were all slightly ill-at-ease, like worshippers in a strange church, confronted with something so far from normal that they feared to show their awkwardness in dealing with it. Almost any word or action could be the 'wrong thing'. But now there came an interruption.

"Pardon me," said the hovering newspaperman, the one without the camera, to Mrs. Bannister. "Are you Mrs. Ballater?"

"Mrs. Bannister," she answered, nodding.

"Can you let me have something for the *Star-Telegram*?" He jerked his head towards Esther. "I guess that's the girl. How old is she?"

He questioned, and Mrs. Bannister answered readily, for some time; he was a tall and personable young man, and his obvious interest was pleasing. There was much that he was curious about—the sort of home Esther had come from, the details of the accident, the plans for helping her now. The group stood silent as the two of them talked: occasionally the others glanced at Esther, and then away again, while Esther stood motionless, waiting for direction.

C

Finally the newspaperman finished his questions with: "What gave you the idea, in the first place?"

Mrs. Bannister smiled. "I just wanted to help her, I guess. It was the village where I was born."

"It's a wonderful thing to do," said the newspaperman cordially, "and I hope it works out." He closed his notebook. "Thanks a lot, Mrs. Bannister."

"Sure you've got that right?" asked Mrs. Bannister. "B-A-N-N-I-S-T-E-R."

His eyes flickered over her face for a second, knowing and yet non-committal. "I'll get it right," he said, after a moment. "Don't you fret."

The things they now did to Esther Costello would not have disgraced a progressive African tribe whose witchdoctors, competing against the unknown, pooled their traditional arts and rivalled each other in inventing new ones.

First they looked at her, outside and in, from every angle; shaking their heads the while, and waggling their beards. They X-rayed her head and her neck: they peered down her throat: they wormed their way into her ears: they stared with bright lights at her eyes. Then they started active warfare. They shaved off nearly all her hair. They fed her strange meals, and starved her for weeks at a time. They took out two of her wisdom teeth. They gave her every variety of shock-therapy that had yet been devised. They tried to startle her with loud noises, they jabbed her with instruments. They removed a two-inch circle of the dome of her skull, and wired it back on again with three millimetres more clearance. They psycho-analysed her, so far as this could be done without answers of any sort, endeavouring to find out what she liked and what she feared. They tried the effect of pain, involving treatment to the soles of the feet, and pleasure, which was focused elsewhere. They gave her chicken-pox on purpose, and measles by mistake. They brought her temperature down to eighty-six degrees, then made her blood boil with fever. They evolved a plan for impregnating her, and then aborting her after three months; but it was thought that, at fourteen-and-a-half, she was a year too young. Instead they dipped her in thermal baths, and planted blisters at the nape of her neck, and gave her generous injections of insulin, and an induced orgasm under pentothal.

As a climax to all this, they subjected her to an immense electric shock which prostrated her for a week. Then they sat back, and waited.

When she came to, Esther Costello could neither see, hear, nor speak.

To the doctors, this appeared a particularly offensive outcome, and they would have tried again, with louder noises, thicker whips. But Mrs. Bannister, following from day to day and month to month the frightful campaign she herself had initiated, had already had enough. Each time she had gone to see Esther in hospital (where the girl had spent nearly a year) she had hoped that the fearful things they were doing to her would justify themselves by success; and each time, when there was only failure to record, she was left with a diminished belief in the rightness of what they were doing, as well as a sense of shame for the past. After the electric shock-treatment, she knew that they must do no more. . . . It did not matter that she was closely involved in this failure, and that it meant the public defeat of all her hopes. There was an end to every journey, whether it was down the road to the post office, or the three thousand miles from Cloncraig to Boston: and people of common sense and normal will know where that end was, and what you did when you got to it. You turned back.

Thanking the doctors, and settling their not inconsiderable

bills, she took Esther home to her Commonwealth Avenue apartment. There she gave an interview to the newspapers, which duly recorded 'NO HOPE FOR ESTHER COSTELLO' (for the name was now widely known), and let the matter drop. Then she sat down to think; and since she felt the need, and did not mind acknowledging it, she drew her friends round to help her decide the next step.

There were only two courses to choose from, once they had abandoned the solace of medical aid: Esther could stay, or she could go. When they came to review these choices, it seemed that the women were for one alternative, and Paul Marchant for another; the division was along lines of female sentiment versus male realism, as traditional and as banal as sex itself.

With mixed motives, Paul Marchant wanted Esther shipped home to Ireland straight away. He produced some of his arguments for inspection, suppressed others; the plain fact was that he had become jealous of her. Esther seemed to take up far too much of Mrs. Bannister's time, and of her money also; Marchant was a comparatively rich man, but if he ever did marry Belle Bannister—the idea flowed on one day, ebbed on another—it would be a pity if her comfortable fortune had been dissipated meantime. He feared that she was making a fool of herself over Esther: a single philanthropic effort was all right, but not one that went on and on. . . . It was hard to put into words his view that Esther Costello had become a damned nuisance; but he did his best, using the phrases he hoped would carry most weight.

"She should go," he declared, with all the brisk finality born of thirty years in the hardware business. "She's doing no good here—a cure's out of the question. It would be the kindest thing of all to send her back."

The three women looked at him. They were all together in the big, comfortable apartment: the noise of traffic along

Commonwealth Avenue, muted by double windows, rose to them faintly. It was a protected world, good to stay in, harsh to leave. If Esther were to be thrust out of it, the women at least would not be able to rest so easy; for those who were allowed to stay thus encushioned must feel, as executioners, doubly guilty, doubly smug.

Mrs. Forbes sighed. "It seems such a terrible idea, to send her back to that village. I think she should stay here in America." She looked across at Mrs. Bannister. "She needn't stay right here, of course. There must be all sorts of homes and hospitals."

"M'm," said Mrs. Bannister.

"She *can't* stay here," said Paul Marchant. "This is a private apartment—you don't want to turn it into an institution." He paused. "And institutions—the real kind—cost money."

Mrs. Tempest, small and bustling, took that one up. "Money shouldn't count at all. The girl's helpless—she's got to be protected. You can't measure a thing like that in dollar bills."

Marchant smiled ironically. He was about to hazard his guess that her late husband, the bank-manager, must be spinning in his grave right now, but he suppressed the remark. With women, you never quite knew what was funny and what was not. . . . Instead he said:

"Belle's not made of money, all the same. You've *got* to measure it up in dollars, to a certain extent."

"It's a terrible thought, to send her back," said Mrs. Forbes, continuing to speak for her conscience. "Aren't there funds or organizations that could help out? How about Henry Ford?"

"He died," said Paul Marchant.

"I mean, didn't he leave money for things like this? Or was it Andrew Mellon?"

Mrs. Bannister broke her long silence. "I took the thing on," she said, with quiet determination. "I'm not going to shrug it off on to other people, just when it gets difficult."

"But you took it on when it seemed likely that she could be cured," objected Paul Marchant.

"Then it's worse still, now," said Mrs. Bannister. But she did not elaborate. She was thinking.

She was thinking of the desperate disappointment which the doctors' reports had brought, and of how best she could equate the future with her hopes and with her conscience. As had happened on the ship, she was aware all the time of Esther, hidden somewhere within the apartment: she knew exactly how the girl would be looking at this moment, sitting in an arm-chair in her small room, with its simplified furniture and its lack of hazard. The bell-push was close under her hand, the way to the bathroom had been memorized for many weeks past, the world for her was blessedly at peace: this day was just like another day, with no more shocks, no more crude manipulation.

Esther was nearly fifteen now, and, having recovered from her time in hospital, was growing very pretty; the slight body had filled out, and it was obvious that she would be, within a measurable number of years, a young woman of singular attraction. It had been all right about her 'growing-up', thought Mrs. Bannister, letting her memory stray: the girl had taken the whole thing for granted, and had dealt with it competently. Mrs. Bannister had forgotten that Esther had lived, as a child, so close to nature, surrounded by farmyard practices and peasant frankness. That worry was over—or rather (she smiled to herself) there was only one other thing to worry about, in *that* connection. . . . It was quite a thought that one day she might have to explain sex to this pretty child. Or would that be unnecessary also?

But, apart from the vague future, what was to be done

now? The newspapers had been pretty good about the whole thing—they might have played it up for the wild-goose chase it was—but that headline 'NO HOPE FOR ESTHER COSTELLO' still rankled all the time, reminding her that she had promised one thing and performed another. It was not her own fault, but that made no difference: if she had assumed responsibility through her good-hearted ignorance, she had assumed it none the less. Over this, her friends were not helping her at all: they only saw the thing as a problem in arrangement, when really it was a moral issue, like the war, like keeping your word to a child. Paul wanted the girl out of the way, because she threatened to become a nuisance in *his* life; the others, realistic in another way, wanted her to rid herself of the responsibility, for her own comfort.

She herself was determined, somehow, to justify what she had done; so that no one could sneer or laugh at her, and the newspapers would see that it was *really* something after all, and Esther would live again.

While they had been talking—and for some time before— she had been thinking of another idea: perhaps the best idea of all, though it was something entirely outside her experience, and would in fact involve a completely new life for her. It had sprung from the conviction that, having brought Esther so far—in time, in space, in hope—she could not now leave her. They were bound together, by her own act of mercy . . . But she was not yet ready to talk about it: before she told them the astonishing proposal, and before she did anything about it, she must do a lot more thinking.

She said: "We're not getting anywhere with this. Let's leave it. How about a drink?"

Mrs. Bannister waited for Paul Marchant in the bar of the Copley-Plaza Hotel. It was the Merry-Go-Round bar, and she sat at a table on the merry-go-round itself, the circular

platform-and-counter which, turning steadily throughout
the drinking day, seemed to be assuring the customers that
the world was a gay and whirling place, with alcohol at its
core.   It was a favourite haunt of Mrs. Bannister and Paul,
and they often spent an evening there, secure in their ten-
year companionship, needing nothing for contentment save
the room idling past them, and lazy, petering-out talk, and
two drinks an hour.   But this evening, she thought, was not
likely to be a contented one; for she had come to her decision
at last, and she would tell him about it in a moment, and he
was not going to like what he heard.

Here he was, anyway.

Marchant came into the bar briskly, saw her at once, and
stepped up on to the platform.

"Hi, Belle!"   He sat down at her table.   "How many
drinks ahead are you?"

"Hallo, Paul."   Now we're both on the merry-go-round, she
thought; but this time he's going to step off, and I'm going to
stay on—maybe for ever. . . .   "No drinks.   I waited for you."

"We'll soon cure that."   He ordered daiquiris, and, when
they were brought, unexpectedly downed most of his at one
gulp.   Paul knows, she thought on the instant, sipping
her own rum less needfully.   Or he's got an idea of what
I'm going to say, and he's going to fight it all he can.   That
was what the quick drink had been for.

She said, as she always did: "How was the day?"

"The day was O.K."   He looked round the room in
search of further comment, and found none.   The bar had
moved through a quarter-segment of a circle before he said:
"It's. time I had a holiday though.   And you too.   How
about it?"

"I'm not sure that I can, now, Paul.   Too many things
to do."

He took that, correctly, for the warning shot it was, and

decided to close with the enemy. After one more quick
swallow, he said: "How's Esther?"

"Fine."

"Have you made your mind up yet?"

"Yes, Paul."

"What's it to be?"

"I want her to stay here."

Marchant nodded to himself, showing no surprise at this
defeating turn of events. His face was serious, and with-
drawn, as if the thoughts he had on this subject were so
different from hers that he did not know how to communicate
them without anger.

"I think it's a great pity, Belle. And I think you're going
to find that out."

"Maybe. It's what I want to do, anyway. I've thought
a lot about it. I just feel that I can't send her back now."

"But what's going to happen? How long are you going
to keep her?"

"There's no time limit. I'm going to see if she can be
trained."

"You mean, you'll put her into an institution?"

"No. I'll have her taught the deaf-and-dumb language,
and whatever they do for the blind—Braille, and things like
that."

"But she can learn all that far better if she's in an
institution."

"No." Mrs. Bannister paused, to marshal her strength.
"Because I'm going to learn it with her."

"*What?*" This, at least, he had never foreseen. "You
mean, talk to her yourself?"

"Yes."

"You must be raving mad! Who's going to look after
her, anyway? She needs a nurse—a companion."

"I'll be that too."

c*

"You must be mad," he repeated.

"I'm not, Paul." She leant across to take his hand—a hand totally unresponsive, a hating hand. "I started this thing for Esther, and I'm going on with it. I don't want her to become a—an orphan again. I want her to have a normal life, in a home of her own. And I'm the only one who can give it to her."

"But you must be crazy," he said, for the third time. He was still flabbergasted, and anger was coming up to aid him. "It means—hell, it means dedicating your whole life to her. It's a full-time job. You'll have to learn everything from the beginning. And the girl's a dead loss, anyway—how can she *begin* to talk?"

"Why not? They've done it with other people."

"But it takes years even to get started."

"That doesn't matter."

"And there's no *need* for it." He drew a deep breath. "I can understand you wanting to give her a chance in life —though I think it's a hopeless proposition—but you don't have to get involved in it yourself. If you do, you'll be tied to her for as long as you live."

"I am tied, already."

"But not like this." He paused. "What about me?"

"How do you mean?"

"How much time will you have for me, if you're going to act as keeper to this girl?"

Mrs. Bannister looked away from him. This was the crucial point, and there could be no evasion of it.

"I know it's bound to make a difference, Paul. At the beginning, anyway. It means I'll have to go to school again, and carry her along with me. We'll have to accept that."

"I won't accept it." His voice was rising. "I'm tired of waiting."

A man at a neighbouring table, sitting with a sulky,

rebellious-looking girl, caught his eye, and called out: "You and me both. But what can we do?"

Marchant smiled briefly, enough for good manners, and then came back again to Mrs. Bannister. "You know how we're placed. We're——"

"We're lovers, and we've been lovers, on and off, for ten years. So what did you mean by 'tired of waiting'?"

"I'm always asking you to marry me."

"I know." She smiled at him. "Dear Paul—you'd get the shock of your life if I said I would."

But he was now very angry, and not to be charmed. "If you do this, Belle, it's the end of us."

"I hope not. It needn't be. I'd like to have your help."

"I'm damned if I'll help you. Of all the crazy ideas. . . . Why should I help you to make a fool of yourself? Do you think I'm going to hang about playing second-string to a half-dead girl who should have been put out of her misery years ago?"

"That's a wicked thing to say."

"It's true."

"I'm going to do it, Paul."

"Then I'm getting out, here and now." He stood up. "I mean it, Belle."

"So do I." She was not angry, but her determination had sharpened enormously as she listened to him. In truth, she had had enough of domineering men, and of emotional blackmail, and of other people trying to refashion her will for her. There had been enough of all those things, in ten years of marriage, to last a lifetime; and no lover was going to reintroduce the routine. . . . "I shall learn to talk to Esther—somehow—and then I'm going to teach her all I can, and bring her up properly. She'll start her life again, where it left off at the age of ten, and I'm going to fix it for her."

"Then you'll fix it without any help from me."

Paul had stepped off the merry-go-round, and, absurdly, was walking along to keep pace with their table. It was all very symbolical, she thought—and much too difficult to work out now.

"I'll fix it," said Mrs. Bannister. "Don't you worry."

"O.K." He turned on his heel. "Have it like that."

"Goodbye," she called after him. "Goodbye, for about a year."

CHAPTER SIX

IT was a curious year, the year that now ensued; a year of retreat, a year of dedication. Paul Marchant, proud and angry, kept to his word and dropped out of her life altogether; and rid of this male complication, and the emotional tie that went with it, she was free to concentrate on the task she had set herself. Many things happened, in the outside world, that might have distracted her: there were the Russians, there was rearmament, there were atom spies, there was a Communist under every bed. But Mrs. Bannister seemed able to turn her back on all such complications: for her, there was only one person, and one idea—Esther Costello, and the need to reach her mind and be reached by it.

Many times, when the fund of patience which this demanded was drawn wire-thin, she doubted the rightness of what she was doing. Her new decision—as with the original one, two years ago in Cloncraig—had been a compound of many factors and many feelings: she had wanted to rescue Esther, she had wanted to finish what she had started, she had wanted to retrieve the public defeat which the newspapers had summed up in the words 'NO HOPE FOR ESTHER COSTELLO'. She might even have needed to demonstrate to Paul that she was a free agent, a personality in her own right, and not dependent on him for inspiration of any sort. . . . But whatever had driven her to volunteer for the job, there was no doubt that it was a slow, complicated, and enormously

difficult affair which would only be solved by complete,
single-minded concentration.

Nor would there ever be a dividend for her, in any event.
That was obvious. Success would tie her to Esther for life;
and failure would be a waste of time so absurd and so morti-
fying that she would never be able to trust herself with a
fundamental decision again.

But still she laboured, and hoped, and watched. When
the amazing results began to come, when Esther grew to
humanity again, it seemed no more than was owed to all the
immense care that had gone before. For years afterwards,
when people talked of 'miracles', Mrs. Bannister was always
secretly annoyed. This thing had been *worked* for: nothing
so lazy, so feeble, so inept as a miracle, had had any
part in it.

The fantastic story started at the local Deaf-and-Dumb
Institute; and there, the first thing they found out about
Esther Costello was that she *could* spell. At Mrs. Bannister's
suggestion, they began with the blessed word 'fire', which
she had been able to 'get through' to Esther while they had
been waiting at the Adelphi Hotel in Liverpool, and which
she had answered so movingly. Then they combined it with
something else: whenever they said 'fire', they tapped four
times in the palm of her hand, for the word's four letters.
This puzzled and defeated Esther for many weeks, until they
began to fear that the whole conception of spelling, which
had been hers five years before, had vanished in the blank
intervening time. But there came a day when she suddenly
smiled, and tapped four times back, and nodded, and tried
to make four separate noises in her throat. . . .

Then they taught her the four letters of the word 'fire',
using the normal deaf-and-dumb sign language on her fingers
and palm.

To 'fire' they presently added 'water'—dipping her hand in a bowl of water, giving five taps, and then going on to the individual letters themselves. The fact that 'fire' and 'water' had two letters in common, 'r' and 'e', seemed to give Esther tremendous pleasure. . . . Next came the word 'mouth', and thus they had, with these three simple words, taught her eleven different letters, including all the five vowels.

These eleven letters took nearly a third of a year to communicate. But after that, progress was a good deal quicker.

Mrs. Bannister learned at the same time, and soon it was she, and she only, who spelled out letters and words on Esther's hand, so that the girl could get used to her touch and they could establish the essential sympathy. They spent hours together, whispering, tapping, pressing the shape of letters on to each other's hands. They learned 'leg' and 'neck', 'face' and 'back': they learned 'chair' and 'table' and 'bed': they moved on to sentences—'I am hungry', 'I want to drink', 'It is time to go to bed'. It soon became clear that Esther was a girl of quick intelligence, and quick humour too: she was seizing on this child's guessing-game, which was so enormously important to her, because it satisfied many things within her—not only her hunger for the outside world, but the lively spirit she had left so far behind. Sometimes she would touch Mrs. Bannister's arm, and spell 'leg', or say 'fire' for 'water'; Mrs. Bannister would grow puzzled and depressed, until a smile on Esther's face told her that the girl was doing it on purpose, that this was the kind of joke with which she had teased other children, five years ago at the age of ten, and she hoped it might still be funny. . . . Whenever this happened, it brought Mrs. Bannister to the edge of tears. The idea that this child could, from her total darkness, conjure up a joke to amuse other people, seemed as wonderful and as touching as birth itself.

There came a day when Mrs. Bannister told Esther what had happened to her in the past.

She had been warned, both by the doctors and by the institute where she and Esther were originally trained, that she was not to do this. They all seemed to have the fixed idea that to explain the causes of Esther's present ruin would shock her, and increase her melancholy beyond a tolerable limit. But surely, thought Mrs. Bannister, Esther had had enough recent shocks to toughen her for life, and there was no melancholy to be increased—the girl was, in fact, now far more cheerful than half a dozen dreary doctors. . . . She might still have obeyed the warning, had not Esther brought the subject up herself. But when this happened, in a moving phrase which remained with her for long afterwards, Mrs. Bannister made up her mind to take the chance.

They had been sitting together in the apartment, having their usual two hours' practice—a daily routine of spelling out difficult words, learning new ones, and trying to increase the speed of their communication. They were now both very quick at this, and already there was developing between them a kind of shorthand—the letter 'R' for 'are', '2' for 'to', 'MT' for 'empty'—which would make it quicker still in the future. All such tricks seemed to bring wonderful pleasure to Esther, as if between them they were fooling the whole pedantic world. . . . There had been a pause in their movements, and then Esther suddenly gripped Mrs. Bannister's arm, and spelled out:

"Where are my eyes?"

Mrs. Bannister frowned, thinking at first that Esther was either 'practising' a sentence with no particular significance, or initiating another of her childish jokes. But the girl repeated the question, and to emphasize it she put up her hand and covered both her eyes, as if with a bandage. Mrs. Bannister paused, and then spelled:

"They were hurt."

"How?" asked Esther immediately.

"There was an——" began Mrs. Bannister. Then she hesitated. 'Explosion' might be too difficult. She altered it to: "A bang."

Esther thought for a moment. Then her hand went up again, and touched in turn her ears and her mouth, questioningly.

Mrs. Bannister said: "Yes."

"How long back?" was the next question.

"Five years," said Mrs. Bannister.

There was a longer pause now, while Esther appeared to be thinking. Five years must seem a lifetime—as indeed it was. . . . Then came another question:

"Will it get better?"

"Yes. Soon." Mrs. Bannister had no hesitation in giving such an answer, though it had not an atom of truth in it. In Esther's blind world, there could be little to live on save hope, and hope must never be denied her.

She had expected that the girl would continue on the same subject, but Esther's next phrase was a surprise.

"The other children."

Mrs. Bannister did not understand at first, and then she remembered. There had been other children with Esther when the 'bang' happened. Perhaps she had been wondering about them for five years. . . . It seemed better to tell the truth.

"They were killed."

There was another long pause, and then a small sob shook the girl, and tears started from her eyes and fell down her cheeks. At a loss, Mrs. Bannister waited, pressing Esther's hand. Then she added: "It was very quick."

Esther nodded. Her face now seemed to be remembering something, something that perhaps she should have remem-

bered before.   She drew the next sentence slowly, as if from
a very old lesson indeed.

"They are in Heaven," said Esther.

Then another quick question:

"Where is my mother?"

"She is far away," said Mrs. Bannister.   "This is a new
country."

"Who are you?"

"A friend."

Now came the longest pause of all, full of the past and the
future, and then Esther leant across and laid her cheek softly
on Mrs. Bannister's.   Both of them could feel the tears on
Esther's face, and presently the girl drew back and, with
a heart-rending smile—half apology, half loving trust—wiped
off the tears with her fingertips.   Then she spelled out, slowly
and with special emphasis:

"You are very good."

And she clutched Mrs. Bannister's hand as if it were a priest's
hand holding the sacrament, as if the two of them were lovers.

For Mrs. Bannister, it was moments like these—as time
went on, there was an increasing number of them—that
seemed at one stroke to wipe away all her besetting worries,
all the drudgery of nursing and housekeeping for so handicapped a human as Esther, all the wearisome job of learning
deaf-and-dumb speech, and becoming, at the age of forty-
five, a backward schoolgirl again.   At the Institute, where
the two of them had been under instruction, side by side,
for so many months, they were proud of Esther—and of
Mrs. Bannister too.   But they were proud of Mrs. Bannister
in a different way: to them, while Esther was a pretty prodigy,
Mrs. Bannister was a paragon of generosity and compassion.
They were sincere, religious-minded people, with a sense of
mission: the whole Institute, indeed, was a model of piety as

well as efficiency: and the sort of thing that Mrs. Bannister
was doing for Esther had, for them, a saint-like quality which
exactly matched their own instincts.

"One day," they used to say to her, "you'll have a great
reward for what you're doing."

"I hope so," Mrs. Bannister would say laughingly. "I
surely hope so."

They meant, clearly, that any reward that came her way
was likely to be in Heaven. Mrs. Bannister was not entirely
sure that this was what she meant herself.

When it was spring once more, and warm, Esther and
Mrs. Bannister tried the outside world again.

Hitherto, they had been very little out of doors: to keep
them occupied, there had been the hours of study at the
Institute, and then the crisp cold of a Boston winter, and the
attraction of the Commonwealth Avenue apartment—an
enclosed citadel that gave them comfort, and freedom from
the difficulty of coping with the demands of the normal world.
But now it was April, and the time of invitation: the spring
air, and the trees along the Avenue, and the sunshine, all
beckoned them to step outside their retreat—and when they
did so, the outside was not difficult at all.

Mrs. Bannister had feared all kinds of embarrassment when
she took Esther out in public, but there turned out to be no
complications of any sort. To the casual eye, the girl looked
normal, and she now walked surely and calmly, with the
minimum of guidance. People sometimes stared, of course,
but it was a friendly stare, not a critical or a malicious one;
and Mrs. Bannister, who had been afraid that she might
seem to be part of a freak-show, found that the world accepted
them as natural elements within itself.

The two of them went shopping: they went out in a motor-
boat on the Charles River: they walked in the sunshine, or

sat under the trees on Boston Common. This last was what Esther seemed to enjoy, above all else. She was content to sit for hours on one of the smooth wooden benches halfway up the hill, her face turned towards the warm breeze that blew in from the sea, her young body stretched at ease, her right hand clasped in Mrs. Bannister's, or flickering as her fingers 'talked'. Often she and Mrs. Bannister fed the pigeons, and there was always a special joy in Esther's face when she could coax one of the birds to perch on her shoulder or her wrist, or even, as sometimes happened, to lie still under the stroking of her gentle hand.

When the bird finally fluttered in her grasp, and then flew away, Esther always spelled out the word 'free'.

She and Mrs. Bannister talked all the time. Esther was now sixteen, and growing lovely: her slight body had filled out gracefully, and her face, warmed and animated, had a young glow upon it that would one day be distracting. . . . She was becoming a woman, and she could not fail to know it: indeed she was immensely curious about all this growing process, and what her face and body looked like, and her questions to Mrs. Bannister darted this way and that as the answers fed her secret thoughts.

More than once Mrs. Bannister noticed Esther touching her flanks and then her breasts, with inquisitive, almost wondering fingers. Once she did this, to Mrs. Bannister's embarrassment, when they were sitting out of doors on one of the Common benches; but luckily there had been no one near to see it, no man to stare or whistle. It came as a shock to Mrs. Bannister to realize, as she did vividly at that moment, that Esther might one day, in marriage, come to know and welcome another person's hands upon her.

Sex. . . . Esther skirted round the question, but the question was there all the time. She knew about babies— babies were just young animals, and human procreation was

for her a simple variation on farmyard practice. That much
had clearly been in her mind already, when she was struck.
What she did not know, and what she was avid to learn, was
her own place in this scheme, her own chance of womanhood. . . . The sentences would come pattering out like the
questions of a shy, persistent child.

"How old am I now?"

"Am I pretty?"

"Am I good to see?"

"What is this dress like?"

"How big is my waist?"

"Tell me about my legs."

And sometimes:

"Are there men near me?"

"Do men look at me?"

"What do they look at most?"

"Is my skirt long enough?"

"Do they look *here*?"

She was, perhaps, more frank than she would have been
if the words had actually been spoken. (So far, all their
conversation was in sign-language: Mrs. Bannister, and the
Institute, were experimenting with the idea of teaching Esther
to 'hear' what was said, by placing Esther's hand on her own
mouth when she talked, as they had first tried, long ago, in
Liverpool; but progress was still slow.) Mrs. Bannister dealt
with the questions as best she could, trying to minimize the
spring. . . . Sometimes she thought: I suppose I was like
this myself, when I was a teen-ager, only I didn't care to
advertise the fact. But Esther still lived in a simpler, childlike
world where a question—any question—was a thing to be
asked straight out.

Mrs. Bannister hoped—without much conviction—that
the answers she gave were enough to allay curiosity. If
Esther, at the age of sixteen, were to start exploring in any

direction, it would be altogether too much to deal with.

It was about this time that they met Mrs. Forbes and
Mrs. Tempest again. Mrs. Bannister had not seen her two
friends for many months; Paul Marchant had much influence
there, and Paul Marchant's theory was that Belle Bannister
was all mixed up, and ought to be left alone till she was
straightened out again. . . . But on one occasion, when
Esther and Mrs. Bannister were sitting on their usual
bench on the Common, the two ladies came upon them
suddenly—so suddenly that neither side could avoid the
encounter.

"Why, Belle Bannister!" It was Mrs. Forbes who took
the lead, as she usually did. "We haven't seen you in weeks
and weeks. Where've you been hiding?"

"I've been around. . . ." Mrs. Bannister bore her friends
no malice for their desertion: there had been more important
things for her to worry about. She gestured to the immobile
figure by her side. "You remember Esther Costello?"

Mrs. Tempest and Mrs. Forbes both nodded. It was just
like Belle to carry it off like this. . . . Mrs. Forbes took a
step nearer, peering short-sightedly at Esther.

"How is she?" she asked. "Still the same?"

"She's improved a lot," said Mrs. Bannister.

As if in illustration, she raised Esther's hand, and 'talked'
to her busily for a moment. "These are two of my friends,"
she was saying: "you met them a long time ago."

"What are you doing?" asked Mrs. Tempest inquisitively.

"Talking," said Mrs. Bannister. "Telling her about
you."

"Land's sakes!" exclaimed Mrs. Tempest. "You mean
she can understand that"—she paused, at a loss—"that stuff?
You mean you can talk it?"

"Yes," said Mrs. Bannister. "We can both talk it."

The two ladies looked down at them, disbelieving, but much impressed.

"She looks well," said Mrs. Forbes kindly. "Say something else to her, Belle. Just to show us."

Mrs. Bannister's fingers moved swiftly.

"What was that?" asked Mrs. Tempest.

"I was telling her to stand up."

As she spoke, Esther rose slowly, smoothing out her dress, and stood patiently erect.

"Land's sakes," said Mrs. Tempest again. "How do you do it?"

"Practice," said Mrs. Bannister briefly. "We've been studying at the Institute."

There was a long silence. Confronted with something so unexpected, and so far outside their experience, Mrs. Forbes and Mrs. Tempest preferred to think only of escape. Esther continued to stand between them, slimmer than anyone, still as a shadow at noon, the proof of something they could not bear to accept.

"You've done a wonderful job, Belle," said Mrs. Tempest, finally and weakly. "Paul will be pleased."

"I think not," said Mrs. Bannister.

The cue was unmistakable. The two ladies stepped back, preparing to take their leave.

"Goodbye," said Mrs. Forbes. "Lovely to see you again."

"Goodbye," said Mrs. Tempest. She looked at Esther. "You know, you and she ought to go on the stage."

"I hadn't thought of it," said Mrs. Bannister coldly.

"You really ought to," said Mrs. Tempest, nodding vigorously. "All that hard work. . . . Goodbye, Belle." She followed Mrs. Forbes down the pathway. Over her shoulder she called: "Or the radio. . . . Better think it over."

It seemed to Mrs. Bannister that she added something

else—something that sounded like 'film contract'. But it
was happily, mercifully lost in the distance.

That was not their only encounter on Boston Common.
It was on this same spot, under the trees in the warm summer
sunshine, that events, for both of them, presently took a fresh
and decisive turn.

They had been sitting on their favourite bench, halfway
up the hill: to Esther, the dappled sun on her face was a
warm blessing, while for Mrs. Bannister the hum of traffic
from the lower edge of the Common made a lazy, soothing
containment for her thoughts. Esther held a pigeon cushioned
in one hand, while with the other she fed it crumbs from a
paper bag: her face was intent and serious, her movements
gently precise. People passed them at a slow walk: more
pigeons, emboldened by sunshine and the promise of food,
fluttered round the bench: children wandered up to watch and
to comment. Presently a tall young man, hatless, in a
flannel suit and a brisk bow tie, glanced sideways at them as
he passed, and checked his step with a frown. Then he turned
back, and stood above them, still looking puzzled. Finally
he said:

"Mrs. Bannister?"

"Yes," said Mrs. Bannister tentatively. Then she recognized him. It was the reporter from the *Star-Telegram*, the
one who had met them at South Station, nearly three years
ago. She smiled, since he was young, and undoubtedly
good-looking, and said: "Hallo, there. . . ."

He smiled in answer. "Remember me?"

"Surely. Are you still on the paper?"

"Yes." His eyes turned towards Esther, and grew puzzled
again. "But. . . . Is this—her?"

"Yes—it's Esther Costello. Didn't you recognize her?"

"Only just." His blue eyes in the pleasant, assured face

were gazing at Esther with frank admiration. "I didn't even know she was still in America."

Mrs. Bannister laid her fingers on Esther's wrist, and spelled out a sentence or two. Esther looked up in the young man's direction, and smiled.

Confused, he smiled back, and said: "Hallo."

Mrs. Bannister shook her head. "No, she still can't hear. Or see."

"Good grief!" His face was now a study in wonderment. "You mean—but you were talking to her. How did *you* learn?"

"I learned. . . ." She smiled up at him, and then, on an impulse, patted the bench beside her. "It's quite a story. Would you like to hear it?"

He nodded vigorously, still looking at Esther. "Sure would. . . . She's beautiful, too. . . ." He transferred his gaze to Mrs. Bannister. "I'm Harry Grant," he said, and sat down at her side. "Tell me what's been happening."

She told him the story, and her own part in it, while he watched her and Esther by turns, and interrupted only to say, at one point: "It's a hell of a thing you took on." There was in his face a most agreeable admiration—and the face itself, Mrs. Bannister could not help noticing, was both attractive and intelligent. . . . Presently she broke off her story, to interject:

"What do you do on the paper?"

"Reporter—leg-man—anything that comes up. I'm still learning."

Mrs. Bannister smiled at him. "What's a leg-man?" She was not beyond flirting, obliquely, with a young man of this quality.

Grant smiled in answer. "The one that does the work. . . ." He turned back to Esther, studying her face and then her figure with an appraisement that was somehow not offensive. "That's a terrific story," he said at last. "I'd like to write it. Would you mind?"

"No," said Mrs. Bannister, after consideration. "Not if you think it's worth it."

"I'll say it's worth it."

There was a pause between them. She saw that he was already thinking hard—sorting phrases, choosing adjectives —and she kept silence momentarily, not wishing to interrupt. Presently Grant said:

"How long did it take you?"

"More than a year. It was slow at the start—I had to learn myself, from the very beginning. Like going to school again."

He said, looking at Esther's pretty face: "You did a wonderful job. . . . Does she know I'm sitting here?"

"Yes. I told her who you were, and she knows I'm talking to someone." She took Esther's hand again, and there was another pause while the two of them exchanged sentences. Then Mrs. Bannister said: "She wants to know what you look like."

Harry Grant grinned at her. "What do you say to that one?"

Mrs. Bannister smiled back, enjoying the moment. "I guess I'll keep that in *our* language."

Grant got up, his expression serious again. "I must go. But I'd like to write it. . . . Can I call you up if I get stuck?"

"Surely—do that. Or come round and see us." She gave him the number of the apartment, and then nodded goodbye. "Nice to see you again."

"More than that, for me." Like an excited child's, his face was beginning to express his wonder once more, and then he checked it, as if remembering some rule about not showing emotion. . . . He said, curtly: "Be seeing you," and walked determinedly away down the path, his body lithe, his arms swinging.

He seemed to take a lot of the sunlight with him.

CHAPTER SEVEN

HARRY GRANT waited in the *Star-Telegram* newsroom, his eyes on the open door leading to the news-editor's office. The news-editor was still tied up, as he had been for the past hour, with some fragrant domestic crisis that involved missing copy, Al Stevens (the paper's resident—though now absentee —drunk), a girl reporter who was trying to cover up for Al, and an editor who for no reason at all wanted a certain story in the paper—not next Tuesday, not tomorrow, but NOW. In newspaper life, it was just another of those rows; but that didn't rob it of a single degree of uproar, on this current occasion.

Grant had waited a long time, but he did not mind the delay. He did not mind anything connected with the *Star-Telegram*—not the endless hanging about, not the time wasted on stories that came to nothing, not having his stuff contemptuously spiked, not irregular hours, not living for days and nights on beer and peanut-butter sandwiches, not even love-nest murders with the gore still gleaming round the edges.

He loved newspapers, and everything that went with them. After four years on the *Star-Telegram*, and two on a local daily in Illinois, he still had, at the age of twenty-four, the dew of Illinois on his desires. They were, simply stated, to be a good newspaperman. Since he had patience, energy, and enthusiasm, all in ample supply, and he could write as well, he was likely to succeed. But no one had told him this, so far. Least of all Ryan, the news-editor, who now—and Grant jumped to his feet—was free.

Grant was one of the few people on the *Star-Telegram* who knocked on any door; when he did so, Ryan shouted: "Come in, for Christ's sake!" as if he had already had his fill of callers on that particular morning. Grant, entering, looked down at him in affection and awe—a stocky, grey-haired man with a tough, square face, sitting solid and compact behind his desk as if it were his favourite, long-held bastion: the man who had grudgingly given Grant this wonderful job, four years before. At the moment, Ryan was shovelling papers—any papers he could find—off his desk into the ring of wire baskets that surrounded him: doubtless, thought Grant, he knew what he was doing, but it was not an orderly process, not the kind of thing you read about in the correspondence courses on making good in journalism. . . . Then Ryan looked at him, glaring upwards under formidable eyebrows, and said:

"Harry Grant. . . . What have *you* lost?"

"Nothing." Most people on the paper called Ryan 'George': a few called him 'Sir' or 'Mr. Ryan': Grant, uneasily poised between these opposing compass-points, had survived four years without calling him anything at all. "I've done the piece on Esther Costello," he went on, tendering the typescript he had been nursing for the past hour. "You remember—I asked if I could write it."

"M'm. . . ." Ryan took the proffered sheets with a non-committal grunt, and then his eyebrows shot up as he weighed them in his hand. Theatrically amazed, he leafed through them. "I wanted a story, not a god-damn novel." Ryan put into the word 'novel' all the venom of the man who, however much he cherished the secret urge, would never get around to writing one. "How long is this epic?"

"About two thousand."

"Two *thousand*? And all art, I suppose?" Ryan made a gesture—not an encouraging gesture—of finality. "Try it

on Features," he said, in the voice of a man saying: Give it to
the first stray dog you meet.

"But it's news," said Grant, who was learning, though
slowly, how to get fifty per cent of his own way on the *Star-
Telegram*. "It really is the hell of a story. . . . Don't you
remember how she came here to be cured, and it didn't
work out, and now she gets along fine, all because of this
Bannister woman?"

"I'm crying," said Ryan. But he still held the typescript,
and he was now looking at the top page. Then up went
the eyebrows again. " 'A good deed in a naughty world',"
he read, mincingly, like a man biting on a lemon. "What
the hell sort of language is that?"

"Shakespeare," said Grant.

"I'm crying again," said Ryan. His fist smacked down
on the desk. "This is the *Telegram*," he said, with horrible
emphasis. "Down the street is the Colonial Theatre. Round
the corner is burlesque. *Here* is a *newspaper*! Choose which
one you want to write for. But for the love of Christ, don't
get them mixed!"

"It isn't all Shakespeare," said Grant rebelliously.

"Shakespeare will be relieved."

"It's a good story," repeated Grant, avoiding battle on
this uncertain ground. "As a story, it has everything. And,"
he concluded lamely, pointing, "it's all there."

"At two thousand words, it damned well ought to be."

Ryan began to read in silence, while Grant watched him
closely. He was still confident, in spite of the unpromising
start, because he had one fact to carry him: Esther Costello
was a wonderful story, worth every word he'd put into it,
worth the front page on most days of the week. . . . Presently
Ryan picked up his pencil, and held it poised over the copy—
an encouraging sign, thought Grant: he must want to print it
after all, if he thinks it's worth altering.

" 'If anyone is a saint,' " read Ryan suddenly, tonelessly, " 'if anyone is a saviour, it is Belle Bannister.' " He looked up. "That's to get the Catholic vote, I suppose."

Grant flushed. "She *is* that sort of woman. At least, she's doing that sort of job, where the Costello girl is concerned."

"I just wanted to know." Ryan began to read again, while Grant, momentarily hating him, stood silent and ill at ease. Perhaps he *had* tried a bit too hard with this story, perhaps the attempt at glowing prose was inclined to fall flat on its face, here and there.... Ryan lit on another phrase that he himself had not been sure of—'a hand reaching down to cherish and nourish a frail plant'—and read it aloud, with acid intonation, before he scored it out.

"We have a separate section for agriculture," he said. "They do pretty well. . . . Don't tell me it's Shakespeare again?"

"No," said Grant. "Not this time."

"Good," said Ryan. "I was getting worried about my education. . . . The trouble with you," he went on, looking up from the copy momentarily, "is that you're not nearly tough enough for this game. You're a sucker for this sort of thing"—he gestured towards the typescript—"you feel it instead of reporting it. It's as if you *want* to get involved in the world's troubles. You're in the wrong job, Harry. You ought to be running a home for old whores."

The first time Ryan had used the phrase 'wrong job', Grant's heart had nearly turned over. Now, after the hundredth or the thousandth time, he simply smiled, and said:

"I'll try it out for a little longer."

But while he waited, Grant pondered on what Ryan had just said. It was partly true, of course—he *wasn't* a tough reporter, he did feel for the people he was writing about, he did suffer for the betrayed, bleed with the murdered, strut with the triumphant. He wasn't tough, and he didn't try to be; instead, he reported with the heart. But he *did* report, with accuracy as well as feeling—that much, he was still sure of, and he thought Ryan was sure of it too. After all, Ryan had kept him on the *Star-Telegram* for more than four years. . . .

Ryan was near the end of the copy now: the picture of the amazing rescue of Esther Costello, the story of faith, love, and compassion actively at work, should be nearly complete in his mind. But now he read in silence, frowning horribly, occasionally drawing in his breath with a hiss. It sounded like surprise, derision, pain—anything but appreciation. Grant wished he'd written the story straight, instead of trying to persuade and to moralize. He didn't think Ryan would print it, after all. There was a spike on one corner of Ryan's desk: a spike that was cleared every morning, to reveal, printed on its base-plate, the one word 'NO'. That was where his story was going to finish up.

" 'This is, for each one of us, a ringing challenge'," quoted Ryan unexpectedly, in the same lemon-skin voice. "Which reminds me, I haven't paid my telephone account."

Grant flushed again.   "All right—take it out."

"No. I like it. Or rather, I don't like it, which means that thousands will."

Grant felt his heart jump, on the instant. "Then you *will* run it?"

"Sure." The news-editor looked up suddenly, and grinned. "Relax, Harry. It's O.K. It's good. Get some pictures as well."

The piece that the *Star-Telegram* carried two days later, under the first-time by-line 'by Harry Grant', was, in its own way, a minor classic of newspaper writing. True, it

was not straight reporting, or anything like it; it took sides,
it demanded sympathy, it aimed straight at the American
heart.   But as a story, it was a triumph, exhibiting brilliantly
the two elements in Esther Costello's progress so far—the
small miracle that had allowed her to live with the outside
world again, and the major personal undertaking that was
Mrs. Bannister's part in it.

It was all there, as Grant himself had said—the first
shattering disappointment, the slow reversal of fate, the
necessary love and faith, the twin emergence of Esther as the
prize pupil and Mrs. Banister as the caretaker of her sanity
and hope.   It was further limelit by three photographs
which, by luck or skill, caught exactly Esther's young beauty,
Mrs. Bannister's handsome competence, and their hard-won
joint communion.   Especially did the last picture, which
showed Esther, open-eyed and mouthed, reacting like an
unfolded flower to something which Mrs. Bannister had spelled
out to her, point the whole theme of Harry Grant's story—
that one human can do for another what Christ Himself
might be glad to admire.

The presentation was so good that the Esther Costello
story was bound to catch alight again.   It made, mainly, a
local sensation, but within those limits it took the town by
storm.

Most people—like Harry Grant—had thought that Esther
had either gone back to Ireland, or was hidden away in
the decent obscurity of an orphanage or an institution; to
learn that the woman who had befriended her in the first
place, and had been defeated, had not given up but had won
her fight in another way, touched the public heart upon a
tender nerve.   There was a solid and persuasive press follow-
up—interviews, leaders, more photographs.   There were
letters to the papers; there was an 'Esther Costello Christmas
Fund' which, though modest in scope, provided toys and

D

Christmas parties for a number of local blind children. The
Institute where Esther and Mrs. Bannister had originally
studied, benefited under at least four wills. Mrs. Bannister
talked on the radio, Harry Grant wrote three more articles.
On the lunatic fringe, Esther signed some autographs, and
received, by post, five proposals—two of them for marriage.
In Massachusetts, at least, the story and the people involved
were favourite public property.

A few weeks later, Mrs. Bannister returned home from
shopping to find some unusual visitors waiting for her. They
were two nuns, sitting side by side, uncertainly, on the edge
of her couch. There was an old one and a young one: forty
years separated them, but they were alike in shyness, softness
of voice, and determination.

The old one came straight to the point—or so she seemed
to think.

"It's our Day," she began, as if that single word 'day'
would explain the whole thing. "The Wednesday after
Easter Sunday. All the parents come, and we have speeches.
We want you to be there—and Esther too, perhaps—and tell
us your story."

Mrs. Bannister, not at a loss, but puzzled, asked where
they came from. The explanations, spoken alternately by
the old and the young nun, took some time, but finally the
matter was made clear. They were from a local convent
school, St. Joseph's: each year they held, after Easter, a sort
of parents' day, when someone—the bishop, or a famous
visitor—made a speech and presented prizes. This year,
having read about Mrs. Bannister, they wanted her, and only
her, to come along and tell her story, which to them signified
love and faith at its most triumphant. Perhaps, repeated
the young nun, Mrs. Bannister could bring Esther as well, to
show the miracle for all to see.

"For it is a miracle," said the old nun, chiming in. "She

had nothing—and now she can speak.   How old is the little one?"

"Sixteen," answered Mrs. Bannister.   She was thinking hard.   Though she did not dislike the idea, and indeed found it attractive, a public appearance of this sort was a new thing, and still far out of her line.   Press interviews were easy, radio a matter of a prepared script; but a public speech—on a platform, with a crowd of people watching and commenting— was an advance into unknown country.   She looked at the nuns: at their long skirts, dusty, old-fashioned shoes, folded hands, odd head-dresses that hid all that women might be proud to show.   The young one was pretty, the old one amiable in maturity.   For a moment she felt rebellious and resentful—they were so far out of touch with life, and yet now they wanted to embrace it, at second-hand, in its most up-to-date form, they wished to eat and drink the latest headlines.

I don't want to tie this with religion, she thought.   It wasn't a miracle, anyway.   But a platform was a platform, an audience an opportunity.   It would be nice to show them. . . .   It would be nice to show them, not that Esther was a miracle, but that she represented four years of the hardest, most complicated work that anyone could undertake.

"She's just sixteen," she repeated.   "I'd bring her in to meet you, but she's resting right now."

"The darling," said the old nun.   She looked at Mrs. Bannister.   "Will you come and speak to us, on the Day, then?"

Mrs. Bannister, crossing to her desk, made a show of consulting her engagement pad.   Then she turned, and said:

"Yes, I'd like to do that.   And Esther can come along, too.   But you must tell me exactly what will happen."

"We'll do that," said the old nun.

"God will bless you," said the young one.

Later, after settling the preliminary details, Mrs. Bannister saw them off from the front door. They drove away in a gleaming new Chrysler station-wagon, labelled: 'St. Joseph's Convent School.'

The young nun called out: "We're just running it in!" and the old one added: "Thanks to St. Christopher," as they drove off.

She wished Paul Marchant had been there to hear that.

Mrs. Bannister was never to forget that 'Day' at the convent. Not only was it the turning-point in her joint life with Esther Costello, marking the hour of which she could say afterwards (though only to herself): "That was when it all started"; but it was a deep emotional experience as well, shattering in its revelation of how the human heart, though wrung and torn by pity, can transform these into a fearful joy in a single uplifting moment. The way in which she and Esther were received, and the way in which their presence worked upon all those that watched, so that in the end there was nothing in the whole vast reception-hall save an embracing love for the two of them— these things dictated the future even while they took shape themselves, as decisive as birth and death within a small family.

They arrived early at the convent, to be met first by an attendant frieze of nuns big and small, and excited children peering round corners at their approach, and then by the Mother Superior, a gracious personage on whom the habit of command sat conspicuously well. Mrs. Bannister had coached Esther very carefully, not only in what she would have to do—which was simple—but in the sort of things which would be going on around her from moment to moment; the girl seemed entirely happy at the prospect, and her manner as they sat in the Mother Superior's office was perfectly composed. It was only later, when they were in isolation on the platform, and Esther was involved in matters too strange for her small ability, that things went wrong—and then, in the end, wonderfully right.

To begin with, the pattern was what Mrs. Bannister had been led to expect. They were ushered on to the platform, above a huge hall in which sat nearly five hundred people —children of the school, parents, priests, casual visitors attracted by the announcement of Esther's presence. Mrs. Bannister took her seat, and immediately began describing to Esther the scene around them: she could not be unaware of the intense, keyed-up interest, down in the body of the hall, in what she was doing, and of the whispers of those who sat near her—visitors, members of the teaching order, local notables. She did not exactly play up to this audience, but she consciously included them in what she was doing; there was in her manner a certain showmanship which her more percipient friends would have recognized. Belle Bannister, they would have said, wasn't missing *this* trick.

The chattering died as the Mother Superior rose to speak: the open-mouthed children, reacting to a voice they knew and loved, settled down to orderly attention. There were some routine matters to be disposed of—the date of the next term, the outstanding achievements of the one just past, some news of former school children now grown-up. Then the Mother Superior introduced Mrs. Bannister and Esther, in a graceful and compassionate speech which could hardly have been bettered, and yielded all to them.

Mrs. Bannister, turning aside, 'spoke' a few more words to Esther, while the audience watched them avidly; and then, to a generous applause, she stood up and began to speak.

She had of course prepared what she wanted to say, but even without her notes she would have found it easy:

she knew already that she was talking to friends. She gave them the story from the beginning, in simple narrative—Esther's accident, the fearful years of neglect, the voyage to America, the trials and disappointments, the final decision that, with great patience and love, had brought Esther to her present situation. There was not a sound in the hall as she spoke: occasionally she turned towards Esther, to point what she was saying, and Esther was always the perfect illustration for each phrase and each word—lovely and immobile, her face tranquil, her blind gaze steadfast; the focus now of a thousand eyes, and hundreds of advancing hearts.

"I will tell Esther about this wonderful gathering," said Mrs. Bannister, nearing the end of her story. "I will tell her that all of you"—she hesitated, and looked towards the Mother Superior, sitting a few paces from her—"that all of you are with her, that all of you are praying for her." The Mother Superior nodded very gently at these last words: a royal acquiescence that no single person in the hall missed. "I will tell her," said Mrs. Bannister, emboldened, "that you all love her."

If the Mother Superior had not nodded again, approving this last claim, it might have exceeded—by a single heart-beat—what was permissible: as it was, every child present, and then every adult, seemed to draw sobbing breath to endorse it. The great wave of applause that followed flowed towards the platform, and then faded as Mrs. Bannister leant towards Esther, and died to nothing as she took the girl's hand in her own.

Turning her head, Mrs. Bannister said: "I am telling her now."

The audience craned forward in their seats, amid an electric silence, to watch her fingers moving. There were some seconds of hesitation and doubt—broken by an occasional sob from an overwrought child—while Mrs. Bannister repeated the words she had spelled: her trembling hands had made her touch uncertain. But there came a huge sigh as Esther's face was seen to soften to a smile; and then a wild outburst of clapping as she leant forward and held out both her arms to the audience she could not see.

Here and there in the body of the hall, voices called to her; here and there, answering arms were held towards Esther, as if to complete an embrace. It was a loving clamour, like the clamour of penitents seeking to heal and to be healed.

Mrs. Bannister happened to catch sight of the Mother Superior's face at that moment, and saw in it a division of desire that was as moving as anything else that the moment could show. She was patently affected by what was happening—so much was obvious; the proud, capable face was softened, the eyes bright with unaccustomed tears. But against that, she was clearly striving to remember that this hall was full of children who were in her charge—and the children must, as a first necessity, be protected against these moments of tempest. Love and tears could always have their place; emotion and hysteria must never do so. . . . But it was not an occasion that could be immediately controlled, and so she allowed it to run much of its course; and then, as Mrs. Bannister watched, her face settled again into its cool competence, and very slowly she stood up.

A gradual stillness rose to meet her; the movement in the hall abated, the sounds fell away to nothing. It was not an easy silence, but it could pass for tranquillity if one forgot what had just been happening.

"All of us must be very grateful to Mrs. Bannister," the Mother Superior began. Her voice was measured, and consciously calm—a sedative voice that served to emphasize the storm of feeling that had just swept them all. "We must thank her, not only for coming here to tell us her story, but for the wonderful work she has done. I want you all to remember"—she was speaking now to her children—"how much love and faith she must have had in her heart, to do all this for another person, a stranger. We must try to copy her—and to copy Esther too, who has been patient, and brave, and determined, for so many long years. You all know that she cannot see you, you know that she cannot hear what I am saying. But Mrs. Bannister will tell her afterwards what has been said, and how much"—she hesitated—"how much we all love her."

Some renewed clapping interrupted her at this point, gradually fading as the Mother Superior held up her hand. There was now a small frown on her face. What she was about to say had been arranged many weeks earlier, and could not easily be altered now; but she was well aware that it was likely to revive and intensify, in an extreme form, the excitement that had gone before.

"There are six children here today," she concluded, "who have won prizes this term, and this is the moment when they will come up to the platform to receive them. The prizes will be presented by—Esther Costello."

At that there was so great a gasp, of joy and fear, throughout the hall, that the Mother Superior felt all her doubts returning. It had been arranged that Esther, in a brief ceremony, should hand to each of the six children the book which was her prize: when they had planned it, it had seemed a simple, natural end to the afternoon. But that was before Esther had so captured their love and pity: now, to many people present, the idea of this blind girl giving a public performance suddenly seemed dangerous—a last emotional stake which might render the whole occasion unbearable.

It might go wrong—which would be terrible: or it might go so right that it would burst its bounds.

As Esther, guided by Mrs. Bannister, stood up and came

forward, the voices and the cheering began to gather again: the whole audience, as if aware that this was a crucial moment, was willing Esther to make it a successful one. The first girl, a small child in a white dress, advanced up the steps of the platform, reached Esther, and took from her hands the proffered book. Above her head, Esther was seen to be smiling. The child walked off the platform again.

The audience sighed, for relief at this simple outcome, and then applauded. Perhaps it would all be as easy as this. . . . Mrs. Bannister put into Esther's hands the second book, for the second child. The second child, nervous, hung back at the edge of the platform: and while she was still some yards away, Esther smiled again and held out the book— forward into space. There was a frightful moment of emptiness, when nothing happened: the smile left Esther's face, to be succeeded by a look of doubt and fear. Then the child, prompted by a nun, advanced, almost at a run, snatched the book from Esther, and clattered down the stairs again, already whimpering.

In the audience, other children began to cry.

Mrs. Bannister took Esther's hand and spoke to her. It was wonderful to see the girl's face regain confidence: it was more than wonderful, it was violently moving—and there had been enough that was moving, for every soul in the audience, that afternoon. Down in the body of the hall, an intolerable suspense grew as the Mother Superior read out the third child's name; on the platform, those in authority looked towards Mrs. Bannister as towards a saviour.

But this time, Mrs. Bannister remained standing by Esther's side, and guided her all through the presentation, with an arm around her shoulder. The applause at the end seemed confused—some for the child (who was unconcerned and co-operative), some for Esther, some for Mrs. Bannister's demonstrated care. It was as if the audience itself was becoming unstable, uncertain of what it wanted to happen. That arm round the shoulder retold, in one single gesture, the whole story which had so moved them all, a little earlier. They wanted it to remain where it was. It was *their* arm, as well as Mrs. Bannister's.

Mrs. Bannister stayed with Esther while the fourth child received her prize. Once again, all went smoothly. Then she sat down, leaving Esther standing alone once more.

By mischance, the fifth child was already crying uncontrollably when she reached the platform. She was older than the others—about fourteen, with a pretty, dark face that now looked hopelessly distraught: she must have been living the past few minutes at some special pitch of intensity. When she was within a few yards of Esther, she stopped dead, as if she could walk no farther. There was a look of pain and horror on her face. It was clear that she could not bear to come any closer to the person who had inspired her pitiful tears.

The Mother Superior, frowning, motioned her forward. She shook her head, all the time staring at Esther who was waiting, patiently, book in hand. The two of them stood thus for a full ten seconds. Then suddenly the girl turned, and darted off the platform, and out of the hall, crying loudly as if pursued.

If anything did pursue her, it was the audience's violent hatred at this betrayal. People like us—so their thoughts seemed to clamour—people with eyes and ears should not fail people like Esther Costello, who have neither of these blessings, and who still make so valiant an effort to play their normal part.

They could not find anything to applaud, at this destroying moment, so they waited in charged silence. They watched Esther fearfully. She still held the book. Someone had to receive it from her.

Mrs. Bannister stood up, and with no further word or sign, took the book from Esther's hands. Esther smiled the smile she had given to the rest of the children. The audience, partners in this public deception, found relief again in anguished applause.

Then the last child, the eldest of all, mounted the steps of the platform as the Mother Superior announced her name. She was nervous—there was no one in the whole room who was not—but she advanced resolutely towards Esther: a tall, slight figure in a white dress, about fifteen years old, walking still with a child's awkwardness. Reaching Esther, she held out her hand, and touched the book she was to receive. Esther smiled, and released it into her grasp.

The book dropped with a frightful thump on the platform floor.

Esther must have felt the impact, or else the book touched her foot, for her expression changed immediately. Her hands groped forwards inquiringly, and encountered the girl's empty ones. There was upon her working face a look of such ruined despair that many people in the audience cried out at the sight of it.

The Mother Superior rose, as did Mrs. Bannister. But it was the child herself who retrieved the whole moment, with sudden, moving grace. She took a pace forward, threw her arms round Esther, and hugged her fervently. Above her head, Esther's face, hardly less childish, melted first into doubt and then into a delighted smile.

They stood embraced for a long moment, while the audience went off its head.

There was some element in the thunderous applause which now followed, that seemed to knit the whole occasion together into an ecstatic success. It was the sort of applause that tried to express everything. There was tremendous relief in it. There was pity for Esther, admiration for Mrs. Bannister,

and thanks for the child who had redeemed them all. There
was a plea for forgiveness, because it was they who had been
the promoters of all this long ordeal. There was, above
everything else, love for Esther Costello, which they must
demonstrate at all cost.

The applause filled the hall, growing, echoing. The
audience began to move towards the platform, where Mrs.
Bannister, Esther, and the child now stood in a line together.
Here and there, people in the first rows stretched out their
hands, trying to touch them. Then those in front started
to invade the platform itself, while the voices and the clapping
still rose in great waves behind them.

It was as if, for this one moment, the whole human world
was flowing towards Esther Costello, striving to reach the
blind girl who was the adored centre of their lives. The
tumult was still at its height when the Mother Superior gave
the signal for the ceremony to end.

In the quiet of the Mother Superior's office, the man—
middle-aged, short, strongly-built—walked up and down with
quick, energetic steps. It seemed as though only thus could
he bear the imprisonment of four walls. Now he glanced at
Esther, who sat quietly in a corner, now at Mrs. Bannister,
who faced him tiredly from the fireplace. He was in a state of
tremendous nervous tension: fresh from the meeting, he had
an exalted look, as if he knew himself to be a better man
because of what he had just witnessed.

"I asked if I could see you alone," he said. He had a
tough, rasping voice, a voice of executive command, but
now it had lost much of its authority, and seemed to be
urging a cause that did not accord with toughness at all.
"That was a wonderful experience for me. I have a little
girl at school here"—he glanced again at Esther—"a little
girl in full health, thank God."

"How old is she?" asked Mrs. Bannister. She had no idea what was coming, but for some reason she wanted to help him, in spite of her feeling of drained exhaustion.

"Just nine years old. . . . That was a wonderful experience for me," he repeated. "I felt as though"—he was groping—"as though I wanted to make a thank-offering—for my little girl, for the gift of sight." He turned aside, blew his nose, and then faced Mrs. Bannister squarely. "You should go all around the country," he said. "Coast to coast. Tell everybody about it."

"That would be a very big undertaking," said Mrs. Bannister.

The man nodded. "I know. And I'd like to help out. You must have had a lot of expenses with this thing already. As well as a lot of worry."

"There've been expenses, certainly. I hadn't thought about it."

"That's because you're a wonderful woman. . . . I'd like to help," he repeated. "You ought to establish a fund. Not just for her. For all the blind." He stopped in front of Esther, looking down at her almost hungrily. "She's such a lovely kid. You saw what we felt about her. Think what you and she could do for the blind."

"That might be true."

"I'd like to help," he said, for the third time. Suddenly he dipped into his pocket, drew out a piece of paper, and held it towards her. Mrs. Bannister saw, without surprise, that it was a cheque, already made out.

"Here," he said to Mrs. Bannister. "Let this be the start of it. You'll have to excuse the writing," he went on, smiling now as if an ordeal were past. "I was a bit shaky when I filled it out."

It reached her hand, and rested there. "But I can't take this," said Mrs. Bannister, no longer unmoved. Her astonished eyes had just noted that the cheque was for twenty thousand dollars. "It's too generous—it's too much. I won't know what to do with it at all."

"It's a lot of money," the man agreed. "I'm not all that rich, either. I guess you realize the way I feel, now. . . ." There was relief and satisfaction in his voice, as if he were reaching out towards her, eager to share the peace he had won. "But I know you'll take care of it all right. For Esther's sake. For all the blind."

PART TWO

CHAPTER EIGHT

WHEN Mrs. Bannister opened the door of her apartment, and found it was Mrs. Forbes who stood outside, she was not especially pleased. But for the sake of an old friendship, she smiled hospitably as she stood aside.

"Come in," she said, "come right in. You're a real stranger. You haven't been round to see us in months and months."

"But you're so famous!" Mrs. Forbes looked closely at her. "My, you're smart these days, Belle. Are you just going out?"

"Soon, yes. We have another meeting tonight, a big one."

"Meetings. . . ." Mrs. Forbes, who had aged somewhat during the past year, sounded querulous and critical. "Seems to me you have too many meetings. You never give yourself a moment's peace."

Mrs. Bannister followed her into the apartment. "There are so many things to do," she said, appeasingly. She did not want to argue, with so much ahead of her that evening. Nor did she want Mrs. Forbes to stay long. "You know how it is. People just love Esther. They come from all over, just to look at her."

"And to hear you," said Mrs. Forbes. But it did not sound very complimentary. "You must have raised a lot of money, with all these talks and demonstrations."

"It's a wonderful charity," answered Mrs. Bannister vaguely. "Anything we can do for the blind. . . ."

"Someone said the other day that you must have collected nearly a hundred thousand dollars."

Mrs. Bannister smiled. "Maybe. Something like that. There are plenty of expenses, though. Travelling isn't cheap. And Esther needs special diet all the time. It's a big responsibility."

"You'd be better with someone to take care of you." Mrs. Forbes paused. "I saw Paul Marchant this afternoon. He asked after you."

"Haven't seen him in years," said Mrs. Bannister briefly. "What will you drink?"

"You've changed, Belle," said Mrs. Forbes. That did not sound complimentary, either. "No, I won't have anything—I only wanted to look in on you. . . . Paul's a real fine man. With all this money, you need a man."

"Sure—if you aim to spend it."

"Now, that's not a nice thing to say."

"But true, though. . . . Money isn't the problem, anyway." Mrs. Bannister sounded somewhat irritated. "People talk as if the whole thing was money, and nothing else. They exaggerate all the time. Taking care of Esther is what counts, first and last, with me."

"Oh, everyone knows *that*. . . . How is she?"

"Very well," said Mrs. Bannister. "She's resting right now. She has to concentrate so much, at these meetings. It takes a lot out of her."

"I'm sure of that." Mrs. Forbes rose. "I really won't stay, Belle—this was just to say hello. Any message for Paul?"

"Give him my best," said Mrs. Bannister. "It's been good seeing you, even for a little while. . . . Now I have to get the two of us ready."

Mrs. Bannister had lost count of the number of their meetings, as she had of a good many other things during the past year. It must now be close on thirty. . . . When she had said, to Mrs. Forbes: "People just love Esther", that had been no more than the plain truth. Ever since Harry Grant's write-up in the *Star-Telegram*, and the extraordinary afternoon at the convent school, Esther Costello had served as a fantastic magnet whenever she appeared.

It was partly her story, partly her glowing good looks, partly the crusading aspect of what these two seemed to have set themselves to do. During the past year, Esther and Mrs. Bannister had travelled very widely, throughout the eastern half of the country, raising funds for the blind; and wherever they went, the sequence was always the same—a warm welcome, a tremendous upsurge of emotion during each appearance together, a final explosion of feeling when Esther took her leave. That was, naturally, the moment when the hat went round. So violent a climax had to be given relief.

Usually, Mrs. Bannister lectured, and then 'talked' to Esther, demonstrating how easily the two of them could communicate with each other. Then Esther would 'make a speech' herself, spelling the words to Mrs. Bannister, who would relay them, sentence by sentence, to the audience. Sometimes Esther would answer questions, using the same relay system. But it did not really matter what she did, as long as she was available to stand there on the platform—deaf, mute, blind, and yet on the other hand young, shapely, and beautiful. For Esther, at seventeen, had blossomed into a startling loveliness that was stunning in its impact.

She was every woman's longed-for child, every man's favourite daughter—or the secret focus of his desires. Everywhere, people came to watch, to hear—and to give.

It was good to be so well-known, so widely acclaimed, thought Mrs. Bannister; it was good to be a ready-made hit, wherever one went. . . . When she talked to the newspapers (and that was on very many occasions), Mrs. Bannister used to describe their activities as 'focusing attention on the needs of the blind': when she addressed an audience, she borrowed the phrase of their first benefactor, the man with twenty thousand dollars to give away, and called for thank-offerings for the gift of sight.   She called for them, and she got them: the money flowed in all the time, from scores of different sources—collections, donations, bequests.   Men dug deep into their wallets, women peered into their purses, children rifled their own money-boxes—all for Esther Costello.   It was astonishing how people responded to this simple urge to give.

They lived comfortably, she and Esther: after all her trouble and worry, after the expenses she had been put to, after all the hard work, Mrs. Bannister felt entitled to a reasonable standard of luxury. . . .   True, she had passed a lot of the money on, to various blind charities; but the rest —and that was plenty—was still there, in the 'fund'.

She hadn't made up her mind about the fund.   It might all be distributed—later.   It might serve as the nucleus of some kind of trust.   It might just be a bank-balance for the two of them.

After all, Esther would never be able to earn her own living.   She had to be taken care of.   One might almost say that this was the first priority, that the 'needs of the blind' started right here, at home.   Mrs. Bannister was still comfortably placed, but it was better to be on the safe side, to build a wall that could *never* be broken down.   She owed it to Esther, in fact, to take no chances with the future.

She went through into the girl's bedroom, to make her ready for the meeting.

The meeting that night was like any other meeting—which meant that it was a heart-warming success from the start. The hall was full, even though an entrance-charge was made 'to defray expenses'; Mrs. Bannister now advertised these meetings under the headline ESTHER COSTELLO ANSWERS YOUR QUESTIONS, and the appeal of this promised miracle seemed irresistible. The audience applauded Mrs. Bannister's brief introduction (she had cut this down to the minimum, since Esther's story was so well-known): they sat still as mice while the two of them demonstrated their methods of talking to each other; they responded generously when, during 'question time', Esther's brave accomplishment became evident.

There was, at the start, every kind of person in that audience —earnest social workers, thrill-seekers, sceptics, bored socialists, cranks from the lunatic fringe, drunks who had wandered in from the cold; but by the time an hour had passed, they were all one kind of person, at the same level of humanity and understanding. They had listened to Mrs. Bannister, watched Esther, seen their exchange of words, witnessed their communion; at the end, the leaven had so worked in them that they were all level in their admiration and their wonder.

From that feeling there sprang, as always, a proprietary joy in this lovely child—for here in Boston, she was their own Esther Costello; they were proud of her and Mrs. Bannister, and proud of a part of America which could, by love and compassion, produce so amazing a triumph.

When, towards the close, Mrs. Bannister introduced the theme: "Give Esther a thank-offering for your own eyesight", the response was brisk and unhesitating. While the three-piece orchestra played soft music of a coaxing kind, the volunteer helpers—girls who had been recruited during the past months—passed round the collecting-boxes; and then, as sometimes happened, individuals in the audience stood up to pledge their support.

Jewellery was passed up to Mrs. Bannister: watches and cigarette-cases reached the platform: ten- and twenty-dollar bills went from hand to hand until they arrived at the small table in front of Esther. Whenever this happened, Mrs. Bannister touched Esther's arm, and the girl smiled blindly and enchantingly—one warm heart greeting another. . . . A man in the audience called out: "Tell her I'm sending along five hundred dollars in the morning!" and the applause lasted throughout the time that Mrs. Bannister was passing the message on to Esther.

At the end of this communication, they saw a fresh smile break over Esther's face, and after a moment's pause Mrs. Bannister said:

"She says: 'Thank you, and thank God for people like you.'"

This generous interpretation of Esther's actual reply— "That's fine"—drew so great a volley of clapping that Mrs. Bannister recognized it as a suitable note on which to finish. She stood up, and stretched out her hands. The music died away.

"We both thank you from the bottom of our hearts," she said quietly and gravely. "For your kindness to us this evening, for your generous help for all blind people. . . . I will tell Esther all about it tomorrow—she is tired tonight, as you can see."

Esther, responding to a covert touch, sat straight up and smiled, while the audience went "Ah-h-h . . ." on a low note of understanding and pity. "You can see how brave she is," said Mrs. Bannister, looking down at her fondly. "Good night to all of you." She leant over, taking Esther's hand briefly. "And Esther says: 'Good night, and God bless you every one.'"

The audience rose, applauding to the last: the volunteers made for the exits, rattling their collecting-boxes; and at a signal from Mrs. Bannister, the orchestra played them out with their farewell number.

It was, as always, *When Irish Eyes are Smiling*.

Esther went straight to bed as soon as they returned to the

apartment: she was always exhausted after these meetings, with their prolonged concentration and the knowledge that she was under the gaze of a crowd of people; Mrs. Bannister's public cherishing of her was not entirely showmanship. . . . Mrs. Bannister looked down at the pale, spent face outlined on the pillow, then bent and kissed her forehead.

"Good night, my darling one," she said, aloud, squeezing Esther's arm in the special grip which was their way of expressing their fondness for each other. "You did very well tonight."

Esther smiled and, reaching up, squeezed Mrs. Bannister's arm in the same fashion, signalling her love. Then her head dropped back on the pillow, and fell to one side. Mrs. Bannister knew that she would soon be deeply asleep. But the girl was, thank God, strong and healthy: she had not been ill for a single day, even during the most strenuous tour. There was never any anxiety on that score. Tomorrow she would be as good as new, and ready for anything.

Mrs. Bannister put out the bedroom light, and walked through into her own sitting-room. The big silver drink-tray had been made ready by the coloured maid, before she left for the night, and Mrs. Bannister poured a stiff highball, and carried it to the fireside arm-chair. The chair and the drink and the warm, comfortable room each welcomed her. This was always the best moment of any day, when the public effort was over, and everything had gone well, and all tiredness fell away. For her, the strain of handling these meetings would never lessen, however proficient she might become— there was so much that could go wrong, quite apart from the skill needed to communicate accurately with Esther. But now it was all left behind, for the rest of the day and the morrow too. Her world contracted, fining down to these small comforts; and gratefully she contracted with it.

It was true, she thought, reviewing the day comfortably—

it was true that Esther had done well that evening. The
applause at the end was the measure of it, not to speak of
the size of the collection. . . . Much of the meeting had been
routine, of course; Mrs. Bannister knew what the audience
had come to see, and the questions they asked—"Are you
happy?" "How old are you?" "Do you remember Ireland?"
—never varied much. She had developed, for these occasions,
a technique of presentation, in which Esther now co-operated
admirably. Among other things, it included a series of code
grips and touches, which told Esther what she should do, at
any given moment.

There was a signal for 'Sit up', there was another for 'Smile';
there was one for 'Laugh', and 'Shake your head', and 'Put
your arm round me'. . . . It simplified both their tasks, to a
very large extent.

Of course, thought Mrs. Bannister, it was a kind of dis-
honesty, if you looked at it one way, since these reactions of
Esther's always appeared spontaneous, always charmed the
audience to distraction. It was immoral, too, on a different
plane; it meant treating Esther like a circus animal, showing
off her tricks, putting her through the hoop while the crowd
gaped. And sometimes Mrs. Bannister improved on things
of her own accord, making up what Esther was supposed to
have said, in answer to questions, or 'translating' her remarks
to suit a particular audience or a particular moment of
emotion. Very often, this was the only way a meeting could
be properly controlled. People soon got bored, if things
started dragging or questions were left in the air.

It didn't matter much, this 'presentation', anyway. In
fact, it didn't matter at all. Basically, the thing was on the
level. She *could* talk to Esther, and be answered by her;
the rest was simply a variation on their joint talents. It gave
the audience what they wanted, what their goodwill and their
support deserved.

The end-result, in any case, justified all this, since the end-result was money: money for the helpless. If one thought of that all the time, a little manipulation need not trouble one's conscience. Indeed, if Esther couldn't think of a good answer on the spur of the moment, then it was Mrs. Bannister's plain duty to think of one for her, and so save the occasion. Who was hurt by that? It was all in a good cause. It was all for the needy.

It had worked well tonight, anyway. The takings had been fine—hall full, good collection, plenty of promises for the future. She hoped that the man who had guaranteed five hundred dollars would come across with it tomorrow. Sometimes they didn't live up to their undertakings—which was a pretty mean trick: not much better than stealing from the blind.

There was a ring at the apartment door.

Mrs. Bannister stirred and sat up, not perturbed. It was probably Harry Grant—he was still a very good friend to them, and often when they had a meeting in Boston he came along to it, and then stopped by on his way home from the *Star-Telegram*. She was always glad to see him. She and Esther both owed a lot to Harry Grant.

But when she opened the front door, she found it was her husband.

Captain Charles Bannister. . . . Mrs. Bannister was conscious of a slightly sick feeling as she saw him standing there—the small, elegant, soldierly man whom she had not seen for over ten years. A cursory glance told her that he had worn well—and that was somehow not reassuring, either.

She said: "Charles. . . . What the hell do you want here?"

"Well, Belle, old thing. . . ." The bold eyes and the gin-croak voice were unaltered, too. "Just came round to look you up. Aren't you going to ask me in?"

"No."

He grinned, as if he had expected nothing better. "Good old Belle. . . ." Then, before she could do anything, his arm came out and he pushed the door back, and suddenly he was over the threshold. "Change your mind," he said, his eyes sharp. "I was at the meeting tonight. I want to talk to you."

She followed him into the sitting-room, feeling weak and unarmed. There was something in his manner she could not place, notwithstanding all the copious experience of the past.

"Snug little place you've got here," he said, looking round him. His eyes wandered to the side-table and the silver tray. "Mind if I help myself?"

She saw, with misgiving, that his suit, though well-pressed, was frayed, and the heels of his shabby shoes worn far down. She shrugged.

"Have a drink if you like. You'll get nothing else from me."

Above the splash of the soda-siphon she heard his voice.

"I was at the meeting," he repeated, as if this explained everything. "Very good show. And that girl's a stunner. You must have taken a dollar or two. Not for the first time, either."

"What's that to you?"

Now he was facing her. "I'm interested in the way people make money, that's all." When she did not answer, he said: "You've got to help me, Belle. Things haven't been going too well."

Things haven't been going too well. . . . Captain Charles Bannister, the nearly-titled Englishman (second cousin of an earl) whom she had married twenty years before had been Mrs. Bannister's first and last excursion into matrimony. 'Things haven't been going too well' might have been the post-lude of their wedding march: now it brought back vividly the small and large dishonesties of their joint past. Charles Bannister, born a few years before the turn of the century, had been just old enough to take part in the First World War. Demobilized in 1919, he had kept his wartime rank (he had explained, once, the somewhat complicated reasoning by which he considered himself entitled to call himself Captain, although not a regular soldier); and it was as Captain Charles Bannister, a well-connected soldier with a slight limp, honourably discharged and now selling stocks and bonds on half-commission in New York, that she had met him, back in 1929.

Though a self-reliant young woman of twenty-five, she was not equipped to withstand so talented an operator as this. They were married within three months of that first meeting.

She realized soon enough where her own inadequacy had led her; nor did it take her long to work out that 1929 was an exceptionally good year for a bond-salesman, however well-connected, to marry a rich woman who still remained rich after the market crash. By then, of course, it was too late: the era of 'Things haven't been going too well' had already been ushered in, accompanied by a dismal fanfare from his bank-manager.

At the time of their marriage, Charles Bannister was deeply in debt: she was deeply in love; at first, the two things cancelled out, to their mutual satisfaction. But that could not last long, since his rescue seemed to be a continuous process, and her love was not. She found that it was not enough to redeem him from pawn when they were married—there was never a moment, subsequently, when he was completely solvent, either in money or in honour.

'Things haven't been going too well.' How clearly she remembered that ominous, lowering phrase. It was the classic warning shot in his armoury, signifying trouble with tradesmen, trouble with his job, trouble with a woman, a

senior executive, a horse, or a cheque. What he did was
never completely outside the law—not so far outside, that is,
that she could not buy him free of entanglement. There was
never an open scandal, simply a moment when he had to
confide his embarrassment ("I'm down to the bones of my
arse, Belle"), when she paid the bill, and he swore to start
afresh.

It was accompanied always by protestations of love and
innocence, explanations which would have strained the
credulity even of a very stupid woman (which Mrs. Bannister
was not), and a display of impudent charm which served only
to recall to her why she had been fool enough to marry him in
the first place.

He still had the charm, she observed now, with a fresh
return of misgiving. Covertly she watched him, while he sat
at ease by her fireside. He had worn well, as she had already
noticed: the clipped moustache, square tanned face, and
grey temples were all as she remembered. Only the lines
round the eyes, and the professional seller's smile, had hardened
and deepened. He must be over fifty now—fifty-two or
three, in fact. He looked younger: he looked attractive
still: he looked spry, confident, at ease with himself and the
world. The fact that he was shabby and down-at-heels
as well would, with most women, only serve to increase his
attraction.

There was still that endearing English accent, too. It was
one of the things she had fallen in love with, twenty years
before, though it had palled at least as swiftly as his other assets.
"Dahling, I a-dawe you!" was one thing, particularly on a
honeymoon: "Dahling, lend me a fivah!" was, particularly
on a honeymoon, something else again.

That alternative phrase, borrowed from his army days:
"Dahling, I'm broke—I'm down to the bones of my arse,"
had never really charmed.

Now, uncertain and ill-at-ease within his remembered orbit, she asked:

"What have you been doing? Were you in the war?"

"Of course I was!" He sounded astonished, even hurt: it was very well done. "What did you think?"

"You know damned well what I thought."

He chose to ignore this. "I was in the Dunkirk show, naturally. Then North Africa and Italy. Then across the Rhine."

"Fighting?"

"Intelligence. . . . I was in the Army of Occupation for a bit, too. That was a really grand show."

"What happened?"

His face clouded. "There was a bit of a mix-up, actually," he confessed, as if he could hardly credit the fact. "Some young fellow made a hash of the mess-accounts. I had to straighten them out."

"*You* did?"

"Yes. The trouble was, I took the responsibility."

"What happened, Charles?"

"They moved me on."

.   .   .   .

They moved me on. . . . That was another phrase straight out of the past. With Charles Bannister, she had found, one was bound to keep moving on, always travelling away from some crisis or near-scandal, towards the certain horizon of another. They had moved on from America, soon after the honeymoon, because of some quarrel (not fully explained) with the broking firm for which he worked. They moved on from England, not once but many times: they were kept moving particularly briskly on the Continent—moving from houses, from hotels, from casinos and bridge-clubs. There was nothing blameable about these crises, naturally: it was never anyone's fault; there was just some sort of misunderstanding,

never clearly defined, followed by a bleak session with an
estate agent, a book-maker, a club secretary, a firm-faced
hotel manager—and they moved on once more.

She paid all the time, of course—but with Charles Bannister,
it seemed, paying was never enough. One had to pay, *and*
get out; that was usually insisted on. There was the small
scandal with the hat-check girl who turned out to be married:
there was the slightly larger affair, involving the doped
racehorse at Newmarket (the English racing people were so
fatuously strict); there was the really resounding row that
stretched right down to South Africa, and the Indian who
had diamonds to sell, and the man from Kimberley who was
the go-between, and the police who, unaccountably, swooped
down on them at Cannes. . . . As usual, nothing could
quite be proved; as usual, she paid, and they moved on.

The climax came in London, just before the war; the
climax was Lady Julia Wroy.

By this time, Charles Bannister no longer pretended to
keep office hours or do any work; she made him an allowance,
and they lived in a flat in Mayfair for which, of course,
she paid the rent. Now, after ten disastrous years, they were
near to separation: he was really costing too much, there had
been too many scenes and crises, too many people were sorry
for her, she had lost too many friends. Even their rare
nuptial contacts had taken on the same aspect of exploitation:
it seemed to cost several hundred pounds every time she went
to bed with him. . . . What tipped the balance against him,
and his resilient, rubber good-humour, and his tailored in-
solvency, and the whole sordid chain of intrigue and lying,
was, surprisingly, a woman.

It was surprising because women had never been a specially
destructive element in their marriage. But there was something in the Lady Julia Wroy episode which finally stuck in
her throat. It was not the fact that he was openly sleeping

with this indolent young whore; there had been a number of such incidents, and flagrant affairs of this kind were apparently fashionable, in the well-connected world in which Charles Bannister still lived. It was the fact that he expected Mrs. Bannister to foot the bill for it.

When she refused—since the girl, nurtured in the bosom of the English upper classes, was very expensive—he embarked on a course of open theft. He pledged her credit at hotels and restaurants. He converted the money for the rent to his own bank-account. He took the servants' wages from her purse. He ran up a series of bills, for food, drink, clothes, and jewellery, which unloosed upon their flat a hideous succession of duns and creditors.

Once they had encountered each other, in different parties, at a night-club. The girl was sitting close by his side, almost in his lap—a half-dressed, haggard blonde with a face like a bored skull. He had waved gaily, and raised his champagne glass towards her. Some time after he had left, an envelope was presented to her, 'with Captain Bannister's compliments'. It was his bill.

Finally, he returned to the flat one night, wept into his whisky, begged for her forgiveness, made love to her until, spent and drowsy, she fell asleep, then took from her jewel-case a diamond bracelet worth fifteen thousand dollars, and left for Antibes—with Lady Julia.

She might have survived even this grotesque betrayal, if it had not been for a single sentence, overheard at a party in London. The comment made her long humiliation spill over at last.

"Poor Belle," this was what she heard, when she paused at the entrance to the room; "Poor Belle—she must be going through hell with Charles."

"Don't be silly, darling!" said the second voice. "She's *American*—it's not like ordinary people."

That had been ten years ago, just before the war. This time, she had paid, and herself moved on, alone. She had not seen or heard of him again, until tonight.

Now she moved restlessly, frowning at her thoughts, and said:

"What are you doing in America?"

He gestured with an easy hand. "Looking round. The old country's absolutely played out, Belle. You wouldn't recognize it. Nothing but the Welfare State—whatever that is—and blasted socialists barging in everywhere. Hopeless. I thought I'd try my luck over here."

She said, again: "You'll get nothing out of me. Let's have that straight, for a start."

"I was at your meeting tonight." Once more it sounded as though the words explained everything to him, and should do the same for her. After a moment he added, in a different voice: "You're on to a pretty good thing there, old girl."

She looked up, to find him staring at her admiringly. She felt weakened by his presence. By God, she thought, for two cents he'd climb into bed with me, even now. . . . It was funny to see him across the fireplace again, after all these years. He could still make her feel like a woman—damn him. . . . She straightened up.

"It's not a 'good thing' at all," she answered tartly. "I've been training this girl, and looking after her, for years, and now we collect money for the blind. It's not one of your damned rackets, if that's what you're thinking."

"Of course not, Belle. I know you wouldn't dream of it." But there was little conviction in his voice: it sounded as though he wanted to wink at her. . . . He rose, and crossed to the side-table, to pour another drink. From there, with his back towards her, he asked suddenly: "Where's all the money, Belle?"

"What money?"

"The money you've collected during the past year or so."

She was feeling weak again. "It's in a fund."

"A trust fund?"

"No."

"Who administers it?"

"I do."

He still kept his back turned towards her. It made his questioning seem detached and judicial, far more unnerving than if he had faced her directly.

"Is it in her name?"

"No. She's blind and deaf and dumb. How could she operate a bank-account?"

"In fact, it's in yours?"

"Yes."

At that he turned to face her once more. His look, she saw, had lost none of its admiration. He said, slyly:

"That sounds a very satisfactory arrangement."

She wished she could lose her temper, but that had never been any use with Charles Bannister. The warm room, and the three drinks, and the man a few feet from her, seemed to be combining to rob her of ten years of self-sufficiency. She could hardly recognize her own voice as she answered him.

"I don't hold on to the money. Now and then I distribute some of it. I gave a donation of ten thousand dollars to the Central School for the Blind, only last week."

He nodded, walking forward, holding his fresh drink carefully. "I read about it. . . . I hoped you weren't over-doing things. . . . What percentage was it?"

"Percentage of what?"

"Of the total takings."

"I don't know what you mean."

E

"Oh yes, you do." He grinned suddenly, intimately: it took her back many years, to half-a-dozen tainted incidents. "Come off it, Belle! I know you're on to a good thing. I just want to make it a better one."

CHAPTER NINE

THEY were still talking, two hours and many drinks later. Charles Bannister, she found, had altered not at all: he was still as persuasive, as self-confident, and as completely amoral as he had ever been. For one thing, he simply would not believe that Mrs. Bannister was not running Esther for her own personal profit; for another, he refused to agree that anything he might have done in the past could possibly come between himself and his lawful wife. . . . There was about him, in spite of his shabby clothes, a special blend of charm, impudence, and determination, which aided both these arguments; and the whisky, Mrs. Bannister realized, was not greatly helping her to establish anything to the contrary.

The fire settled lower in the grate: outside, the traffic-noises along Commonwealth Avenue died to nothing; here, waylaid in her own home by a man she had loved long ago, she battled for a sane outcome to an absurd and crucial situation. But as the time went by, she battled less and less effectively. Charles Bannister had altogether too much on his side. He had the past, which for all its iniquity had included also the indelible tenderness of first love: he had the present, summed up in the brash confidence of an attractive man; and he had the future, which appeared to involve, for good measure, a guarantee of blackmail.

Alcohol, fear, and her own silly heart were making these things irresistible.

"Don't tell me," he said authoritatively at one point, when they were still arguing about her good intentions: "don't tell me that you set out on this money-making effort with the idea of turning everything over to charity. I'll lay you anything you like that you've done nothing of the sort. You said yourself that you've been building up a bank balance. You must have been spending a lot of the money, too."

"Of course there've been expenses," she said defensively. "Esther needs all sorts of things, all the time—food and clothes and medical treatment. There were the training fees at the blind school, as well as all these operations and tests, for months and months, when we first arrived. I'm entitled to deduct for that sort of thing."

Even as she spoke, she heard an echo of his own wheedling voice, out of the past, saying: "But *dahling*, I only *borrowed* it. . . ."

"Of course you're entitled." Swiftly he changed his ground. "You're entitled to a suitable standard of living, and a decent return for all the trouble you've taken with Esther. That's only fair. . . . The question is, of course"— he hesitated, delicately—"how *much* you're entitled to, for all you've done for her, and the way it's changed your whole life. *I* maintain"—here he sounded incredibly honest and fair-minded—"*I* maintain that you're entitled to a hell of a lot. Why, you've given up everything for her!"

"I don't want a hell of a lot."

"But you haven't exactly stinted yourself, even now, have you?" He looked round the room, touched the arm of his chair, sniffed at his drink, all in one appraising gesture. "All this is snug enough, Belle."

"I've had 'all this' for years," she said scornfully. "Otherwise you wouldn't have married me."

"You mean there've been no improvements?" he countered. "Are you telling me you *haven't* stepped things up since Esther came along?" Mrs. Bannister was silent. "Of course you have! You lost quite a bit of money during and after the war, didn't you?" he went on, maddeningly shrewd. "I don't say you went broke, or anything like it, but things certainly weren't what they used to be—wrong stocks—investments in the Far East—that sort of thing. Now you're building up again—and good luck to you, I say. But what I maintain is that you could do a lot better—and you deserve to."

"How?" She knew she should never have asked him such a question, which seemed to make her an accomplice with one single syllable; but she was intrigued by the idea he had produced. She honestly did not think that she had done so badly. . . .

He brightened. "It just needs organizing, that's all. We want to make Esther a world figure, not simply a home-town celebrity. Just think what we could do with national and international publicity, with world tours instead of just local ones. There's no limit to it. She's a winner, that girl—a real winner! But she needs handling properly, on a really big scale."

She said: "Freshen up my drink again, will you?" And then: "No, Charles—I don't like the idea and I don't want to do it."

"Why not?"

"It's too much trouble, for one thing."

"*I'll* look after that."

"That's what I'm afraid of. . . . Hell!" she exclaimed, annoyed, "why should I agree to any of this, just to give you an easy living? That's all it amounts to."

"I hate to see a good idea going to waste."

"You hate to pass up a chance of getting money for nothing."

He grinned. "It's the same thing."

Mrs. Bannister shook her head. "We still talk a different language, you and I. No, Charles," she said again: "I don't want to make any changes. I'm doing very well as it is."

"Yes, indeed. . . ." There was so sudden an alteration of tone and inflection in those two drawled words that she looked up, to find him staring at her fixedly. "That's exactly what people are going to say."

"What do you mean?"

"That you're doing very well as it is." It was extraordinary how significant, how evil her own words sounded, when Charles Bannister got to work on them. "Mrs. Bannister doing very well—it'll make a good headline."

"There'll be no headlines," she said, secretly appalled. "There's no occasion for them."

"I'll make the occasion." The thing that had been in his manner from the very beginning, the lurking thing in the background which she had not identified, now emerged into the open. She recognized it at once: it was a threat, a completely confident threat. "A word or two in the right quarter could make a lot of difference to you. Even a hint that you're holding back some of this money——" he gestured. "It would kill you—stone dead."

"They'd never believe you."

"They'd never believe *you*—unless you showed all the accounts, and gave the full figures. Are you prepared to do that? Can you stand an investigation? You know damned well yon can't! You're breaking every law in the States! Mrs. Bannister doing very well——" he repeated her fatal phrase, with yet more crude sarcasm. "Gives nearly ten per cent to charity, keeps rest."

His absurd English voice, aping a newspaper report, might have been funny if it had not mirrored so brutally her encroaching terror.

"You wouldn't dare."

He put the fresh drink down beside her without answering: then he straightened up slowly, standing above her with no trace either of humour or of weakness in his face.

"There are a lot of things I'll dare, if you don't see this thing my way, and do as I want. The real truth about the Esther Costello donations—that's one good story. *I'm* another."

"You?"

"Yes. Mrs. Bannister's husband returns." Again that absurd newspaper caricature, which once more clawed at her heart. "Mystery Englishman surprised by wife's activities. *Sues for divorce.*"

"What? You must be crazy!"

"Sues for divorce," he repeated. "And not only because of the Esther Costello racket. What about this man you've been going around with, for years on end. What about Paul Marchant?"

She stared, horrified at once by his ruthless look and by his knowledge. "How long have you been in America?"

"Long enough to find out that. . . . By God, I'll sue him for alienation!"

She laughed wildly at that. "Where will that get you? You've slept with more women——" she broke off, at a loss for detailed words. "You'll get precisely nowhere, if you try that divorce idea."

"Possibly not. But the scandal will finish you. You know it only needs to be mentioned—like the rumour about swindling. . . . And there's *another* thing."

He paused, so that she was forced to look up at him again, fearful of what more could be coming, wondering how high he would build his wall of blackmail before it broke and overwhelmed her. She knew from the past that he would use any weapon to get what he wanted: the deadly knowledge stole away all her strength.

"There's another thing. . . ." The smile on his face was the smile of years ago—sly, vulpine, wholly corrupt. "America isn't the only place I've travelled to, since the war. I was in Ireland, a couple of months ago. Looking at some horses. D'you know where I landed up?"

"No." But she did know.

"Cloncraig," he said.

"What of it?"

He came straight to the point. "The Costello parents are still there, both of them. They've heard about Esther, though they don't know how to get in touch with her. They'd like to see her. They'd like"—his fingers flickered—"they'd like a cut."

"They've absolutely no right to it." For some reason this last piece of news shook her as nothing else had been able to: the whole carefully cherished structure of herself and Esther seemed on the verge of toppling in ruins. "They gave up all claims to her, years ago."

"Did they?"

"Of course they did."

"In writing?" She was silent. "You never adopted her, did you? She's still their child, legally. If she's earning money"—he smiled briefly, mirthlessly—"which wouldn't be very hard to prove—they're entitled to a share of it. They're very poor," he went on, with loathsome concern. "The law courts *love* poor people."

"But I've done all the work." Already her voice was nearly breaking with despair. "I've taken all the trouble."

"Too bad. . . . But it's been a labour of love, surely, Belle? In fact, I'm almost sure you said so once, in a newspaper interview. People remember these things. . . . You know, you'd better have another drink."

As he said that, and turned from her, lifting the pressure of his own accord, she was suddenly and totally wearied of the whole thing. This was a battle she knew she could not win. It was true that a single breath of scandal—whether about Esther or the money or her own marriage—would be enough to destroy everything: and the idea of Esther's parents coming on the scene again was the most desolate prospect of all.

Charles had all the cards—and he had something else, too. She knew now, with a kind of hopeless self-derision, that he was not 'a man she had loved long ago': in spite of the ruinous past, she was still in love with him.

While he was busy at the side-table, she said unexpectedly, soberly:

"Why are you such a bad man, Charles? I never did you any harm."

She had thought that this would make him pause, but he answered immediately:

"I've told you, Belle." His back, towards her again, gave his voice reason and normality, against all the known facts. "I just want you to make the most of this girl. She's a gold-mine. We can make a lot of money for ourselves— *and* for the blind. That's why I was—putting the pressure on."

In spite of herself, the word 'was' fell like a caress, promising her a respite from all threats, all danger, as soon as she agreed to what he wanted.

"But you must have planned it all—a long time ago."

He shook his head. "No. . . . Cloncraig was a pure coincidence: I really was there to look at some horses. Then I heard about you and Esther, and I travelled over here to see what the form was. It was all as simple as that."

She realized that, tactically speaking, his quiet, seemingly honest tone was a brilliant variation: it alternated with his recent threats as perfectly as a wave that breaks and then recedes, completing a natural pattern, leaving the sand bare and white for the next footprint. . . . She realized, too, how confident he was, and how well equipped to deal with her at any level. She realized that she had no weapons left: he could destroy her if he wanted to, and he would do so if she

E*

stood in his way, since he had nothing to lose thereby. The only thing left to discuss was terms.

But he was before her, even there. He said, suddenly, coaxingly:

"You're still a damned good-looking woman, Belle."

'Still' was not the ideal word, but it did not wholly spoil this sentence. . . . She knew now that the tide was running hopelessly against her. He could ring the changes too expertly: the whisky, the man, the discarded threats were weaving a chain that could only have one end. She felt herself sinking into a haze of soft relief, becoming a woman again, abandoning everything to him.

As he came towards her, she said: "Being good-looking never did me much good, where you were concerned."

"I've learned my lesson." His voice was gentle, and his next words fell into place as aptly and inevitably as that receding wave. "How about giving it another try, Belle?"

"But what about the girl?" She was getting mixed up, caught between the battle she had just lost, and the swift change of feeling that was putting the two of them on a plane of sensual accord.

"I'll take care of that."

"You'll spoil it all if you overdo it."

"I won't overdo anything."

She sighed. "It's a long time since we've been together like this."

"I won't overdo anything."

CHAPTER TEN

THE things they now did to Esther Costello would not have disgraced a twilight advertising agency whose executives, competing for a new account, were determined to leave no avenue unexplored, no stone unthrown, no throat uncut. With Captain Charles Bannister—no stranger to personal exploitation—in charge, they got to work on Esther with at least as much energy, determination, and optimism, as had the doctors, when she first arrived in America. Happily for them, personal exploitation proved a much more exact science than medicine, where Esther was concerned.

When Charles Bannister said that he would not overdo things, he had been completely sincere: he had meant, of course, that he would be careful not to move too fast, not that there was any sort of ceiling to his ambitions. Mrs. Bannister should have known this: indeed, in her more sober and reflective moments, she *did* know it; but at the beginning, secure and ecstatic in an Indian summer of love which, at the age of forty-six, she thought she could no longer attain, she was caught off her guard—and after that it was too late.

Charles Bannister was a skilful lover: it was the sort of thing he had been paid to be, for very many years; and in the present case he applied his skill long enough to establish himself firmly in the saddle. Once there, once Mrs. Bannister was committed to his plans for a bigger and better Esther Costello, there was no retrieving the situation.

Whenever she protested, in the early days, against some

particular extravagance, he threatened—though always elegantly—to withdraw his favours. Soon there was no use in her protesting anyway, since the machine had started turning and could not be stopped; and presently there were no favours to withdraw, because the Indian summer had burnt itself out, and would never return.

But to begin with, she had no great suspicion in her mind that Charles Bannister would overstep the mark: chance had rescued him from penury, and it seemed he must realize that Esther Costello could give them both a substantial living, without too gross an effort on his part. In fact, against all the odds she continued to trust him. . . . Even when he was first introduced to Esther, and, surveying her admiringly, had said: "She's a damned attractive girl—wish I were a few years younger!" Mrs. Bannister had not got beyond thinking: 'Oh no—he wouldn't do *that*. . . .' Embalmed in unexpected love, she had forgotten how many times she had used these precise words in the past, and how many times the outcome had astonished and shamed her.

There were plenty of ghosts for her to call on, if she cared to, a whole gallery of hideous memories; but she was blind to them at the beginning, and by the time she awoke to reality, reality had won itself too long a start.

First, said Charles, when they were at the planning stage, first there was some ground to be cleared.

"We must definitely fix the parents," he told her. "The mother's a stupid peasant, the father's a drunk; but they *have* got a nuisance value. We don't want some crooked Irish lawyer ferreting about, later on. . . . We'd better adopt the girl, formally."

"Will they agree to that?" she asked.

He shrugged. "It's bound to cost a bit. . . . But I know a man in Dublin who can fix it up for us. He'll talk them into accepting a small pension, in return for giving up all rights to the girl. We can't afford any mistakes, once we get properly under way."

Thus it was arranged; and the 'man in Dublin' presently reported that the Costello parents had agreed to Esther's being legally adopted. They didn't seem to have much idea, he said, of what the girl was really worth. . . . When this was satisfactorily disposed of, Charles Bannister touched on his own position.

"We'd better tell people," he suggested, "that I was in the war, and then I had some British Government job that took me travelling round the world. Now that's finished with, and so we're together again."

"What about Esther?" said Mrs. Bannister. "She's liable to be jealous."

"You needn't go into any details, with her," he answered. "Just say that I'm a friend of yours, and that I'm helping you with general organization. She'll soon get used to my being around."

"But she'll know——" Mrs. Bannister hesitated. "She'll know that you're living here—and everything."

He grinned. "She needn't know about *everything*," he said. "Not unless she climbs into bed with us one morning." He laughed again. "Not that I've any real objection to that."

"Now, Charles. . . ." But in spite of the past, she still did not take the remark, or its implications, seriously. "There's no need to put everything in technicolour."

"Well, explain it to her how you like. Perhaps it might be better to tell her the truth about us—some of the truth," he amended. "As long as she realizes that I'm in charge of things, helping the two of you to organize yourselves. . . . . And," he went on, less agreeably, "as long as everyone else realizes it."

"How do you mean?"

"I mean Paul Marchant," he said bluntly. "And any other of your friends who want to interfere."

"I haven't seen Paul in months," she said defensively. "Well, I have."

"When?" She was very surprised. "What happened?"

"He called round when you were out," said Charles Bannister. "Wanted to know what was going on, and who I was. Damned cheek. . . ."

"What did you say?"

"I said I was the husband," he answered. "The husband in the story, who comes back and kicks up a row, *if necessary*. Then I asked him who he was."

"What did *he* say?"

"He said he wasn't anyone special, and I said: 'I agree', and that was really all. Somehow I don't think we'll see him again."

"But I'm very fond of Paul."

"Too bad. . . . It was just one of the things that needed organizing. Like the parents. Like my position here, as far as Esther is concerned. I want to clear the ground, and then get to work."

The precise way in which he would 'get to work' was the subject of many discussions between them: in those simpler days, she accepted most of his ideas without argument, and, when he seemed to grow too cynical or opportunist, she put it down to the hard life he had been leading recently. . . . In some ways, she encouraged him to plan these extensions to their activities; she cherished the vague idea that the busier he was, the less likely to get into trouble.

"We want to raise the level of the whole thing," he said once. "Esther's pretty well-known in the east, already; we want to extend the lectures and the personal appearances, till she can go anywhere, coast to coast, and be sure of a hearing. Then we'll think about a world tour."

"But it can't last for ever," said Mrs. Bannister doubtfully.
"Not on those lines. People will lose interest, unless it's
tied to something definite. We ought to make it a million-
dollar appeal, or a hospital for the blind, or something like
that."

"I'm working on that," he told her briskly. "But we
don't want to fix any definite sum, and we don't want a specific
building either—otherwise we run out of attractions as soon
as we've reached our target. We want something big but
vague—something like an Esther Costello Corporation. It
will collect money for the blind—and we'll have a free hand
to allocate the money ourselves."

"We'll need some other people, to make it look right,"
said Mrs. Bannister. "The public like a lot of names."

"One can always buy names," he said. "Take a look
at the cosmetic advertisements. . . . As long as we retain
effective control, it doesn't matter how many guinea-pigs
there are on the board."

"Church people are a good bet," she said, after a pause,
prepared to be helpful. "Bishops, clergymen. . . . In fact
we might give the whole thing a religious angle. It still
draws the crowds in America—and the confidence."

"What sort of religion?"

"Well, Esther's a Roman Catholic, technically. So am I,
for that matter."

"Charles Bannister considered the point.

"No, not R.C.," he said finally. "It's too sectional—you
make too many enemies at the same time as you make friends."
He smirked. "It's really too early to try to get her canonized."

"Charles, please! . . . Something else, then. What about
Methodist?"

He shook his head again. "Not even that. Religious
people are so damned clannish. . . . Better keep it vague
—like the Corporation itself. It gives us a lot more scope.

Don't forget," he added, "that she's got to have a *universal* appeal." He smirked again. "It would be a pity if we left the Jews out of a thing like this."

"It's a big job, however you handle it," Mrs. Bannister commented. "Are you still sure you want to go ahead with it, Charles?"

"Yes," he answered. "That's one thing I am sure of."

In those early days, they were on a level plane of intention. But it was not long before she was left far behind, whence even her protests could not reach him.

They started with a tour to the west coast; it was an obvious extension of their activities in the east, and they had, to guide them, a path already well beaten by boxers, wrestlers, burlesque artists, religious sectarians, and lecturers on English literature in the seventeenth century. . . . Their westward tour lasted over three months, and they were fortunate in many things: in the weather, the absence of other attractions, and the fact that, though this was the farthest from home that Esther had ever travelled, her fame had already preceded her.

It developed into a triumphal progress, covering over twenty major towns and many hundreds of miles; wherever they went, Charles Bannister, travelling ahead, had been able to arrange meetings, demonstrations, radio broadcasts, TV appearances—all the accompaniments that buttress fame. His task was not difficult, since most people on their journey had heard of Esther, most editors were ready to give her space, most local charitable bodies were eager to co-operate. By now, Esther Costello had caught on, and the Esther Costello Guild had won itself a niche in the American mind that ensured for it, and for her, an uncritical welcome and a solid body of public support.

The Bannisters had thought it best to regularize (in their own sense) Esther's position, before they set out on their tour;

and the Esther Costello Guild was already a reality. Besides
themselves, they had co-opted on to the board of trustees the
kind of people who invited the confidence of the simple and
spiked the guns of the inquisitive: the Guild, as set out on its
letter-headings and throw-away leaflets, looked good from
every angle save that of a chartered accountant. The Board,
in addition to the Bannisters (who remained in full control),
consisted of four other advisory members. They were a
bachelor earl, somewhat discredited in England, whose sexual
foibles were not yet common property in America; a Mid-
Western bishop, ill-advised by an ambitious chaplain; a
ranking city politician who commanded a large and sym-
pathetic local following; and an old-time aviatrix ('Birdwoman
No. 1'—'First Lady of the Skies'), over whose wandering
mind Charles Bannister had, at some crucial moment in the
past, established an effective hold.

With this crew to hallow its activities, the Esther Costello
Guild declared itself open for business. Business, from the
very beginning, was brisk; and it gathered momentum until,
by the time they reached California, traditional home of
lunatic causes, they were a riotous and golden success.
California took them to its heart; and in particular, Hollywood, seeming to recognize in Esther someone in its own
idiom, a manufactured creature whose appearance could set the
crowds gaping—Hollywood accorded them the full treatment.

It was scarcely flattering to be thus identified, but it
produced notable results. They held a series of five public
meetings, all crowded out and all conspicuously profitable.
Esther was interviewed continuously, via Mrs. Bannister.
She signed autographs, and her guided hand was the feature
photograph on scores of front pages. She toured the film-
studios, and met selected film stars. ("How terrible!" said
one of these, struck by Esther's basic tragedy. "She's never
seen any of my pictures. . . .") She left her foot-prints, in

cement, in front of a famous theatre, in between those of a collie dog and a cowboy's horse. (It was suggested that she made her eye-prints instead, but this was not a feasible proposition: the nose intervened.) She was the centrepiece of a fabulous party given by a world-renowned studio magnate, at which there were three separate brawls among the guests, and a hold-up by one of the hired waiters. She received a proposal of marriage from an ageing Roumanian prince who was seeking, by means of this—his sixth—union, to repair fortunes shattered as long ago as 1906.

The Hollywood climax, in fact, produced immediate dividends, as far as money and publicity were concerned. But in particular, it produced, in Charles Bannister's hotel suite, one April evening, a man called Jack Lett.

Charles Bannister was alone, and rather tired, when the caller's card was brought to him; Esther and Mrs. Bannister had already gone to bed, and he was thinking of doing the same, aided by a highball long and strong enough to serve for half-a-dozen night caps. 'Jack Lett—Novelties', proclaimed the card, in an unusual form of script reminiscent of second-century Chinese: the name meant nothing to him, and the word 'novelties' conjured up a vision of coloured paper hats with 'Kiss and Tell" inscribed upon the brim. . . . But there had been many such visitors, some of them worth seeing: it was part of a pattern of success which Charles Bannister had no wish to vary. He said to the waiting bell-hop: "Send him up," and added a touch more whisky to his highball. He would go to bed in half-an-hour instead of a quarter.

He did not go to bed in half-an-hour, or anything like it. Jack Lett was not that kind of man, and the occasion proved to be not that sort of occasion.

The visitor who presently shouldered his way into the room was a tough, bustling, stocky character who looked like a salesman's dream of himself next year. He was small, square, olive-skinned, alert: he carried, clenched in one over-burdened hand, two fat brief-cases, and a green hat with a curly and aggressive brim. He came forward briskly, almost running, the other hand outstretched, and said:

"Captain Bannister?" His voice was like his hand—outstretched to clasp the customer. "Hope you don't mind my butting in this way—I wanted to meet the brains of the organization!"

Charles Bannister frowned. This was the sort of moment when he reminded himself that, but for a trifling irregularity, he might have been commissioned in a Guards' regiment. He said coldly:

"I'm Captain Bannister, yes. What can I do for you?"

"It's the other way around, Captain." Not put out by this chilly greeting, the man laid down his hat, and the brief-cases, and smiled at Charles Bannister as if the latter had just paid him some extravagant kind of compliment. His voice— harsh and yet winning, warm as a patch of carpet in the sun— filled the hotel room. "It's what *I* can do for *you*. . . . I'm Jack Lett. You've seen my card. It says 'novelties', and it means just that." His hand darted out, seized the nearest brief-case, and drew something from it. "Now just tell me how you like this."

'This' was an ornament made of coloured plastic. It had the same shape as the trio of monkeys—one guarding its eyes, one its ears, one its mouth—familiar to most people over the cautionary directive, 'Hear no evil, see no evil, speak no evil'. But the three figures were not monkeys: they were human, and female; and the face of each was a very fair imitation of Esther's. At the base of the ornament was the legend: 'BE LIKE ESTHER COSTELLO'.

In the pause that followed, Jack Lett said: "It's just an idea, Captain. I've got lots more like it. I wanted to try this one for size."

In spite of himself, Charles Bannister could not help feeling a trifle sick. He was ready to agree that the ornament was, in a way, simply a 'novelty', a commercial demonstration of Esther Costello's known personality; but there was something in the three figures, and the hands over the eyes, ears, and mouth, which seemed an indecent comment upon her. It was akin to a Christmas-time advertisement which had shocked him when he first saw it: 'Unbeatable Value in Plastic Crib Sets—4 Animals, 3 Wise Men, Manger, Mother, Babe: $1.98.'

Aware of his hesitation, Jack Lett was already talking fast. "I've got plenty more ideas like it. You needn't take this one. I think we might do business. That little girl of yours" —he raised his fingers, and kissed them, like a head-waiter over the sauce—"she's a natural. I've been to all your meetings. Everybody's talking about her. You want to cash in, Captain—in a dignified way, of course."

"Dignified," repeated Charles Bannister, looking at the three figures. And then: "You had this specially made— have you got a factory, or what?"

Jack Lett shook his head. "No, sir. I deal in ideas. I had it made by a friend of mine, because I wanted to illustrate an idea for you. I've got lots more. I thought we could do some business together. Are you interested?"

"I haven't thought of it," said Charles Bannister, untruthfully. "All we've done so far is to have these lectures and demonstrations—raising money for the blind."

Jack Lett nodded energetically. "And very fine work, too," he said. "I haven't yet had the pleasure of meeting Mrs. Bannister, but it was clear to me, from watching her, that she's a fine woman, a deeply religious woman, devoted to the interests of this child."

"Yes, indeed," said Charles Bannister.

"Then we can do business. . . . It's fine work," he repeated, "but there's never any harm in building up a side-line. It always helps with the publicity." His hand darted into the brief-case again. "Have a look at this."

This was a large toy dog, made of brown felt—an Alsatian. Round its neck was a collar with the words: 'Esther Costello's Seeing Eye'.

"It barks and whines," said Jack Lett. "We could sell a million. . . ." He seemed to be bursting out of his clothes at the thought. "Lots of money for the blind, and a little for me. . . . I thought up a game, too," he said, and plunged down again. "Now this could sweep the country. It's like Snakes-and-Ladders—you know how *that* works." He pro-duced a board, and unfolded it. Its details were too intricate for Charles Bannister to take in all at once, but he saw that the board was marked out in a progressive series of squares, forming a pathway leading to the centre, which was labelled: 'Sight, Hearing, Speech'. He read the words: 'Meet Mrs. Bannister—Go Forward Six Squares', and farther on: 'Trip Over Steps—Go Back Four'. Swallowing, he said:

"I think we'd better both have a drink."

Nodding yet more vigorously still, Jack Lett said: "Sure thing, Captain—I knew you'd be interested," and then, as Charles Bannister turned to the side-table, he went on: "I thought of a cracker-jack advertising slogan. For that break-fast food—can't remember which one it is. Say to the kids: '*You* are lucky—Esther Costello cannot hear it go snap, crackle, pop.' Don't see why they shouldn't buy it. . . . Here's something else again."

Charles Bannister turned with the drink in his hand, wondering what more could be coming. He saw that Jack Lett was now nursing a doll.

"The Esther Costello Doll," he explained with pride. "The eyes open. . . ." He tipped the doll, and pointed. The eyeballs had been painted white. "The mouth moves. . . ."

He squeezed the neck, and the doll's lips moved—soundlessly.
"There's nothing to the ears," he said regretfully. "But the
rest is authentic. The hair is nylon. The kids will be wild
for this one." He took the proffered glass. "Here's to the
future. We could certainly make it a bright one."

As he drank, Charles Bannister's only thought was: 'Belle
isn't going to like this at all.' But it was not a consideration
that had a great deal of weight by now.

It was very much later when Jack Lett took his leave:
much later, and much farther on. Between them, they had
come to a provisional agreement. Lett was to use Esther's
name on various products and toys, all of which had to be
approved by Charles Bannister. "Preserve dignity," said the
latter, by now somewhat drunk as well as inspired. "Very
important. . . ." There would be a royalty on each article
produced. The use of her name would be exclusive to Jack
Lett. Advertising would be tied up with their tours and
lectures. The range of products could be widened limitlessly
—anything from children's hot water bottles to Esther
Costello shoes—'Walk with confidence'—'No false steps'—
their ideas poured out, matching the whisky. They were
in the mood in which victories are plotted, empires built,
presidents nominated, Africa carved up. But Jack Lett's best
idea came towards the end.

"We want to get the kids really organized," he said
dreamily. He had mellowed somewhat during the long
session: he now sounded like a benevolent uncle planning a
birthday for them both. "Form a nation-wide club—the
Esther Costello Junior Club—something like that. Get them
to collect money, help at the meetings. Dress them up.
Like Hopalong Cassidy." His eyes brightened. "Sell them
a uniform—Irish type—an apron with a shamrock, a green
hat: the Esther Costello outfit. Like Hopalong Cassidy."

Charles Bannister started to speak, and Jack Lett raised his hand. "You don't have to worry," he said. "We'll keep it dignified."

"I was going to say," said Charles Bannister, "that I just thought of a good name for them." He raised a portentous finger, emphasizing the punch line. "Not Hopalong—Tapalong. Because she's blind. The Tapalongs." He began to improvise, feeling articulate and brilliant. "The children all start as Junior Tapalongs. Then they collect money, or fill in a card with stamps, or enrol a lot of members, and they get to be Senior Tapalongs, or Grand Tapalongs, or something."

"And Esther," said Jack Lett, catching his mood, suddenly bursting with it, "can be at the top of the tree, the hidden secret figure in the middle. The Mystic Colleen Tapalong. Like the Shriners. . . . Charlie," he said—and Charles Bannister no longer winced—"Charlie, you're a genius."

'Genius' was not among the many words which Mrs. Bannister used, when confronted with these plans next morning. For one of the few times in her joint life with Charles Bannister, she was lividly angry, and she made the fact clear, in a stormy interview which they both remembered for long afterwards. More memorable still was the fact that it was the last time that she opposed her husband, where Esther was concerned. Thereafter, defeated, she let him have his way.

But before she got to that point, many things were said that widened for ever the gulf between them.

"You can't do it, Charles," she said, again and again. "I'm not going to allow it. It's not fair to Esther. She's happy, everything's going well, we make plenty of money. Why spoil it with all this"—she searched for a word—"this exploitation?"

"It's not spoiling it," said Charles Bannister. He was

liverish and irritable after the long session of the night before, and he felt in the mood for a showdown. Very soon the moment for that would come. . . . "I'm just extending it a bit, that's all."

"Extending it? It's the rottenest idea you've ever produced —and that's saying a hell of a lot! No, Charles," she shook her head vehemently. "You've got to leave things as they are. I'm not going to have the kid ruined like this."

Charles Bannister ground out his cigarette, and looked across at her coldly. "You're going to do exactly what I say," he told her, in his most even voice. "Let's get that straight. *I'm* running this show. We agreed on that, a very long time ago."

"We didn't agree to a lot of trash like this." She motioned contemptuously towards the litter of objects that lay between them on the table: the dog, the doll, the snakes-and-ladders game, the trio of monkey-like figures—all of them forlorn, ugly, and indecent in the morning sunlight. "Just look at them. . . . If you had two cents' worth of shame in you, you'd throw the lot out into the street."

"Well, I haven't that two cents worth, and you should know it by now." His voice was tough and edgy. "We're going ahead with all this"—he gestured, as she had done, but with satisfaction instead of disgust—"with the toys, and the trademark, and the club as well. It's a natural development of what we've been doing in the past. We'd be fools not to expand when we've got the chance. . . . Jack Lett is working on it now."

"But it's so—so undignified." Faced with his intransigence, she sought for an argument valid within the framework of his own reasoning. "People won't like it. They'll turn against her."

"This is America," he answered, offensively. "They won't turn against her, because it's how they expect a girl like Esther to be handled. For their money, she can do anything except a strip-tease act at the Hollywood Bowl. . . . Jack Lett has the right idea."

"Jack Lett, Jack Lett!" Suddenly she was nearly screaming, feeling herself being robbed of all she hoped for. "Who the hell is he, anyway? He sounds like a pimp."

"We need a pimp." He was completely uncompromising, completely unaffected by anything she might say: it had always been his deadliest weapon, and now it was routing her. "A commercial pimp to back up what we're doing ourselves. So far, we've only been playing with Esther. . . . That idea of a children's club is a stroke of genius."

"It's a stroke of swindling." Now she could hardly find the words she sought: her mouth, ugly with anger and weakness, worked with difficulty round the tumbling syllables. "I'll take her away from all this—I'll hide her. You won't do this to her."

"I'll do anything I want, anything I choose." Suddenly he was standing up, looking at her with intense hatred and disdain. It was the moment of onslaught. "All those arguments I used, when I first arrived here—they're still as good as they ever were. You've been evading all the charity laws, for years on end—you *know* you have—and as for the Income Tax people"—he grinned suddenly, sardonically—"it's murder, out-and-out murder! You can't fight me, Belle, and it's no use trying. You'll either do exactly as I say, or you'll have a divorce on your hands, and an inquiry into the finances of this whole thing. Whichever way it goes, you'll be finished."

"I'd rather be finished." But already there was a fatal edge of defeat in her voice. "Esther will crack up anyway, if you make her do too much. She's terribly tired, right now."

"That's your part of the job. . . ." By this stage, the subtle alchemy which decides all battles, for or against, had nearly

worked itself out: the colours in the crucible had changed, and
they both knew that Mrs. Bannister was in retreat. "You
keep her going, I do the managing, Jack Lett handles the
commercial side. If she's tired, for God's sake deal with it!
Give her benzedrine. Hire a doctor. Get a nurse." His
contempt as he spoke these words was obvious, and loathsome;
she knew that he was thinking, as he had thought and said
many times before: bloody Americans—that sort of fixing is
all you're good for. . . . "Your job is to keep her fit—and it's
the least of our worries, anyway. Look," he said reasonably,
and she knew it was his old trick of seeming to relent on the
crest of victory, "give it a chance. Jack Lett and I will do
a moderate amount of promotion, on the new lines. Just
wait and see what happens on the journey home."

"It'll spoil everything," she repeated, feebly.

"It'll make us. . . . Just you wait and see."

The journey home, to New York and then to Boston, was
indeed a spectacular success. That 'moderate amount of
promotion' which Charles Bannister had proposed, left
nothing to chance: everything about it—bookings, advertising, radio time, personal appearances, local contacts—all
were handled with a degree of skill and a sureness of touch
which convinced him, more strongly than ever, that Jack
Lett's inclusion in their organization was not a mistake.
Before they set out, Jack Lett went on ahead, bearing not only
the tidings of the Esther Costello Club (which had been
launched in Hollywood), but with invoices for several hundred
thousand Esther Costello products, already ordered in advance,
and a cabin trunk full of samples to drum up further business.
He made good use of his time; and from the very start, as
they retraced their steps in his wake, the idea caught on.

The dolls sold, the dogs sold, the monkey-figures sold like
hamburgers at a race-track; the Snakes-and-Ladders game

(renamed 'Tapalong') became a current epidemic, and Tapalong tournaments supplanted everything save Canasta in the national consciousness. But it was the Esther Costello Club—for girls only—which set all hearts a-beating. Here also they kept the name 'Tapalong', and the proposed sale of uniforms to members: the latter rose in grade from Junior Tapalong to Seeing-Eye Tapalong, in accord with the number of members they enrolled, at a dollar a time. The uniform also followed the line that Jack Lett had planned: it consisted of a white linen apron embroidered with harps, and a kind of beret in the form of a three-leafed shamrock, with 'Tapalong Club' printed on the border, and the stalk hanging down at the back.

Originally, Jack Lett suggested wooden clogs to complete the outfit; but medical opinion was against this. Instead, there was a bunch of three keys, worn on a chain round the neck, and labelled 'Sight', 'Hearing', and 'Speech'. The keys came in five different metals, from aluminium alloy to gold, according to the grade of the member. They were of special significance, and there was a complicated kind of ritual attached to their handling at meetings.

By the time the party reached New York, the club was solidly established; and the rally which they held there set the seal on what was already a national institution. Four hundred club members, in their uniforms, made up the guard of honour: Esther 'spoke' for over an hour; and at the end the collection, taken up by children wielding green shamrock bags at the end of long white wands, brought in nearly twenty thousand dollars.

"White wands?" said Charles Bannister later, querying a modest item in the expense account. "Why white?"

"She's blind," said Jack Lett cheerfully. "It's quite legitimate."

New York was the peak of triumph, Boston the warm

clamour of home-coming. Esther had left her adopted town as a local celebrity, whose name in a Boston headline rang a familiar bell with most readers; she returned, six months later, as a national asset with a coast-to-coast following. Jack Lett, going on ahead as usual to prepare the way, found that there was little to do save co-ordinate Press publicity for Esther's arrival, and then for her first big meeting; the Boston branch of the Esther Costello Club was already established, and, thanks to his local agents, sales of the various games and toys were booming. There was no doubt that Esther Costello had arrived.

But there was no doubt either that, in spite of the nation's acclaim, she was still Boston's own; and Harry Grant of the *Star-Telegram*, who met their party at the station, and subsequently wrote up their arrival in a two-column, half-page spread, hit the gong squarely when he headed it 'HUB'S FAVOURITE DAUGHTER HOME'. Secretly, Mrs. Bannister had been worrying about what he might say: she had noticed him looking somewhat askance at the Tapalong Guard of Honour on the platform, and to her mind he must surely be thinking that the whole thing had become far too streamlined, forfeiting altogether the gentler atmosphere of Esther's first appearances. She had feared some acid kind of comment. . . . But he must have decided to let it go, for he made no mention of this aspect.

Only in his longer piece, when he covered the welcome-home rally, was there a slight hint, towards the end, that he remembered a more subdued Esther, a less slick entourage, a simpler pity.

The leader-page account of this meeting—the greater part of which was later distributed by Jack Lett, in photostat form, to 150,000 schools throughout the United States—marked the crowning moment of Esther's triumph. It was a good piece, halfway between reporting and comment; even

Ryan, the news-editor, who had hesitated about giving Grant
a free hand, was pleased with it.   It told of the ovation which
the packed audience accorded to Esther: of the emotional
climax as she rose to 'speak' and answer questions; and of the
mood of lyrical adoration in which the audience bid her goodnight.   Of this last, Grant spoke with special tenderness.

"There they sat, together on the platform," he wrote,
in a passage which had Ryan frowning throughout: "Mrs.
Bannister in white, Esther in pale blue.   The girl was
obviously tired, after her long ordeal—she was white-
faced, and listless.   By her side, Mrs. Bannister was a
compassionate and wonderfully loving figure.

"Presently it was time to say goodbye—and for Esther,
after the 'speaking', the questions, the effort of communication, it seemed a moment of grateful release.
Our eyes returned again and again to this young girl
who was and is the centre of an extraordinary miracle.
To us, she seemed all things: young, lovely, accomplished
—and fatally stricken.   There can have been very few eyes
among us quite free of tears as we watched her still
figure.

"We in the audience wished her goodnight.   Here and
there a voice, sometimes a man's, sometimes a woman's,
called out: 'We love you, Esther.'   Mrs. Bannister was
constantly speaking to her, telling her all that was said.
We hoped that she was passing on to Esther *everything*
—our love, our admiration, our hope that perhaps some-
day, somehow, somewhere, in spite of all the odds against
her, she might come back to the world again.

"Then she left the platform, gently guided by the
wonderful woman who is her eyes, ears, and tongue.
The audience surged towards her with their hearts full,
striving to give her a last moment of warmth and love.

The children in their strange uniforms, which we must now accept as part of the Esther Costello legend, formed round her at the door. Then she was gone.

"Gone—but leaving many lasting things behind her: leaving tears, emotion, hopes, pity, love.

"Dispersing to our homes, we remembered her as our own Esther, an Irish waif adopted by this city, given hope here, given contact at last with the outside world, by the loving care of a great woman.

"That is all that need matter to us. Forget the 'Esther Costello' toys, forget the dressed-up children and the stagey presentation. These are extras—new additions to our own central, simple figure.

"May such things never obscure her, never spoil the Esther Costello we know, love, wonder at, and pray for."

This story, like Harry Grant's first one of the year before, started a series of other manifestations that were a long time dying down. Esther was *Time's* cover story, a couple of months later: she was named 'Woman of the Year' by another national magazine: her photograph adorned a hundred thousand calendars put out by a Child Care organization. Korean veterans named her 'The Girl We Would Most Readily Give Our Eyes For.'

As a final accolade, her childhood history, her extra-ordinary progress, and her present pinnacle of love and fame, were condensed for eleven million people in a magazine specializing in potted profiles.

The article was entitled: 'BLINDNESS CAN BE FUN.'

CHAPTER ELEVEN

THE suite at the Bristol was wonderfully luxurious, by any standard: Mrs. Bannister, no friend of England, was prepared to admit that where comfort was concerned, some British hotels could give America a smart sort of lesson. The sitting-room looked out over the west of London, allowing her a wide view of rooftops, the trees of green and distant Hyde Park, the hazy warmth of an English summer in town. When she turned from this view to the room again, its elegance and receptive colouring completed a picture with no flaw in it.

Even her husband, lolling deep in an arm-chair as if he had lived in the Bristol all his life, and Jack Lett, shirt-sleeved, murdering a cigar as he paced up and down, could not spoil her sense of well-being. If she had to be in England, this was the town to be in, this was the hotel to stay at, this was the time of the year to make the visit.

It was after lunch: Esther was resting: there was no meeting that night, and therefore no more cares for that day. Lunch, as usual, had been a very good one. At that moment, in spite of the strenuous routine that underlay everything they did these days, in spite of one other factor that lay in the back of her mind, she wanted nothing changed.

Charles Bannister said: "Sit down, Jack, for God's sake. You're making me giddy."

Jack Lett turned, on the ball of one foot, like a dancer. He looked, as he always did, bustling, energetic, forceful: the coiled mainspring of the Esther Costello enterprise. He was putting on weight, thought Charles Bannister, surveying him. And, by God, he could afford to. . . .

Jack Lett looked down at him. "Only way I can think," he said briskly. "And I've got plenty of things to think about."

"What things?" asked Charles Bannister. He did not really want to know: he was contented, slightly muzzy, after the drinks and the long lunch. But he was never prepared to give Jack Lett a free hand, within any part of the organization: he tried always to make the point that Lett's work was only a small proportion of the total of their activities, even though it was clear that the business side of the Guild, the actual selling of Esther Costello products, was looming larger and larger every day.

He remembered that Jack Lett had taken to calling himself Business Manager, and he frowned, and repeated: "What things?" as curtly as he could. Esther Costello was still a Charles Bannister promotion, and she was going to remain so.

"Australia, chiefly," answered Lett. "It seems a hell of a long way to go, just for three weeks' tour. We ought to make it longer."

"That's a policy matter," said Charles Bannister briefly, like a nurse dismissing a child with 'You'll know when you're grown-up'. . . . "Before I mapped out the tour, I had to decide the total amount of time we could spend away from America. I didn't want to make it more than six months, at the outside."

"Why not?" Jack Lett was like Bannister himself, in being impervious to snubbing, unabashed by protocol. "A year wouldn't be too long. I've got a lot of selling to do, before we get back from this world trip."

"In a year, people in America might have time to forget Esther." Charles Bannister, irritated by being lured into discussion, slopped out some more brandy into his balloon glass, and sipped at it, frowning. "That's something I want to avoid."

"But she's making other friends, all the time. It evens out. And America won't forget her so soon, anyway. Not with the kids' clubs working on it the way they are."

"It's dangerous, none-the-less. America is still our top priority. That's where the money is."

"Not all of it. We haven't done so badly here. Look at the Albert Hall meeting. A sell-out."

"Oh, the *meetings* are all right." Charles Bannister's tone was spiteful. "But what about sales? What about the uniforms?"

Jack Lett shrugged. "Goddam British. . . . They don't seem to like dressing-up."

Standing by the window, Mrs. Bannister broke in, with an old argument. "We never really needed to leave home," she said to her husband. "We were doing all right, just on the American basis."

The two men smiled at each other. On this point at least, they were in full agreement.

"Esther's big enough to be a world figure," said Charles Bannister complacently. "This tour will make her just that. Look what's happened here in London—a riot. Look at the Press coverage. They may not buy the uniforms, or the games——"

"Games are O.K.," Jack Lett chipped in. "Twenty-two per cent up on last week."

"—but they do come to the meetings," Bannister continued, ignoring him, "and they do give to the Guild. The same thing's going to happen in Australia, New Zealand, South Africa, Canada—wherever we go. We'll come back to the States on top of the wave."

"With a lot of money, too. . . . A guy asked me yesterday what we did with the profits."

F

"I hope you told him," said Charles Bannister austerely.

"What!   And land us all in jail?"

"We make very substantial donations to charity, and we are building up the Guild all the time." Charles Bannister's voice was positively Victorian in rebuke. It had not proved possible to exclude Jack Lett from the financial side of their activities, and he had an accurate picture of it; but both the Bannisters tried to avoid open discussion on the point.   It tended to weaken their authority. . . .   "We have absolutely nothing to hide."

"And we're all living at the Bristol."   Jack Lett grinned, not innocently.   "Come off it, Charlie, like the British say —you're not talking for the suckers now."

"We are living at the Bristol because it is comfortable for Esther."

"So central, too. . . .   Jesus, who are you trying to convince?"

Charles Bannister frowned.   "We depend completely on the public's confidence. It's very important that all our actions should be above reproach. I deprecate"—he said, looking exceptionally statesmanlike—"I deprecate any loose talk on the subject."

"Then you'd better make a big donation to some blind charity.   And create a lot of noise about it, too."

"Our prime duty is to the Guild.   We have to place it on a solid basis, first."

Jack Lett grinned again, glancing round the room.   "This basis looks solid enough to me. . . .   Look, Charlie, I'm only trying to help.   I've no complaints myself: my side of it is a gold mine—we both know that—and I don't want to interfere with yours.   But if people really started talking, it would kill us all.   That's why I say, come across with a pretty solid donation now, while we're in England. It'll pay us a dividend, in the end."

"I think he's right, Charles," said Mrs. Bannister. "Surely we can afford a few thousand dollars."

"Of course we can afford it. The central Guild fund now stands at"—he checked himself—"at a very substantial figure. But I don't want people to get into the way of thinking that we can answer every call on us. We have to build up a solid reserve.

"I think," said Jack Lett, "that you ought to distribute not less than twenty per cent."

"There's no point in going to extremes," answered Bannister coldly. He stood up, brandy glass in hand: dapper, correct, well-tailored, very English among these crude transatlantics. "It's a policy matter," he said, swaying slightly, repeating the magic, exclusive phrase. "You can leave that sort of thing to me."

Jack Lett turned towards the door, shrugging it all off. "Well, I've got to meet a man. . . . Are we having dinner here in the hotel?"

"Yes. . . . I thought we might take Esther down to the restaurant. People like to see her."

"She's tired," objected Mrs. Bannister. "And we've got that farewell meeting at the end of the week, before we sail."

"She doesn't look tired," said her husband. "She never does. Wonderful girl." His tone was dwelling. "I'd like to take her down to dinner. It makes me feel twenty years younger, just to look at her."

Mrs. Bannister stared at him, speculatively. "That would make you thirty-five, Charles."

"A man is as old as he feels," he answered largely. "Wonderful girl," he repeated. It was the brandy talking. "Best-looking girl in London. No wonder people stare at her." His voice, unguarded, slurring, had a lickerish edge to it. "In fact, I stare at her myself."

I stare at her myself. . . . Mrs. Bannister, strolling in Hyde Park in the late afternoon sunshine, pondered the remark, and all its implications. She knew that it was true, and she knew it could be disastrous.

There was no room for ambiguity, in at least two things. Esther *was* lovely—now, nearly twenty, she was in the full tide of her glowing beauty. Charles *was* a completely unprincipled man, accustomed to taking whatever he wanted. Put the two of them together. . . . It would not matter to him that Esther was defenceless. It would not matter to him that she was as innocent as air. It would not matter that, at his age, such a liaison would be especially degrading, even apart from its grotesque cruelty. If Charles felt like it, he would do it.

She knew now that he did feel like it. There had been many indications, some faint, some strong, all of them conclusive—if one knew Charles Bannister.

It was a pity they were in London. She looked around her at the green of the Park, the red buses and the traffic through the trees, the lovers and the children lying on the grass. It should have been wonderful, but all it meant was that they were now in Charles's own setting—he was securely at home in this town, and he grew in stature and authority with every day they stayed there. Already, he was quite beyond her control: he drank far too much, he lived (as they all did) at a pitch of extravagance which endangered their reputation. (She remembered an item in his expense account, 'Car Hire, Ascot: £46'. They were collecting money for the blind.) But there could be no argument with him: this was his own home-ground, where he felt he could do as he liked. He had been poor here, now he was rich: it meant that he would take whatever he chose. Part of what he chose was going to be Esther.

Mrs. Bannister stood stock still, miserable, jealous, and

afraid. She had come a long way with Esther: a loving way, a tiring way, a triumphant way. Now the whole thing was in fearful danger—because she had been so successful, because Esther, her own creation, was so lovely and so vulnerable. Now the girl was likely to be destroyed, for the second time.

As usual with Charles Bannister, there was nothing to be done about it.

She collected her thoughts, and began to retrace her steps, across the Park towards the hotel.

She let herself into the suite quietly, closing the door with a furtive hand. She crossed to her own room, still treading softly, and entered it. She did not switch on the lights. Instead, she walked to the window that gave on to the balcony, and looked out, enjoying, as always, the view of London at dusk. There was magic in the lights, entrancement in the pale night sky above the rooftops: the traffic noises far below whispered like a nocturne. Then a slight movement on the balcony outside caught her eye.

A few yards along, level with Esther's room which adjoined her own, a man was crouching.

She knew now why she had entered the suite like a conspirator; she knew that the man was Charles, and she knew what he was doing He was looking through the curtains into Esther's room, where Esther was either in bed, or dressing for the evening.

Sick at heart, powerless before evil, she opened the communicating door and went into the next room. Without surprise, she saw that Esther was standing before her wardrobe, naked, feeling for some underclothes on one of the upper shelves. Her slim body, reaching upwards, had a flawless grace.

Not looking towards the window, ignoring the gap in the curtain, Mrs. Bannister touched the girl gently on the

shoulder, and then began to help her. She felt herself
trembling, and her protective back, now placed between
Esther and the window, seemed to be on fire.

Mrs. Bannister had no idea what to do, except never to
leave Esther undefended. She had the desperate hope that
if she could only stave off the crisis until they left England,
it would make a vital difference: once out of London, Charles
Bannister would surely shrink again, and lose his dangerous
quality, and become manageable. She blamed herself for
not having foreseen this disgusting turn of events—or rather,
for having foreseen it and yet decided that it could not
possibly happen. She remembered a thousand things that
had been pointers, as sharp as needles, towards the present
situation.

They had been living too close together, all the time. She
had seen Charles eyeing the girl, letting his eyes slide down
from throat to waist, from waist to thigh, unguarded in lust,
secure in Esther's blindness—and she had still thought:
he *can't* intend to do a thing like that. She had noticed him
helping Esther, leading her forward with an arm round
her waist, once fondling her neck as he helped to fasten
her necklace. She had allowed him to hold the girl's hand
and arm for an hour or more, trying—or pretending to try—
to communicate with her as she did herself.

She had watched him exploit all the furtive contacts to
which Esther was exposed, under the cloak of 'guidance'
—hand on elbow or shoulder as she went through a doorway,
hand on waist or thigh as her chair-cushion was adjusted.
She had seen her husband meanly taking advantage of
all these opportunities—and then seen his eyes and face
change, as he became aware that he was being watched.

She had observed all these things, for many months past;
and she had done nothing, because she had hoped that

the ugly affair would resolve itself. Now she was not sure that there could be any solution, save in flight or in the last dishonour—for him to slake his body at the blind fountain he desired.

Peace lay over the Bristol suite. They were due to sail in a few days' time on the Australian leg of the tour; most of their luggage, already packed, had gone down to the steamship offices, and their rooms now seemed bare and impermanent, waiting for them to leave. It was a suspended moment, a moment of silence and uncertainty.

Mrs. Bannister, packing the last of Esther's clothes, went down the short corridor and into the girl's bathroom, to sort out the toilet things she would need on the voyage. The room was clean and bright, the sunlight falling on the polished tiles and reflecting long, mote-filled shafts from there on to the ceiling; it was an enclosed hygienic box, lined with mirrors, steam-warmed and perfumed, a room for nakedness, relaxation, private security.

With her hand poised to open the medicine-chest above the wash-basin, Mrs. Bannister heard a slight movement behind her. She turned, startled, but found nothing—nothing save the wind rustling the water-proofed curtains that hung round the shower.

They were still trembling slightly, slurring against the tiled wall, as she turned back again. Then, on the instant, it was she who was trembling, as she noticed something else about the bathroom.

It had a single window, and that window was closed. There could therefore be no draught, to make the shower curtains move.

When, turning once more, she called out: "Charles. . ." she could hardly articulate, so tightly strangled was her dry throat.

The curtains moved again. Charles Bannister's face appeared between them, inquiringly. He was not taken aback: he was even smiling.

"Hope I didn't startle you," he said. "I was just looking at this tap. It's leaking."

For a split second she thought of accepting the absurd explanation, and passing the whole thing off. Then the tide of her fear and horror returned to engulf her, and she swallowed and said:

"You were waiting here to watch Esther."

"Don't be absurd, Belle." There was still no embarrassment in his voice: she could not remember a better performance, in all their long years together. "What on earth would I do that for?"

"You wanted to watch her." Mrs. Bannister's voice was choking with disgust. "It's her own bathroom. She always uses it. But, *I* came in instead."

"The tap," he said briefly. "Only you call it a faucet. It leaks. I'm fixing it."

"You were hiding behind that curtain, waiting for Esther."

"The *faucet*. It leaks."

His face between the shower curtains was gravely controlled: only his words were false and lying, not meeting her own at all. It was as if they were drawing farther and farther apart: it reminded her of a nightmare, when one person strives to behave normally, while another conducts some insane antic. The two of them could never meet, never eliminate the hideous ground that lay between.

In the face of his bland and insolent assurance, her own excited loathing was beginning to look foolish. For the thousandth time in her life—even now at this special pitch of guilt—she could not prick his guard.

"If you hurt her, Charles," she said at last, intensely, "it will finish everything. I'll go to the police."

His face, mildly surprised, regarded hers steadily.

"I don't know what you're talking about." He stepped between the curtains, and out on to the cork floor: she saw that he was in his shirt-sleeves, and carried some kind of wrench or spanner in his hand. He held it out to her. "See?" he said amiably. "I was fixing the tap."

"You were waiting for Esther."

He shook his head, as if the situation were beyond him. "Very well," he said cheerfully, "I *was* waiting for her. With a spanner. I always use a spanner. The adjustable kind—so convenient for little girls."

"You filthy bastard!" she shouted at him, suddenly beyond control. His unabashed and smiling face, mature, experienced, elegantly framed by the iron-grey hair, was more than she could stomach. "Is there any rotten thing in the world you wouldn't do?"

"The tap," he said quietly. It was the lunatic, nightmare answer once more. "It leaks. I was fixing it."

"If you harm her," she said, "I'll kill you!"

"I wouldn't harm her." She saw that he was now laughing quietly. "Not with my little adjustable spanner. Never. . . . I'm *much* too fond of her."

It was like a siege, a siege with the enemy already within the ramparts: a jungle with the bandit waiting in silence beneath the trees, ears cocked for the snap of a twig. It was like the doors double-locked for the night, and the burglar within; it was the zoo gardens at dusk, with the gates closed and the cages left open. It was the food, gratefully swallowed, that will swell and choke in the throat; the welcomed caress that turns to throttling.

That particular night, the night before they sailed, Charles Bannister got drunk at dinner; otherwise Mrs. Bannister

F*

would never have left him alone in the hotel. But by nine o'clock he was snoring on the sitting-room sofa: she had some friends she wanted to say goodbye to, and she welcomed the chance of leaving him, with a clear conscience, and going out. The unrelaxed surveillance of the past few days had been getting on her nerves.

Esther was in her own room, with the door locked. Jack Lett would be back from his party before very long. There was nothing that could go wrong. . . . She could still hear Charles's steady snores as she let herself out of the front door.

Esther had laid down her Braille edition of *David Copperfield*, and was drowsing in bed, when she felt the draught from the open window strike upon her bare arms, and ruffle her hair. For a moment she was puzzled, and then she decided that Mrs. Bannister must have come in, as she had promised to do, and opened the balcony window to the cool of the night. She waited without anxiety for the touch on her shoulder which would be her familiar greeting.

The greeting did not come. Instead, the draught on her arms died to nothing again, and she felt the vibration of uneven footsteps on the floor near her bed. She raised her nostrils, and sniffed. There was the cigar smell—and the queer smell that Mrs. Bannister said was whisky—and then the smell of a man. . . . She drew the bedclothes high around her shoulders, and waited uneasily. This was something outside her experience.

It was the first of many such things. There began to take place around her a series of movements which at first puzzled and then terrified her. There were twitchings on the bed-clothes around her shoulders, a furtive hand in her hair, then on her shoulder, then exploring beneath the covers themselves. At this last, she whimpered soundlessly within her throat, and stretched out her arms, trying to ward off something she could not see and did not understand. Her arms touched nothing—and while she was thus groping, other arms came up beneath her guard and clutched her round the waist.

The bed moved sharply as someone lurched or fell against it. A living weight materialized upon the lower half of her body. Then there was a fearful pause, with nothing in her world; and then a hand closed on her bared breast, and another began to fumble and pluck incomprehensibly at her thighs. She fought and cried out, and continued to fight and cry all through the crude disposal of her body; but the scrabbling hands and the rest of it soon lost their incomprehensibility— they were suddenly, loathsomely tied to whispers and sniggers heard long years ago, to her own questionings, her own warm desires.

When she had screamed and fought and lost her blind battle, she bore all things under a crescendo of pain; but there was still a small margin of horror left when presently she found that she could *see* the shape of a man leaving her, and *hear* the sound of his moaning breath.

So Esther awoke once more to the full delights of the world.

PART THREE

PART · THREE

CHAPTER TWELVE

AUSTRALIA loved her. Perth, Adelaide, Melbourne, Sydney
—they flocked to her meetings, joined the club in hundreds,
gave with both hands. Esther was presented with a half
life-size toy kangaroo, containing a cheque for two thousand
Australian pounds tucked into its pouch. She was 'rescued'
by life guards on Bondi Beach, and given an ovation and
a shower of silver coinage as she was carried up the
beach. She was photographed against a background of
Sydney Harbour, with the caption: 'Wishes She Could
See It.'

"Too bad you had to delay the trip," said a man in
Melbourne to Mrs. Bannister. "Doesn't seem to have made
much difference to the public, though."

"We just *couldn't* leave England," said Mrs. Bannister.
"You know how it is when you get tied up."

New Zealand loved her. Auckland, Wellington, Christchurch—they drove in from hundreds of miles around,
just to spend an hour at one of her meetings. They gave
her a stuffed kiwi, with a purse full of sovereigns in its beak.
She was photographed holding out her hands towards one
of the hot-spring geysers, under the heading: 'One Natural
Phenomenon Meets Another'. In Wellington, fifty members
of the Southern Cross Tapalong Club drew her car all the
way from the railway station to her hotel, on a blazing
hot day which prostrated eleven girls under the age of
fourteen.

.   .   .   .

South Africa loved her. Johannesburg, Durban, Bloem-
fontein, Cape Town—it was impossible to keep the crowds
away, even with policemen well-schooled in the art of mob
control. Her progress up Adderley Street in Cape Town
rivalled the visit of the Royal Family. She was given the
freedom of Johannesburg, a Zulu shield and spear in Durban,
and a walking-stick decorated with pure white beads in
Pretoria. In the Orange Free State she was taken down a
gold mine, and photographed holding a gold ingot, with the
foreseeable caption: 'Golden Girl'.

When she patted a half-naked negro child in one of the
Transvaal locations, hundreds of native women burst into
chanting praise of what seemed to them a spectacular ex-
hibition of humanity.

"What held you up?" asked a reporter in Johannesburg.
"We were expecting you three months ago."

"We had to delay our start," answered Mrs. Bannister.
"Esther overtaxed her strength in London."

Canada loved her. Quebec, Montreal, Ottawa, Toronto
—wherever she appeared, she was greeted as though she
brought a long-awaited message from another world. In
Quebec, six thousand French-Canadian children acclaimed
her with songs round a camp-fire. In Toronto, the Maple
Leaf Tapalongs staged a picnic excursion to Lake Ontario,
with fireworks, which brought in nearly eleven thousand
dollars. She was made an honorary member of the premier
ice-hockey team, and photographed with four red-tuniced
Mounted Police under the heading: 'Mounties Get Their Girl'.
In Montreal, an over-zealous Canadian patriot who called her
'an American brat' was almost lynched by the crowd.

America loved her for coming back to them again.
Chicago, Cleveland, Washington, New York—it was a

triumphal progress, ecstatic, warm-hearted, as if they had to make up to her for her nine months' exile among the barbarians. Even Jack Lett, who had always been worried about the long time spent abroad, had no complaints about their welcome. The Chicago branch of the club (Windy City Tapalongs) greeted her at the U.S.-Canadian border with a mile-long torchlight procession which gave the police and the fire department a completely sleepless night. She was presented with a miniature churn made entirely of butter —there had been some talk of how sorely she had missed this commodity in England. Washington (prompted by Jack Lett) planned to give her the millionth flask of Esther Costello Healing Oil, at a presentation ceremony under the shadow of the Capitol.

Harry Grant of the Boston *Star-Telegram* met them at Washington airport.

"Expected you a lot earlier," he said, smiling at Mrs. Bannister as he shook her hand. "You were a long time in England—they said you almost went into hiding. Is there a story there?"

"Not a paragraph," said Mrs. Bannister decisively. "Esther just had to rest before the world tour. . . ." She looked up at him: it was fine to see his tall, rangy, unexpected figure, after all the strange places and the thousands of miles of travelling. "But what are you doing in Washington?"

"Covering the welcome home. . . . It's a nice break from Boston." He looked across at Esther, standing immobile under the wing of the aircraft as the flash-bulbs exploded. "And pretty good to see you all again."

Harry Grant had not always felt that way about the assignment. Four days before, when Ryan, the news-editor, had called him into his office and told him to cover the latter half of Esther's homecoming, from Washington to

Boston, he had been ready to argue about it. Yet another two years on the *Star-Telegram*, with little measurable progress to show for them, had given an obtrusive edge to Grant's self-confidence. If you said 'yes' to everyone, he had learnt, no one said 'yes' to you. . . .

"Esther Costello?" he repeated, on a rising note, as if Ryan had said: 'Write a very long piece about Father Christmas': "Esther Costello? What's new there? People know the story by heart, already."

"She's been away for nine months, raising all kinds of money," answered Ryan. He liked Harry Grant for sticking his chin out a bit, but it wasn't going to interfere with his assignments on the paper. Not yet, anyway. "That makes it a triumphant homecoming. I want you to go along with them, and cover the finish of the tour, from that angle. Intimate story of Boston's own heroine. Blind Goddess Returns—we haven't used that one yet."

Harry Grant frowned. "I hope we never will. . . . You mean, all the way to Washington, just for that?"

"And New York as well. You'll love it."

"I'm not a travelling man. . . . It's the same old story, in any case. I can write it from here."

Ryan looked surprised, even hurt: it was his least con- vincing expression. "I thought you'd jump at it. It's *your* story, Harry. You've done more than anyone else to put Esther on the map."

Grant shrugged. "More's the pity. . . . I think she's a racket, anyway."

"How?"

"Oh, I don't mean a *racket*, like protection or the horses. The girl's a marvel, and she makes all the money there is for the blind. It's just"—he gestured irritably—"it's not like it was at the beginning. It's too organized, too much of a circus."

"That's what brings the money in."

"Sure. But it isn't *Esther*. There's too much streamlining —managers, Press hand-outs, clubs, uniforms, those lousy dolls. . . . And then the meetings themselves—it's too much of an act, all the way through. Sure, it raises money! But she's *too* helpless, *too* clever, *too* radiating. Too many people pay to come in, too many people cry. . . . Of course it's a miracle, but the miracle's been crowded out by too many other things—at top prices." He paused. "Can I write it that way?"

"No."

When Harry Grant had gone, Ryan switched to the next job; but his thoughts kept returning, now and then, to their discussion, and the return was not comfortable. Basically, he agreed with what Grant had said about Esther Costello: she *was* a racket—like everyone else, from the tubercular to the legless veteran, who was exposed for charity; and the charity-angle didn't alter the fact of racketeering, either. Esther was now one of an accepted company, whose role in life was to excite, first disgust, and then a liberal pity in the passers-by. She had joined the ranks of the beggars with sores, the polio victims dragging themselves along the streets, the old women with no noses, the children marching on their stumps.

There had been regular gangs of them in the Bible, Ryan recalled: roving bands of halt and maimed, who collected wherever there was a crowd, and were always good for a parable or two. . . . They used to hang around Christ, in those days; now they haunted the cripple-care agencies or (if they were properly handled, and could fix the police) the busier sidewalks.

One could not blame the victims themselves, when they cashed in on their handicaps. The world owed them something, for playing such crude jokes upon them. . . . Esther Costello, for example, could not be blamed for her

blind eyes, her hideous voice which was now being trained
to ape human tones; and she was entitled to extract from the
world, which had thus punished her, the reward of free upkeep.
But there *were* bad characters involved, and they were the
people who had elected themselves as the showmen: the
barkers who pointed to the crippled legs, and told the passers-
by to look at the noses, and held the sores up to the light,
while they rattled the tin cup with the other hand.

Such to his mind, was Mrs. Bannister, who rode to glory
on triple chargers: Esther Costello's inhuman squeaks,
stunning good looks, and immensely talented silence.

But the public liked it that way, and the *Star-Telegram*
had to be sold to the public. It would have been fine to
let Harry Grant write the kind of piece he wanted; but that
wouldn't have fitted the formula, and the formula sold the
paper, and the paper paid the salary list. . . . With newspapers, nothing operated in a vacuum—least of all, Truth.
In the background of all Ryan's thinking, there was an editor,
self-modelled on Napoleon, who enjoyed giving orders and
dictating policy; and at *his* back was a proprietor, like God
at the time of Creation, who surveyed the whole thing as an
eagle and occasionally snatched it up in his beak and shook
it. Ryan himself had an ulcer, and a wife who saw herself,
inaccurately, as a spur to greatness. He would never be
an editor: he just had a job to keep, a good job. Grant might
be an editor. Esther Costello was undoubtedly a racket. . . .
Ryan turned back to his desk again, leaving the ethics for
someone else to pick up.

Harry Grant, being a good newspaperman, did his best
with the assignment, using the method of attack laid down
in the manual of instruction—that was, to dig out what
was new about it, and then to send as much of that as the
paper was likely to print. It was waste of time, he knew,

to write what he really thought about the 'streamlining' of Esther Costello, the slick presentation of her which never took a false public step: he couldn't describe, for example, Jack Lett's particular part in the promotion. He *could* write that Esther seemed to be more popular and successful than ever, and that she and Mrs. Bannister had evolved a completely new technique: Esther could now 'hear' Mrs. Bannister's voice, by placing her hand on the other woman's mouth, and she could produce in return an approximation of human tones—a kind of high-pitched, monotone gabble which Mrs. Bannister then translated verbatim to the audience.

He could write of the enormous ovation they received in Washington, and the preparations for the corresponding welcome-rally in New York. He could write of his own privileged position, living in the same hotel with the family, sharing their private as well as their public life. He could not add that the hotel bills must be fantastic, or that Captain Charles Bannister now had a valet, thirty-seven suits, and a complexion like a badly-executed sunset.

But though there was much that would never be set down in print, this did not stop him observing and correlating the facts. He was far too good a reporter to miss the likely items, even though they would not be used this side of the Last Trump. There were always things you noted down, although you knew they would never see the printed page, and never be heard of outside the local Press Club bar. A President getting drunk, a Queen reproving her husband, someone dropping the Sword of Stalingrad—these were items too hot to print, in the prevailing climate, but not too hot to file away. During the time he spent with the Esther Costello organization—that was how it must now be phrased—he assembled a valuable collection of these, for his private filing system.

He observed that Mrs. Bannister now ran the whole thing: Jack Lett was preoccupied with production questions, and Captain Bannister was now an infinitely subdued character who never made a single concrete suggestion, and drank his way steadily through each succeeding day. It was not a comfortable household, but at least it had a predetermined protocol which cut mistakes to the minimum.

He observed that Jack Lett, handling the toys and games angle, was making a fortune, both for himself and for the Guild. The Tapalong Club system was an intricate structure, extremely well organized on a world-wide basis: the subscriptions alone, remitted direct to the Guild, were a huge item in the balance sheet, and the royalties on the sale of uniforms added up to a fantastic total.

He observed that this balance sheet was a somewhat haphazard affair; though the donations from the Guild to outside charities were substantial, there was an enormous margin left over, undistributed and never allocated to any specific object.

He observed that 'expenses' covered a lot of ground, much of it scarcely charitable.

He observed that Esther was not happy: that Mrs. Bannister was never quite free of anxiety: that Captain Bannister did whatever he was told, with a beaten dog's obedience; and that Jack Lett was careful not to identify himself with the various meetings and the 'presentation' of Esther, only with the sale of her various brand products. He did, however, put in a certain amount of overtime as Mrs. Bannister's lover.

Harry Grant could not use any of this, but he tried his utmost with the printable material. The tour progressed: New York built up to a legendary triumph; he filed a lot of stories, and Ryan telexed that he was pleased with them.

Then two things happened. They should have cancelled each other out, but they did not. He found himself suspecting that Esther Costello was a fake. Not just a racket, but a straightforward fake. And he found that he was falling in love with her.

The two things happened side by side: sometimes it was difficult to tell when he was watching Esther with suspicion, and when with love. . . . Love gave him wonder and desire; suspicion gave him three separate items which finally sent him racing home to Boston, ahead of the party, with the hottest news story of the decade.

The first item that pricked his attention was so slight that only afterwards, when he was reviewing his monstrous suspicions, did it make its true weight felt. He had been sitting in the lounge of their hotel suite in New York, with Charles Bannister in the opposite arm-chair. The time was after lunch, which meant that Bannister was far from sober; the two of them had been talking idly, about the big meeting which was scheduled for a few days ahead, when Esther came into the room. She looked young and cool in her print dress, and not for the first time Harry Grant found himself appraising her as a woman, instead of a protected human being outside the normal tide of desire. To examine her thus was very agreeable.

When she sat down, smoothing her dress, he winked at Charles Bannister, and said:

"She really is a honey, isn't she? Just look at that figure!'

Grant would never have said this, if he had not been slightly drunk himself, and surprised by his sudden feeling of attraction for Esther. But the girl really did look beautiful, on that summer afternoon; her face was studious and beauti-fully formed, her body graceful, her legs a delight. . . . It seemed to Grant an enormous pity that he could not tell her so himself.

He was very much taken aback to hear Charles Bannister say, in tones of the utmost discomfort:

"You oughtn't to talk like that about her!"

As well as surprising him, it angered Grant to be thus rebuked by this second-rate, drunken hanger-on, and he countered roughly:

"What the hell? She can't hear, can she?" The girl, sitting immobile across the room from him, had the grace and the inaccessibility of a marble statue; her useless beauty reproached him, and he was driven beyond what he would normally have said, to Charles Bannister or to anyone else. "What does it matter what I say? I wish she *could* hear. I'd like to tell her she's got the best-looking body in New York!"

"That'll do, Grant!" There was a drunken embarrassment in Charles Bannister's voice that again took him aback. "Just shut up about her, will you?"

"What's your worry?" Grant felt like taunting him now. "Not getting jealous, are you?" He looked again at Esther, at her oval face and composed brow. He thought again: I wish she *could* hear—I'd tell her a thing or two. . . . "If this is what they mean by a blind date," he said, with appalling crudity, "I'd choose it every time."

"By God!" said Charles Bannister furiously, "I wish I were a few years younger. I'd thrash you for saying that!" As he spoke, Esther rose from her chair, and felt her way out of the room. "You see," said Bannister, watching her exit, nearly beside himself, "you see what you do with your filthy tongue! Why can't you keep quiet?"

Grant stared at him, no longer angry or malicious, but amazed at the sense of his words. None of this added up. . . Then, as he looked, he saw a spectacular blush appear on the other man's face, rising above his collar and suffusing his neck, cheeks, and brow in a rich wave of red. He looked like a small boy who has made some violently uncouth noise in church. Thereafter Bannister rose swiftly to his feet, muttered something, and shambled from the room without another word.

They neither of them referred to this occasion again. Grant, indeed, felt rather ashamed of himself: he did not in the least want to talk like that about Esther, even to himself. . . . He supposed that Charles Bannister had the same feeling, and that some queer drunken inconsequence had made him choose the words he did.

The words themselves had not made sense, but the instinct behind them was clear and valid enough. . . . Grant did not think about it again until much later.

The second item concerned himself and Esther alone.

Grant had now taken to studying Esther as closely as he could: he told himself that it was a reporter's interest, he knew it was something like a lover's. He spent as much time as possible alone with her: especially did he enjoy sitting opposite her in the comfortable silence of the suite, watching her reading Braille or doing embroidery at which she was now expert. It gave to their time together a gentle domestic significance which he found very attractive; and in some strange, undefined manner he received the impression that she liked it that way herself.

Indeed, if the idea had not been nonsensical, he would have said that often she was watching him covertly, and enjoying his company as he did hers. Now and then, with no one to hear, he would say aloud: "You're lovely, Esther. I wish I could tell you about it"; and as if the thought could communicate itself to her, she seemed to react to his words, and her face would soften to a marvellous sweetness. Once

he said: "I'd like to kiss you. I will, too, some day. . . ."
And it was as if she could hear the loving, urgent words,
so shyly confused did her whole face and manner become.

One day, after asking Mrs. Bannister to explain the plan
to her, he took Esther for a walk, alone, in Central Park.
Her hand in his was soft and close; as they strolled along
slowly, they might have been normal lovers, normally happy.
When they returned to the hotel, Esther passed a message
of special thanks to him, using her sign-language through
Mrs. Bannister. Whenever Grant was there, Esther would
not use the frightening, unco-ordinated speech which she
now produced for the entertainment of the public.

She then went through to her own room, with Mrs. Bannister
by her side. Harry Grant noticed that she had left behind
her on the table the small handbag she had been carrying,
and with a lover's instinct he picked it up, intending to take
it along to her room. But as his fingers closed round it, it
slipped from his grasp and dropped to the floor.

It fell open as it hit the ground, and out of it dropped a
pair of dark sunglasses.

That night he went to sleep frowning. In his dream, a
man, unidentified, whispered to him that Esther could see.
He said, astonished: "How do you know that?" and Ryan,
appearing suddenly across an enormous desk, answered
acidly:

"The sunglasses, you dope!"

When he awoke, the resemblance was only shadowy.
But it was still there: and with the utmost unwillingness
he began to work out what it could mean. His appalled
speculation had to battle all the time with his love; but in
this case his love—however protective, however increasing—
could not win.

The third item was, for him, conclusive proof.

By this time, Harry Grant knew himself to be deeply in love with Esther; and he knew also that he was on the verge of uncovering a monstrous swindle of which she was the centre. It was no longer a battle between loving her, and uncovering this deception of hers: he was now determined that he would love, and uncover, at the same time, and so rescue her from her frightful situation.

He realized, of course, that she could not be innocent in this affair, and must indeed be completely involved in it; but he was convinced in his heart that she must be under constant pressure, from Mrs. Bannister and the others, in all that she was doing.

The third item concerned a mirror.

There was in the hall of the New York hotel suite a mirror of an old-fashioned type, a long cheval glass adjustable to any angle. Once again, Harry Grant had come up from his own room, one floor below, to spend the afternoon with Esther; and as he passed the mirror he moved it, locking it at a new angle so that he could see his whole reflection. Then he went through into the sitting-room.

Presently Esther opened the door and came in. He went up to her, took her arm, and started to guide her towards her chair. Then, when she was settled, he returned to the door in order to close it. Something made him look at the cheval glass again. When he did so, he saw that his head and shoulders were no longer reflected in it: the angle of the mirror had been readjusted to suit a much smaller person.

It must have been moved within the last few moments; and the only person to go anywhere near it had been Esther.

She was, of course, a head shorter than he. In fact, she scarcely came up to his shoulder.

With great care, Harry Grant now chose his moment and his man. It seemed essential for him to clinch his suspicions, by a counter-check within the organization. . . . The man, by a process of elimination, was to be Jack Lett; and the moment, whenever Lett was off his guard. Mrs. Bannister, of course, would never talk: Charles Bannister was hard to get hold of, harder to pin down; and Esther was not the person whom Grant wished to trap. . . . The opportunity came after Esther's final New York meeting, one of those triumphant occasions which left its sponsors spent and exalted at the same time.

The immediate excitement, the flash-guns and the autographs, gradually died away: by midnight that night, Esther was in bed, Mrs. Bannister safe in her room, and Charles Bannister had got lost in a down-town club and was unlikely to come to the surface before daylight. Only Jack Lett remained; Jack Lett, and Harry Grant, sitting together in the deserted suite, contentedly lowering a bottle of Scotch whisky.

The moment, for Grant, was now propitious, since Jack Lett was more than usually complacent after a profitable finale to their New York stay; and Grant let it run on for a few minutes longer, patiently attentive to the other man, as Jack Lett enlarged on the evening's triumph. The more he talked and the more whisky he downed, the more easily would Grant throw him off balance, when the time came for the surprise question.

Lett was at the very top of his form: confident, bouncing, full of commercial sunshine. He had, that evening, clinched some production deal which guaranteed his future for a long time to come.

"Harry," he said, setting down his half-empty glass, "Harry, there's no ceiling to this thing, at all. You saw them this evening, howling their heads off before the show was halfway through. We signed up over three hundred new Club members at the end of it. That means more uniforms, more badges, more everything." He grinned. "The boys back in California will be working overtime— and they'll be loving every minute of it."

"Very gratifying," said Harry.

"You bet it's gratifying!" Lett downed the rest of his drink in one prodigious swallow, and began to pour himself another. As usual when he was pleased, he seemed to be outgrowing his clothes, expanding physically as his thoughts soared. Grant wondered what his blood-pressure was. . . . "She's a wonder, that girl. And Mrs. Bannister too: a fine, devoted woman. Between them they've put blindness on the map—and it's going to stay that way."

"What's the total club membership, now?"

"It's difficult to say, the way the thing's growing all the time. It must be around the half-million mark, I guess."

"Still trailing Hopalong Cassidy," observed Harry.

"You stick around!" answered Lett energetically. "They've got themselves a long start, that outfit—but we're only just hitting our stride. Esther will have them all beat, by the end of next year. Yes sir!" he repeated: "She certainly has put blindness on the map."

He raised his glass. In the moment of silence, Grant said: "How long has she been able to see?"

Jack Lett, who was drinking (as Grant had intended him to be) when the question hit him, gulped wildly at his glass, upsetting half of it over his coat. His eyes bulged, as if the pressure of whisky had been forced up directly behind them. His face, never very healthy, took on a greenish tinge. Then he set down his glass, with a shaking hand, not bothering to mop up what he had spilt, and said:

"You must be crazy!" His voice was a ludicrous, whis- pering parody of its normal tone; all bluff, all bounce, all confidence had been knocked out of it. "What do you mean, 'how long'? Esther *can't* see."

"How long?" said Grant. "I'm just asking *that*."

Jack Lett stared at him, his face blurred with doubt and indecision. It was easy to read his mind. He could not guess exactly how much Harry Grant knew; but it was enough that the one central fact had been confidently voiced. If that item could thus be thrown into the ring, then all their swindling world must be falling in ruins. But he tried once more, feebly.

"You're way off the track, Harry." His voice had a politician's lilt. "Esther's as blind as—as Charles Bannister, right this moment."

Harry Grant looked at him. It was a look of complete loathing and disbelief, and it gave the other man no margin for denial, no shadow of hope.

"I *know*," Grant said at last. "Get that, and cut the crap. I *know*. How long has she been able to see?"

Jack Lett, swallowing, said: "Since London."

There was a long silence. Harry Grant, watching this defeated man who had so easily surrendered, was conscious not of victory but of a sick disgust at what he had learned. So it *was* true, all that he had suspected—the whole thing *was* a swindle, and Esther *was* a liar, double-dyed, inhumanly dishonest. But of course she must have been cruelly forced. . . .

"What happened in London?" he asked finally when the harrowing silence had stretched far beyond his choice.

"I don't know at all," answered Jack Lett. The question told him of an essential gap in Grant's knowledge, and he now made a swift effort of recovery, raising fresh defences as fast as his slick brain and weasel tongue could work. "Some accident, I guess. I only learned about it a lot later. . . . You know me, Harry—I just sell the toys and the uniforms. I'm not part of the main organization at all," he continued briskly—and Harry Grant wanted to sock him for it. "The meetings are nothing to do with me. Just the toys—that's my line. . . . There's never been any guarantee about Esther being blind, with them, has there?"

"You bastard," said Grant.

"All right—so she can see!" Lett was now accumulating a horrible jaunty self-confidence, drawing round him the chips of his cast-iron assurance. "What's the difference, anyway? We're making money for the blind, aren't we?" He saw that Harry Grant had risen, and he rose too, his face derisive and yet quailing at the same time. "We're all in it together—*you're* in it, too. . . . Get wise to that, Harry: you make money, writing all that stuff about it—and you're another one who'd like to lay her, aren't you? . . . I was getting out, anyway," he said, suddenly fearful, falling back a swift step as he saw Grant's expression. "I've made my dough. I'm satisfied."

"You bastard," said Harry Grant again. He was cool now, and the hand that reached out to grasp Jack Lett's collar was cool, and the clenched fist that hit the other man full on the mouth was especially cool, cool with fury, coolly accurate. Lett's lips glowed suddenly crimson, and he fell back, cursing; and the cool fist caught him again, between his ear and his streaming jaw, and he toppled backwards, senseless before he hit the ground.

"You bastard," said Harry Grant, looking down at him. Though the room was suddenly cleaner, because Lett was no longer in it, in any active sense, Grant had a moment of flaming anger, of fury that Esther had been entrapped (as she must have been) by so swinish a gang. Then, since there was nothing left for him to hit, he relaxed, and his arm fell to his side again.

It stayed there only for a moment, until he turned, attracted by a new sound. This time it was the door. It opened awkwardly, and Charles Bannister appeared, framed within it like a blotchy painting of a man in evening dress.

He was clearly drunk, but that was not going to matter. That was just his bad luck.

Grant advanced towards him. "*You* bastard," he said softly.

"Extraordinary remark to make," said Charles Bannister owlishly. His eyes swivelled round, took in Lett's still form on the ground, rose again with foolish surprise. "I must say——" he began, but that was not a sentence he ever finished. Grant's fist caught him flush on the chin, and he collapsed backwards, like an elegant sack whose outlines had suddenly melted into rags.

Harry Grant stepped over them both, and made for the outer door. The whole suite was now very silent, as if waiting for his next move.

He did not know what that was to be. He found that he was still shaking with rage. He was far too angry to work any of it out, too confused and shocked to decide what to do.

"Tomorrow," he said, addressing the air outside the suite, haranguing the elevator. "Tomorrow. Wait until to-morrow. Then I'll break the whole story."

CHAPTER THIRTEEN

GRANT could never decide why he did *not* break the whole story next day, or what it was that sent him to Boston, on the midday plane, instead of filing the full account of what he had discovered, from New York. All his normal newspaper instinct urged him to send the story then and there: all his second thoughts—crowding in on him even as he walked down the single flight of stairs to his hotel room—told him to delay.

There were many such thoughts, many conflicting reasons for waiting. Lying awake that night, and watching the dawn through the curtains later, he tried to sort them out.

Perhaps he was delaying because it was too big a story to handle, without direct consultation at headquarters. It was not that he wanted to throw the whole thing in Ryan's lap: he really felt he needed the older man's comment and criticism, his sustaining presence, before he made up his mind how it should appear in print.

Perhaps it was because he was ashamed of his behaviour, and wanted to put a distance between himself and the night's crude action. Violence could never be the answer, to anything: it was satisfactory to have clipped Jack Lett so squarely on the jaw, and pleasing (as a neat, back-handed piece of repartee is pleasing) to have rounded it off with a complimentary poke at Charles Bannister. But the physical acts did not settle anything, they disposed of nothing save the immediate urge to express his disgust. The whole thing needed dealing with on quite another plane.

Perhaps it was something queer that had gone astray,

something in Jack Lett's phrase about 'laying', which continued to nag him, and made him want to clear a space for thought.   There was one single word—he could not remember which—that remained stuck in his brain; an object in cloudy aspic, too deep to be distinguished.   He felt he could not write the full story until he remembered it.

Perhaps it was his love for Esther that stopped him filing the story immediately: his emerging, protective love that wanted above everything to shield her from the tremendous scandal he was about to unloose.   A little delay could do no harm; and it might clarify her position, presenting it in a new and innocent light.   How fearful, how vile, if he wrote a straightforward piece about the swindle, with Esther as the wicked centre of it, and then found that he had overlooked some angle which explained or even cancelled her part in it.

He could not think what such an angle could be; but it *might* be there.   For his peace of mind, indeed, it must be.

Perhaps the real reason was Mrs. Bannister, next morning.

Harry Grant had spent much of the war in the Navy; and now, a phrase from that war—'Close watertight doors' —returned irresistibly to mock him.   For, next morning all safety doors had been slammed, all clips screwed home: the ship, mortally hit, was putting up an atavistic struggle for survival.   Next morning, when he came up to the suite, prowling for facts, intent on straightening things out, he found himself completely blanked off from all further contact.

First, Jack Lett had disappeared.   "Gone back West," said the floor-waiter, an old friend of Grant's who had the habit of gossip.   "Took the first plane out.   Big contract coming up, I reckon."   Then, Charles Bannister had gone to hospital—"for a thorough check-up," said his personal valet, and added caustically: "Not a day too soon, either. . . ." Then, Esther was incommunicado, he   behind locked doors over which Mrs. Bannister's secretary stood guard. "She's not well at all," said the latter, an earnest, negative woman, who travelled everywhere with them. "Mrs. Bannister wants her to rest. She can't see anyone, I'm afraid."

Finally, there was Mrs. Bannister herself. Grant met her in the same big sitting-room where he had had the late-night session with Jack Lett: the room, now sunny, was purged of its overnight shocks and shadows, neutral in this sordid battle. He stood up as she came in—and while she was still halfway towards him, it became crystal clear that, before he flew back to Hollywood, Jack Lett must have talked. Here, the watertight door had slammed shut on a direct order from the bridge.

"She's not well, Harry," Mrs. Bannister repeated, when he asked to see Esther. There was an arrogant finality in her voice which marked a new stage in their relationship. "I don't want her to meet anyone."

"I'll bet you don't," he answered—but he did not speak aloud. There was a temptation to lay all cards upon the table, but he could not quite bring himself to do so. He looked at Mrs. Bannister—at this smooth, tough, competent woman who was surely the mainspring of the whole horrible racket. On her appearance, he could not fault her: she was as well turned-out, as well made-up, as well presented as she had ever been. She looked as though she knew she was actively enjoying this warm summer morning: enjoying it because she knew she could handle it, and him, and every-thing else, with complete, exclusive authority.

Only her eyes, which seemed to notice every move and take account of every shadow, had a jungle awareness which betrayed her fear.

"Where's everybody?" Grant asked.

Mrs. Bannister smiled briefly, a smile so mirthless and so brittle it might have cracked the corners of her mouth.

"Still asleep, I guess," she answered. "You know what these big meetings are like."

"I wanted a follow-up story on last night."

"It'll keep. . . . Why not take a walk, Harry? Fresh air will do you good."

"Can I see Esther after lunch?"

"Maybe. But I want her to have a real, long sleep. . . . Tomorrow would be better."

They were staring at each other now: wary, circling like animals that fear the final grapple. Grant remembered his crude words of last night—"I *know*—cut out the crap—I *know*"—and they were on the edge of his tongue again; but he could not use them could not take the plunge into the mire. He wanted to think, he wanted to talk to Ryan. . . . He said, instead: "O.K., then—see you later," and made for the door. He felt and walked like a retreating coward.

Mrs. Bannister watched him all the way, steel-eyed, as if a single false step would be his doom, and her finger were poised over the button. It was a relief to have the closed door as a shield for his back.

Grant walked out of the hotel as he was, leaving his baggage and his room intact, and drove to La Guardia, and caught the noon plane for Boston.

Ryan, the news-editor of the *Star-Telegram*, did not blink an eyelid while Grant told him his story. He was not surprised at what he heard: he had not been surprised for thirty years: he had lost the capacity. Surprise was for other people—for the *readers* of newspapers. Of course, he believed instantly what Harry Grant was telling him. He believed, firstly, because he trusted Grant and knew he was a good newspaperman. But principally he believed his story because it was the sort of thing that was always true.

Of course Esther Costello could see, hear, and speak. That was what people who collected vast sums of money on the plea of being blind, deaf, and dumb, could inevitably do. It was the natural second paragraph to any twentieth-century charitable hand-out.

Only very simple people—that was, newspaper readers—would ever be surprised by it. Ryan himself knew well that there was no limit to the corruptibility and baseness even of normal human beings: there was nothing, thinkable or unthinkable, that one man would not do to another. They seduced each other, raped each other, cheated each other, sold each other. They killed, mutilated, drugged, and maimed: they slandered, swindled, and traduced. They could smile engagingly, even as they betrayed, even as they dropped the poison into the cup.

In America, a negro accused (wrongly, as it turned out) of rape, had been castrated and burned alive. In England, an idiot male child had been kept chained in an attic, sleeping on newspapers, fed on bones, for eleven years before a complaint was made—to the health authorities. In France, a woman took a lover on the kitchen table while her children looked on, and told her twelve-year-old daughter: "You can watch, but you oughtn't to start till next year." In Germany a doctor had been ready to gas his fellow-men in batches of a hundred at a time, with a squad standing by to salvage their clothes, their shoes, their hair, and the gold in their teeth, before their corpses were rendered down for soap and glue. In South Africa, a white farmer killed the negro girl he had got with child, cut off her head, and disembowelled her of the tell-tale foetus, while his wife held a torch for him to see by.

Such things were part of the human pattern: they were the things that people did to each other, the things that made up a front page. Harry Grant's news, though promising, was nothing out of the way. Except, of course, as a story:

in that category, it was a good one, though it still needed readying.

He said: "We'll have to have a lot more facts, before we can print."

Grant nodded.   Obscurely, it was the answer he had been hoping to hear: it relieved him of responsibility for not filing the story straight away, it made sense of his hesitation.   Of course, the story needed more facts to support it. . . .   But for honour's sake he had to argue the point.

"Surely we've got enough to go on.   The spectacles, the mirror, Jack Lett's confession——"

"Lett won't testify," Ryan interrupted.   "I know these smart operators—and so do you.   They're like bookies.   Try to put them on the witness stand, and they're three states away, under a different name and a false beard, before the case comes up."

"But I can testify to what he said."

Ryan smiled.   "You're a reporter," he said.   "A man with a story to sell to the public.   You're the biggest suspect of all."

"Suppose we run the story, and let them climb out of it. I know—*we* know—that they can't."

Ryan shook his head.   Across the desk, he looked like a rock of sanity—a disbelieving rock.   "Not for this newspaper," he said, after a moment.   "The editor doesn't like it, and I don't like it either.   If you print news that way, you can print anything.   Suppose we run a story"—he hesitated, though for a few seconds only—" 'Churchill is England's Number One Communist'.   We sell a lot of copies, then it turns out we're wrong, and we have to say we're sorry. Plus a million dollars to make the fact clear. . . ."   He shook his head again, more vigorously still.   "Not for the *Telegram*."

"But this story's true."

"Sure. We just want proof. Proof that no one can knock down."

"What sort of proof?" Grant knew, even as he asked the question, what Ryan would answer.

"There's only one sort of proof, Harry. The girl herself. You'll have to go back to New York, and get the story from Esther."

"She won't be on view."

Ryan smiled again, sardonically. "You're on the *Star-Telegram*—and this time it works a different way. You've *got* to get her story, somehow. Find a way. Phone her up —bribe the secretary—knock Mrs. Bannister out—hide under the bed. You know the story's there. Go out and get it."

"They're due here in Boston, in three days' time."

"So much the better. Wait here for them. Catch them on their home ground."

Grant was astonished to hear his own voice saying:

"I'm hoping she's innocent."

There was a long silence in the office. Across the desk, Ryan's strong, square face below the crew-cut grey hair was devoid of expression. Finally he said:

"Innocent is a big word. It's the biggest there is. It'll need to be, in this case."

"I mean," said Grant, with difficulty, "I hope she's been doing all this because she was forced to."

"Me too. But ask her. She'll talk to you." Ryan's eyes flickered upwards suddenly. "Won't she?"

Grant felt himself blushing vividly. "I reckon so."

The news-editor nodded again. "There's always an angle." But the words were not cynical: they sounded, indeed, like an attempt at comfort. Ryan was sitting back now, at ease, understanding, immensely human. "It's a great story, Harry," he said gently. "We want to do it *just* right."

CHAPTER FOURTEEN

How to see her? Harry Grant, sitting in an air-cooled bar on Tremont Street, on the day that Esther Costello was due to return to Boston, had still not found the answer to his problem. There were too many things in the way: too many facts, and too many thoughts. Esther would be living at the Commonwealth Avenue apartment: she would be guarded with triple vigilance by Mrs. Bannister, who must guess that he would be back in Boston himself; and she might be unwilling to see him anyway. He recalled, with prickling shame, some of the things he had said to Esther, aloud, when he thought she could not hear. There had been something about a good-looking body, something about kissing. . . . It could well be that she would be scared of him for that reason, leaving out of account the fact that he planned to expose her.

He had had some vague idea of 'rescuing' her. Suppose she did not want to be rescued, by him or anyone else, and in fact looked on him as an enemy?

Suppose he were his own enemy as well? He had got on to a good story: the best that had ever come his way. If he broke it, he would break Esther as well. He loved her, and there was a war going on inside his head, a war of love against the story. He knew that the story would win, because he was that sort of man, in that sort of job. But the contest was a near thing, and he hoped with all his soul that the story might somehow be published without shaming and destroying Esther.

Ryan had had the same idea. In spite of his tough

armour, Ryan was a man of compassion; and when he
had said: 'We want to do it just right,' that had been
one of the things he had meant. If it were humanly
possible, he wanted Grant to break the story, and rescue
and absolve Esther at the same time. It could be done—
but only if she had become party to this fraud because of
some unspeakable duress. It was tied up with that missing
word, the buried motive that he could only discover by
talking to Esther.

He turned to the bar again, and ordered another drink.
Then the door swung open, and a man walked in, unsteadily:
a middle-aged sagging man with a face as rumpled as his
suit. It was someone Grant knew well—Al Stevens, the
Star-Telegram's staff drunk. By the look of him, he was not
out of character, at that moment.

Grant said: "Hi, Al. . . ." and Al Stevens blinked at him,
and answered, for some reason: "Shame on you, Harry."
It fitted in so well with what Grant himself was thinking that
he felt his face flushing. But it was only old Al Stevens, aiming
at some target within his own muddled head. . . .

"Have a drink, Al," he said uncomfortably.

"Too early," answered Stevens, and almost in the same
breath, to the barman: "Two Scotch. On the rocks."

The drinks slid deftly across the counter: two tumblers,
ice-filled, two jiggers of whisky, a glass of water for a chaser.
Stevens raised his, sucked half of it down, and blinked at
Harry again. "Cheer up, kid! You're still on the pay-roll,
aren't you? What's new?"

"Nothing much." Grant, sipping his drink, stared at Al
Stevens. He liked the other man, but he hoped he would
never come to match him. This was where you ended up,
if you drank too much and fell down on your assignments.
Stevens had fallen down once, years ago, spectacularly: he
had become tangled up with a girl in London, and had

G*

missed (among other things) a possible scoop on Edward
VIII's abdication. He had got drunk to cure it, and had
been the same way ever since. Harry Grant hoped he would
never fall down on a story like that.

He had such a story now—and such a girl as well.

Stevens knocked back the rest of his drink, and hammered
on the bar. "Two Scotch, my good man," he said to the
barman. The barman, pouring the fresh drinks, winked at
Harry. No one ever got sore with Al Stevens. It had
ensured his ruin.

"What's new?" asked Al Stevens again.

"Quiet day," answered Harry. "A knifing in Scollay
Square, Tommy Manville got married, Princess Margaret
didn't get engaged. Run-of-the-mill stuff."

"You were in New York," said Stevens, out of the blue.

"Yes. Esther Costello." It was difficult now to pronounce
her name simply. "Just got back."

"Swell girl," said Stevens vaguely. Then he frowned,
at some unrelated thought. "They were talking about a
big robbery, back in the news-room."

Grant nodded. "Sure. Some old dame at Cambridge.
Jack Owen's covering it. Man walked up the fire-escape
while the family were at dinner, emptied the old girl's jewel-
box, walked right down again. Not a clue, not a print.
About twenty thousand dollars' worth of stuff."

"She was too rich, anyway. . . . It beats me why that
sort of thing doesn't happen more often." Stevens looked
around him: the bar, deserted, was very silent, the air-cooling
system humming gently. "Anyone," he said—and to Harry
Grant his voice seemed to come from a long way away—
"anyone living in one of those old houses, with a fire-escape
at the back, is asking for trouble."

.   .   .   .   .   .

Harry Grant parked his car up the Avenue, a block away

from Mrs. Bannister's apartment building, and settled down
to wait.

It was eight o'clock, and getting towards dusk. He
might have to move nearer to the front entrance, when it
grew dark; but for the moment, he would see clearly enough
if Mrs. Bannister left the apartment. There was no reason
why she should leave tonight—their train from New York
had got in at six, and the household might now simply go to
bed; but she *could* go out, for a late dinner or a visit to a friend.
If not, he would have to try again next day. He dared not
attempt the fire-escape route, up to the third floor and Esther's
own room, unless Esther were alone in the house. He was
taking a big chance even then, but there was no other way of
finding her alone. If Mrs. Bannister went out for any reason,
she would be sure to lock her front door. The fire-escape,
leading up to the Bannister apartment—one of six in the
small block—was all that was left.

He waited. The traffic thickened up for the late movies,
then slacked off again. It grew darker: the street lamps
came on, and the couples walking along the Avenue—
advancing from one pool of light to another, like men
cautiously stalking a hilltop—quickened their pace instead
of strolling. The clock on the dash moved slowly: nine
o'clock, a quarter-past, half-past. At nine-forty-five, stiff
and cramped with waiting, Harry Grant moved his car
half a block nearer the entrance.

Almost immediately, Mrs. Bannister came down the front
steps, paused under a lamp, then got into a blue-grey sedan
(which Grant now recognized as hers) and drove off down
Commonwealth Avenue towards the centre of town.

Grant's throat went dry as he watched the bright gleaming
tail-light fade and then vanish: for a long time he could not
move, though his brain was urging him, with a 'Now—
now——' like a hammering pulse. Again it was the war that

was closely recalled: the sudden thickening in the throat
that meant zero-hour, and the need to set course for the
beaches, with no more cover, no more excuse for delay. . . .
Swallowing his fear, Grant got out of his car. In those
bad old days, he had always forced himself to think: Before
another five minutes have passed, I'll be there, and it will
all be over—the beaching, the scythe of lead aiming at my
guts, the promise of murder: I've just got to exist for the next
five minutes. Now he thought: Round the block into
the parallel street at the back, up three flights of iron steps, and
I shall have landed on *this* beach.

He turned his back on the brightly-lit entrance, and
walked steadily for the corner and the beginning of the narrow
street that ran behind the apartment block. A few minutes
later, breathing fast, he had traversed the paved garden
masking the service entrance to the apartments, and his
foot was on the first step of the fire-escape.

There were lights within the building, all the way up:
the rusty iron ladder zig-zagged across the centre of it, with
a small platform at each stage: to the right of every
platform was a kitchen, to the left a back bedroom. Each
lighted window beckoned his eyes irresistibly. At ground
level, he saw a man stooping over the refrigerator in the
kitchen, and a couple, negligently dressed, kissing in the
bedroom. Now there's a situation, he thought, stepping
upwards past the static, dubious tableau: in that set-up,
who is married to whom? Is that the husband who is
hungry, while the lovers grab a quick chance?—or is it the
lover who waits his turn, and meantime settles for a cold cut?

He would never know: his steps, agreeably firm, almost
brave, carried him upwards, to the next floor. Here the
bedroom was in darkness: in the kitchen, a coloured girl
sat at the white enamelled table, eating something from a
wide plate, reading a magazine propped up by its side.

Save your eyesight, Chloe, Grant thought, stepping lightly past, making for the last, the crucial flight: tomorrow's *Star-Telegram* should have a real story for you. . . . His throat went dry again as the mounting steps turned for the last half-flight: his head came level with the back of the Bannister apartment, then he stood in silence, conscious of his thudding heart, on the small platform outside the kitchen door.

All was in darkness, save for another glass-framed door which he knew to be the entrance to Esther's bedroom, at the far end of the platform. He inched his way along the railed space, giddy with the height and the black void beneath him, and peered round the edge of the lighted door.

He saw Esther immediately. She was sitting in an armchair, half-turned towards him, reading. Her eyes, of course, were open, and attentive to the printed page. The book in her hands was a normal edition of *The Robe*.

It seemed to Grant that he would shame them both if he delayed in watching her. With love and pity in his curled knuckles, he tapped on the glass of the door and, turning the handle, stepped within her room.

At the sound of the opening door Esther had raised her head slightly, though not enough to meet his eyes: now she froze, going through a routine which was horrible and moving at the same time. Harry Grant had never seen a person become blind and deaf before, but this was what Esther did: immensely wary, like an animal alerted by a sudden noise, she seemed to retreat within her own body, drawing over herself a hood of impotence. The book dropped to her lap: her head took on a wooden fixity, and her eyes the cloudy film of night. She was no longer a lovely girl, reading a book in a warm room. She was Esther Costello.

Harry Grant, seeing her thus forfeit all her life at one glacial stroke, found himself trembling, with fear and shame. What had they done to her, that she could have come to accept such imprisonment?

He took a pace forward, standing above her chair, and said:

"It's all right, Esther—I know."

She did not stir. He had not thought that she would, at one single sentence from himself: the armour of her pretence was now too much a part of her. He leant over, and touched her arm above the elbow. He had feared that she would carry the fraud another step, and produce a sudden stagey start. But she did not move at all.

It was enough for him: it told him that she had given up. He said again: "It's all right, Esther. Jack Lett talked. I *know*."

Esther raised her head slowly. As she did so, she seemed to melt back into womanhood again: her eyes, focusing honestly on his for the very first time, had a depth and grace that went straight to his heart, and her whole face was lit with yielding tenderness.

She said: "Thank God, Harry," and, rising, went directly into his arms.

Everything was to be for the first time. It was the first time he had heard her natural voice, which was low and gentle: it was the first time he had touched her body, which was a young delight. Holding her close, feeling her tremble and then cease to tremble, waiting for her to raise her lips to his, he had only one single, thankful thought.

He was lucky. There were enormous, fantastic complications to every aspect of this. But he was very lucky.

Her mouth came up, meeting his gently. It must be the first time for her, he thought, conscious at once of the shy assent of her lips. How warmly, how sweetly she does it. . . . Then Esther drew back, and smiled, and murmured:

"You *said* you were going to kiss me."

He grinned ruefully. "I must have said a lot of things. . . . Oh, Esther. . . . You're so lovely. . . . What have they done to you?"

"I'll tell you. . . . It's wonderful to be able to talk to you."

"It's wonderful to hear it. Your voice is—is like singing." He kissed her again. "I said I was going to kiss you. I didn't know it would be like this."

"I used to wonder what happened to the noses. . . . Your arms are so strong," she went on softly. "I never felt arms before."

"Really never?"

Turning slightly from him, she said: "Why did you ask that?"

He was momentarily confused by some wariness in her voice, and in the feel of her body. "No reason. . . . Because you're so lovely, I suppose."

"Then you *don't* know?"

"Know what?"

She seemed to be sinking her head lower on his chest, as if afraid of their eyes meeting. Her voice, no longer confident, was suddenly troubled and tense.

"That I should have said: 'I never felt arms before. Except.'"

"Except what?" he asked, puzzled when she stopped on the single word.

"Except what I have to tell you." There was something in her tone that was like a cold breath entering the room. He knew then that she was on the verge of an appalling revelation—that this was the missing word, leering at them both over the near horizon. He did not want to know about it—he only wanted to hold her and kiss her. But that was not to be their pattern.

"What did they do to you?" he asked again.

"All things." Harry noticed, as she spoke, that Esther still had a trace of brogue in her voice. It had outlived and survived ten years of silence, as everything about her— her loveliness, her warmth and softness—had outlived the horror of her infirmity. "We can talk now," said Esther, bravely determined, her head coming up again. "She's out—some welcome-home party or other. There are things you have to know."

"But why did you do it, Esther? Why did you pretend? And what happened? You *were* blind, weren't you?"

"Oh yes, I was blind and deaf and dumb. Then there was a—a shock."

"What sort of shock?"

He was watching her closely, holding her at arm's length and he saw creeping into her face a tide of shame and distress that almost answered him. Immediately something clicked into place—the forgotten phrase that Jack Lett had used. Jack Lett had said, coarsely: "You're another one who'd like to lay her." *Another*—that was the word he had been groping for, ever since.

He said: "Jesus, Esther. . . ."

She nodded. "It was force," she said.

"Jesus. . . . Who?"

"Bannister himself."

"When? In London?"

"Yes."

"But what. . . ." He was confused and appalled: he had the key now, but the key was filthy and ugly, and would not turn for him. "But what did you—what happened after? When did the pretending start?"

"I'll tell you." Esther drew away from him, and sat

down on the bed, motioning to him to join her. She was grave now, and pale: her eyes held his urgently, as if she were praying that he would listen, and believe, and forgive. "It's a long story, Harry. There's plenty of blame in it— blame for me, and for him, and for her. But I thought I was doing right."

"I love you anyway," he said, touching her hand again. "Love you and believe in you."

"That's good to know."

"Now tell me."

So, trustfully, with no more hesitation, she began to tell Harry Grant her story. She talked steadily and bravely for a long time, with her hand clasped in his hand, except when he strode the room in rage and torment, and her eyes holding his, save when he could no longer bear to meet them. This was what she told him, and what she implied, and what he guessed at: this was the missing part of her fearful history.

It was force, Esther said again, with a submissive determination which Harry Grant found cruelly moving—as if, unreassured, he might come to the conclusion that she had made a freewill offering of her body. . . . It was force; and for a long time afterwards she lay like a flower cut down, while around her the London household hummed like some noisome piece of carrion. It was force: there was even some surgical repair to be done, a tribute to Charles Bannister's prowess of which, later on, when drunk, he was inclined to boast. Just now, he did not boast; indeed, he hardly seemed to exist at all—spending long hours laired up in his bedroom, slipping down furtively to the hotel restaurant or the bar, appearing briefly in doorways and passages, with the branded look of absolute guilt in his face.

Jack Lett would not speak to him; Mrs. Bannister, after,

her first crude onslaught, did not acknowledge his presence
at all; Esther was no longer in his world. He could not be
excluded from the party, since he was a grossly material
witness; but as far as any human being could be disregarded,
that was his current fate.

Meanwhile, there were plans to be made, arrangements
to be altered or abandoned. To begin with, the Australian
trip, said Mrs. Bannister, must be postponed.

"What do you mean—*postponed*?" asked Jack Lett, to be
met by a look from Mrs. Bannister so complicated and
stealthy that he let the question lie unanswered. He had
much to lose by a public confession that Esther was no
longer abnormal in any way; he hoped for some fortunate
outcome; and after meeting Mrs. Bannister's glance he
trusted her to find it.

He had come to rely on Mrs. Bannister in a great number
of ways; this, apparently, might be yet another of them.

She herself was in turmoil: pity, rage, and fear held her
enchained. She could not believe that even Charles Bannister
would have done so fearful a thing. She was wildly jealous,
although she had not cast a glance in his direction for months
and knew that he must have been totally drunk to have thus
entered the lists of love. But above all she was possessed
with fear—fear that the story would leak out, fear that
everything would now be lost, and that all her hard work and
self-dedication, all the riches that the future had promised
them, would come to naught. Mrs. Bannister had never
been a predominantly greedy woman, but she was certainly,
by now, an ambitious one; success had hardened and enlarged
her will, and (mindful of the past) she was seeking also an
impregnable financial security.

Having gone far towards attaining it, having in the process
been accorded a mantle midway between celebrity and
saint, having worn it with assurance for years on end, she

could not give up her position without a frenzied struggle.

Such were her thoughts, such her aching desire, as she considered what to do next. When she had said to Jack Lett that the Australian tour must be 'postponed', she had not really considered how the trip could ever be undertaken at all. Esther was in the doctor's hands—a doctor so obscurely skilled, so dubious, so marginal, that there had been no need to swear him to secrecy: she had recovered all her faculties: she now possessed, according to their standards, no assets at all. But Mrs. Bannister had said 'postponed' instead of 'cancelled', because she could not bring herself to surrender. The fat years, the years of homage and acclaim, had corrupted her too deeply. Somehow she must salvage the triumphant past, and build on it again.

The tour was accordingly put off 'for at least three months': they took over a house in the country, about fifty miles from London, and settled down in absolute obscurity. Esther they gave out, was exhausted, by a schedule which had proved altogether too much for her strength. She must have complete rest. There could be no visitors, no interviews, no public contact at all.

Having thus taken care of the immediate problem, answered sufficient questions, and secured her breathing-space, Mrs. Bannister gave her mind to the future.

The small Buckinghamshire house was very quiet: the country noises, the distant traffic from the by-pass road a mile away, barely reached within its walls. In a room at the top of the wide creaking stairway, Esther lay, absorbing all the riches of the world again.

Her body was healing, and she had much to enchant her eye and ear. It was astonishing how many things she had forgotten, in the ten years of darkness.

There were some sounds so delicate and alluring—like a

bee at the honeysuckle that framed the window, or a cat
mewing in the yard below—that she felt like laughing with
joy at their emergence. There were some sounds so loud
and violent—like an aircraft passing low over the house, or a
man shouting at some animal—that she was ready to weep
at their ugliness. There were some things so strange to see
again—like food, or a mirror—that they frightened her:
there were things so welcome—like Mrs. Bannister, and the
bars of sunlight moving across the wall—that joyful laughter
came near to her heart once more.

Everything was much smaller than she had remembered:
in ten years, her childhood world had shrunk amazingly.
The horse she could see through the window was a pigmy
horse, nothing like the Irish farm-horses when she was a child;
the bed she lay in, unlike the vast double-bed she had once
shared with her brother, felt scarcely big enough to contain
her. In those old days, the adult world and all that was in
it had seemed to threaten and overwhelm; now it was a
small world, a reassuring world of companionable things.
Only occasionally—as when aircraft passed overhead, or
summer thunder filled the sky—was she reminded that
human beings might still revert to the stature of children.

To begin with, it was a happy time: learning to see, learning
to hear, learning to speak again. She saw Mrs. Bannister
and Jack Lett nearly every day. They would come up
to her room, together or alone, and talk to her: telling her
of outside happenings, answering her eager questions.
Gradually she was brought up-to-date with the missing
time—and especially the last few years, when the successive
triumphs had begun, and grown. She knew already what
Mrs. Bannister had done for her; but what Esther herself
had been able to do for other people, the total love and faith
she had called forth—these were new things she had never

fully comprehended before, things that now made her proud
and happy.

Yet there came a day when Mrs. Bannister began to talk
of less agreeable matters.

"All the work you used to do," she said to Esther one
evening, when they were alone together in the sitting-room
downstairs: "all the meetings, and the money we collected—
they did such a lot of good for the blind."

"Yes, you told me—and I'm glad," said Esther happily.
"But you should be very proud, too. It was all your work,
wasn't it?"

"It was *our* work," corrected Mrs. Bannister. "Neither of
us could have done anything without the other. . . . It
seems a terrible pity," she went on, picking at the linen cover
of her arm-chair, "that everything must come to a stop now.
The blind will suffer, all over the world."

She continued for some time in the same strain, persuasive
yet never insistent, until Esther, feeling vaguely guilty, said:
"But couldn't we go on, in some way? Go on talking,
and collecting money?"

Mrs. Bannister shook her head. "It wouldn't be the same
thing at all. In the old days, people came to the meetings
and gave money, because you were so blind and helpless,
and so clever at the same time. That was what reminded
them of all the other blind people, and made them want to
help. Now there'll be no feeling like that left."

Esther said nothing.

"Even the toys and games and dolls," said Mrs. Bannister,
filling the pause, "will be no good now. Even the Club
won't make sense any more. The name Esther Costello
won't mean anything to anyone, as soon as people know
that you can see and talk. It means the end of all that. I'm
afraid Jack Lett will just have to fold up."

"But aren't you glad?" asked Esther uncomfortably. "I

know it was a terrible thing that it should happen that way"—she blushed vividly, and shivered at the same time—"but it means—it means everything to me."

"Of course, darling!" Swiftly Mrs. Bannister reassured her. "It's everything to me, too. But you can see what a difference it will make, as soon as we tell people."

"Don't they know, already?" asked Esther. "Haven't you told anybody?"

"No," said Mrs. Bannister. "I've been ashamed to."

"You mean"—Esther felt herself flushing again—"because of—of your husband?"

"Oh, no!" answered Mrs. Bannister. Her hands were busy again. "*He* doesn't matter. It's you I worry about."

"How do you mean?"

"It's such a terrible thing to have to tell people, about any girl. I've wanted to keep it a secret."

"But it wasn't my fault," said Esther, now somewhere near weeping.

"Of course. *We* know that. But it's not an easy thing to convince people about, honey. You know what they always think—*and* say. . . . If only we didn't have to tell anything about it. But never mind!" she ended brightly. "We'll find some way of fixing it."

That was the first of many such talks: some ended on a hopeful note, some in tears, some near to open disapproval. Mrs. Bannister, forecasting the future for Esther's benefit, set out, step by step and mood by mood, to produce as many different ideas as possible, and to ring the changes on them with remorseless skill. There were many sections to this varied tapestry, many subtle contrasts of light and shade. There was the loss to the blind, the loss to Jack Lett, the loss to herself—and above all, the shame of confession. Without doubt, Mrs. Bannister had promising material to work on. Esther was a young and simple girl, just emerging into the normal world for the first time, in circumstances of the utmost horror: she had been totally dependent on Mrs. Bannister—dependent for sight, sound, and voice—for years on end: she loved this strong woman who now seemed so unhappy. . . . Sometimes Esther could hardly bear to watch her distress, so deep and abiding was her gratitude for the past, so lively her sense of obligation.

Mrs. Bannister and Jack Lett were very close to one another. Indeed, on many occasions they were in a position to talk in intimate darkness.

"I think she's coming round to it, Jack. Something tells me it's going to be O.K."

"It's still the trickiest thing I ever heard of, Belle. Even if she does agree to it, she'll have to learn the whole routine over again. *And* make it look as convincing as it used to be."

"She'll do that. . . ."

"Suppose there's some slip-up?"

"There'll be no slip-up. . . . As soon as Esther agrees, we'll really go into training."

"You must have been doing some fast talking."

"Yes. And it had better be left to me, from now on. I know all the angles, and she's very fond of me."

"Even so, there can't be so many arguments to use."

"Oh, there's a lot to be said for carrying on, the way we used to do. Esther knows already how much good we did for the blind."

"You're a wonderful woman, Belle. I've always thought so."

"And there's another thing," said Mrs. Bannister to Esther. "There's the police."

"The police?" Esther looked at her in alarm: the word

to her conveyed only guilt and crime, a man with a gun stalking a murderer down the length of the village street. "What's it to do with them?"

"You see, we haven't yet told them about you and Charles. That was an illegal thing he did. We could get into trouble for not telling them about it."

"But it wasn't my fault," said Esther. Already she had used the words many times. "You know that well."

"I'm afraid it makes no difference. In fact, it makes it worse. It makes two crimes instead of one."

"Two crimes?"

"What Charles did to you was a crime. And not to tell about it was a crime. If we confess it now, there'll be no end to the trouble."

"But what can we do, then?"

"What I said last night. Say nothing. Behave as if nothing had happened."

"But I don't understand.   How can we do that?"

"I've explained the idea to her," said Mrs. Bannister to Jack Lett, in the warm darkness of the bedroom.

"What did she say?"

"She said she was afraid."

"Her and me both. . . . Christ, if we ever get found out!"

"We won't be found out."

"You'll have to train her, Belle. Train her like for the Olympic Games."

"As soon as she agrees, I'll start."

"She hasn't said yes, then?"

"No. That's tomorrow."

Power, greed, and vanity were at the core of Mrs. Bannister's hard determination; against them, Esther Costello—young, frightened, ashamed—had nothing to set save her isolated will; and this had been softened and eroded far in advance, by the years of dependence, the years of love.

"You *must* trust me, Esther. I tell you, this is the only way."

"But it's so terrible. And so difficult. I don't think I could ever manage it."

"After all I've done for you," said Mrs. Bannister.

"Ah, I know that! But I'm not clever enough for it."

"You just don't want to do it."

"I do, I do! But I can't!"

"After all I've done for you," repeated Mrs. Bannister. "Rescued you, brought you up, spent all those years looking after you, teaching you, acting as your eyes and ears, giving up everything for you. And now this. . . . It's no good crying, Esther," she said grimly. "The time for tears is long past. You should have thought of all the consequences, before you and Charles——"

"But he forced me," said Esther, with desperate unhappiness.

"Whichever way it happened, it happened. Now you can see and hear—and as a consequence we're all ruined. It's a fine return for all I've done."

"But the other thing is cheating," said Esther.

"It's not. It's helping the blind. And me. And Jack Lett."

"And I've only just started to see and hear."

"That will make it easier. There's less for you to forget."

.   .   .   .   .   .

"It's O.K., Jack," said Mrs. Bannister. "She's going to do it. We start tomorrow."

"What's the routine?" asked Jack Lett. "You mean, she's got to learn *not* to see and hear again?"

Mrs. Bannister nodded. "Yes. And we can help her, too,

in lots of ways.   With earplugs, maybe.   And we might have
to work out something for her eyes, unless she can really
make them go blank, of her own accord.   We might even——"

"What?"

"Some kind of operation.   It depends if she can't do it
all on her own account, by pretending."   Mrs. Bannister
sighed in the darkness, and murmured: "It's not as if she
were losing it all for the first time.   It wouldn't be as bad
for her as for ordinary people.   And we want it to be completely fool-proof."

"You're a wonderful woman, Belle. . . .   I guess I'll leave
it all to you."

The next few weeks were the most miserable that Esther
Costello had ever known, in a life which had held far more
than its due share of inhumanity and pain.   Even in the
months following her original accident, when she had groped
about like a stricken animal, there had been nothing to
match her present situation.

Then, there had at least been some sort of hope, even if
it were only the irrational, tearful hope of a child.   But now,
after a quick glimpse of the happy world, she was being
pushed back into the darkness again—and this, in circumstances which she knew to be shameful, and which might
prove criminally fatal to her.   It was no wonder that her
small resources, which had flowered briefly during the weeks
of convalescence, could often scarcely sustain her in her
ordeal.

She was going through with it for many reasons, but
chiefly for love—love of Mrs. Bannister, who in ten years of
close and cherishing care had established an unassailable
command over Esther.   Formerly, it had been a benevolent
authority—a mother-daughter relationship compounded of
utter dependence on one side, watchful care on the other.

Now it was something different, though it worked just as surely, just as unassailably. Now it was power in operation: the power of one human being to compel another to do something she knew was wrong and evil, because her defences against such compulsion had been razed to the ground long ago.

Esther was doing what she was told, for love of Mrs. Bannister, to whom she owed every single thing in her life. She was doing it also for the blind, who would suffer, all the way round the world, unless she continued to work for them. She was doing it for poor Jack Lett, who had sunk so much money in his various agencies and factories, and would be ruined if the Esther Costello Club, and all the other affiliations, had to be disbanded. She was doing it because of the police, whom, in her ignorance, she saw as continuously hunting for her, unless she could conceal the crime she had shared with Charles Bannister. She was doing it for shame—the shame of a shy and completely innocent girl who had to confess to a huge public that she had been raped by a man of fifty-five.

She was doing it because she was facing, alone and without allies, the most formidable barrage of persuasion she had ever known in her life.

But whatever the reason, whatever drove her to compliance, it was certain that she had much to endure; for the things they now did to Esther Costello would not have disgraced a team of Hollywood make-up men setting to work on some definitive version of the Bride of Frankenstein.

As a preliminary, the doctor who had done the original repair work upon Esther, came to live in the house.

He was a small, off-white man whose nervous over-the-shoulder manner was doubtless well grounded in the past. He was about fifty, with plump hands and a suppliant smile; his papers—at least, the papers he carried with him

—showed that he had practised as a dental surgeon in Cyprus, a gynæcological consultant in Tangier, and a neurologist in Cannes. He gave his name as Dr. Worthington. He seemed to be Egyptian.

The hour produced the man, and this without doubt was a vile hour.

Dr. Worthington's role was executive: he was to bend his talents towards the physical re-handicapping of Esther, supplementing Mrs. Bannister, whose sphere was re-education in sensory anæsthesia. . . . It was of course essential that, whenever she was under the public eye, Esther should never betray herself: the loud noise, the sudden light, the wish to respond to some special kindness or acclaim—these must never be allowed to make any impression on her. Much could be done by training, by schooling Esther—as is done with police horses—to ignore any outside manifestation; but to aid in thus dulling her senses, Dr. Worthington, who was of an inventive turn of mind, weighed in with a number of experiments.

It was not possible to make Esther completely deaf again, but by means of ear-plugs she could be rendered abnormally hard of hearing, so that she became disinclined to listen to people talking. She could not be made blind; but an ingenious form of contact lens, clear when viewed from the outside, opaque when looked through from within, ensured that she saw almost nothing of the outside world, while to the spectator her eyes appeared to be still unclouded. Complete dumbness, to avoid the danger of her answering questions when caught off her guard, was not possible to achieve without the sort of operation which Mrs. Bannister still shrank from; but Dr. Worthington was able to perfect a form of injection which, by constricting the inner muscles of her throat, made speech painful for a number of hours afterwards.

These things were simply aids to training—the training

which Mrs. Bannister instilled into her, day after day, and
which gradually she came to accept, with a hopeless resigna-
tion that was perhaps the most effective frame of mind for
what they planned to do with her.

"I think she can cope with it now," said Mrs. Bannister.
"It's taken all of three months, but it's been worth it."

She was sitting on the sun-porch in the cool of the September
evening: the garden below, still green and inviting, was very
peaceful, and the house behind her fulfilled its promise of
still tranquillity. Opposite her in the other easy chair, Jack
Lett nursed his drink, and watched the swallows circling and
dipping low over the lawn: between them, Dr. Worthington,
in an inappropriate business suit of pin-stripe blue, was
manicuring his nails. Somewhere within the house, Esther
lay resting and Charles Bannister lurked, half in shadow,
half in tentative sunlight, wondering if anyone would speak
to him that evening. . . . There had been many such days,
during the past few months; but now they were sharpening
towards a definite outcome.

"You've done a wonderful job, Belle, a miracle," said
Jack Lett, appreciatively. His chief role during their retire-
ment had been to make a series of remarks of this sort, at
suitable intervals: it had taxed neither his vocabulary nor his
patience, both of which were in any case sustained by lively
hope of the future. "Soon as you say the word, we'll get
going."

"She's ready, any time," answered Mrs. Bannister. "Don't
you think so, Doctor?"

Dr. Worthington lowered the gold-plated, miniature
scissors with which he had been trimming a cuticle, and
creased his face into a smile. "She is as ready as she will
ever be." He had a pronounced lisp. It might have been
endearing. It was not. "The girl is well trained, and"—he

waved a fleshy hand—"the little arrangements I have made will keep her out of trouble."

"All the same, I wish you were coming along with us, Doctor," said Jack Lett, not for the first time. Originally, it had been planned that Dr. Worthington should be one of their party; but some trifling circumstance of the past now made it inexpedient for him to apply for a renewal of his passport. It had come as no surprise, but it was certainly a disappointment to them all. "I'd feel a lot happier," Jack Lett went on, "if you were there to look after her. What happens if she breaks one of those lenses?"

"There's no reason why she should break them," answered Dr. Worthington. "However, I shall arrange for some spares to be sent after you—and in any case, Esther will soon be able to do without them." His lisping version of the word 'Esther' was particularly unreal. "The eyes become conditioned. . . . The ear-plugs are a simple matter—nothing to go wrong there —and the injections"—he gestured again—"are beyond any mistake. You should do well."

Mrs. Bannister nodded agreement. "*I'm* not worrying," she said energetically. "Hell, it's only a routine! We've done it hundreds of times before. You've got to remember that people take the whole thing on trust, anyway. She's Esther Costello. It's like"—she paused, searching for a suitable parallel—"it's like the Royal Family, here in England. Everybody's with them, from the start. If they trip over the mat, people just look the other way, and say 'What funny weather for July'. . . . She's Esther Costello. Sure, there's a lot of people looking at her all the time, but they're all ready-made fans, whatever happens."

Dr. Worthington inclined his head. "Dear lady, you are right." The words 'dear lady' should have sounded gallant and complimentary. They did not. "What I have done for her is a safeguard. The real strength is in the girl herself—and all the work that you and Mr. Lett have done in the past. That is still there. You need have no worries about it, no worries at all."

"Just as long as you're sure," said Jack Lett. It was not his job to cast a shadow on the rosy future. He turned towards Mrs. Bannister again, voicing a query which had not yet been openly discussed between them. "Do we take the old man along, Belle?"

The question had been in the back of Mrs. Bannister's mind also, ever since the initial crisis: now she faced it with candid realism. She loathed Charles Bannister, for all that he had been in the past, for seducing her from the simpler life which had been hers when first they met again, after their ten-year separation, and especially for what he had done to Esther—the crown of his career. But in their expedient, confederate world, loathing was not enough. "You know I don't want to," she answered, "but he's still part of the outfit. People have got used to him, by now: they expect him to be there. They're liable to start asking questions if he's not."

Dr. Worthington joined in again. "That is so. He is part of the thing you have built up. He need not worry you at all, now. But he should be there."

"Just so long as he doesn't start getting ambitious again," said Jack Lett hardly.

"He won't do that." Mrs. Bannister was emphatic. "You've seen him, Jack. Pearl Harbour isn't in it. He's finished. . . . We'll take him along, as part of the scenery. He won't bother us—or Esther."

"It would be very serious if he *did* bother Esther, very serious indeed," said Dr. Worthington. "There would be a danger of a complete breakdown, in that case. . . . But as you say, he is finished." He grinned horribly. "Like a horse that has that little operation. There is no more interest."

"That's a load off all our minds," said Mrs. Bannister.

There was a slight sound behind them, and they all turned. It was Esther. She stood in the doorway between the house and the porch, groping with uncertain fingers for the edge of the frame. She looked as she had always done in the past: young, fresh, startlingly beautiful—and helpless. She was staring at them, and not seeing them at all.

"Come in, honey," said Mrs. Bannister. "We were just talking about you."

Esther gave no sign that she had heard a single sound. She continued to stand there, her fingers grasping the door-frame, considering the hazards of the next step. It was clear that she was wearing Dr. Worthington's full regalia, and that because of this she was Esther Costello again.

Much heartened, and with an interested look on his face, Jack Lett, who was nearest to her, reached out and tapped Esther on the arm. Her start of surprise and shy confusion was as good as anything they remembered from earlier, happier days.

Mrs. Bannister turned to Dr. Worthington. "Congratulations, Doctor," she said warmly. "You've done a fine job. . . . I don't see that we need to worry over anything."

On that long tour covering thousands of miles and scores of crowded meetings, Esther really did very well. It was true that all her audiences were uniformly on her side, and had come there especially to acclaim her; but they were sharp-eyed human beings as well as disciples, and they would have been quick to notice anything odd or suspicious in what she or Mrs. Bannister did. Esther must have been stared at, examined, appraised, touched, watched, and hailed by a quarter of a million people, in Australia, New Zealand, South Africa, Canada, and the United States: she had to appear on platforms, at parties, on balconies, in the streets, at missions and institutions and schools: she had to give a flawless public performance, without respite, for six months on end.

In the whole of this time, with all its dangers and crises and chances of disaster, she made only two discernible slips.

The first was in Christchurch, New Zealand. There, she was received privately by the Archbishop, and afterwards, accompanied by His Grace, she faced an audience of four hundred schoolchildren and a battery of Press cameramen. The hall in which she appeared was somewhat gloomy: the flash-guns, when they exploded in quick succession, had therefore an unexpected and dazzling brilliance.

This may have taken her by surprise: or it may have frightened her: or it may have been too much for Dr. Worthington's strange lenses. But a photograph in the *Christchurch Courier* next day showed Esther with her hand on a small child's head, and her eyes tightly shut.

The occasion had been religious. "She must have been praying," said the more devout readers. "How very sweet."

"You know," said the man who took the photograph, later, "if it wasn't a silly idea, I'd say that she was waiting for my flash-gun, and she blinked."

The second mistake was more serious, because it involved a definite, observed action on Esther's part, which could only be explained by the fact that she could see perfectly well. But luckily it took place in South Africa, and the only witnesses were confused and inarticulate negroes whom no one treated seriously in any case.

The party was staying in Johannesburg: it was the day after a huge meeting in the City Hall, at which Esther's lovely face and flawless performance had worked their usual magic. The richest city in the southern hemisphere had lived up to its other, less publicized reputation—that of being the warmest-hearted also: the collection after the meeting made even Jack

H

Lett blink, and the promises of support for the future were a golden guarantee of success. But the morrow found Mrs. Bannister and Esther in a very different *milieu*—one of the miserable shanty-town locations outside the city, where sixty-five thousand negroes lived in an atmosphere of disease, squalor, filth, and crime not easily matched anywhere in the world.

In this particular location there was a soup-kitchen run by a big local charity; and it was this that Esther was to visit, partly as a publicity excursion, partly because Mrs. Bannister had been genuinely surprised to learn that such an institution existed anywhere in South Africa. "By God, there *are* human beings here!" she had exclaimed to Esther, when she had heard about it: relying on South Africa's newspaper reputation abroad, she had imagined that no single white human being in the entire country would ever raise a finger to help a black man. "We'd better have a look at it, honey—it'll be something to tell the folks."

So it had been arranged. But what Mrs. Bannister had not taken into account was the effect, upon Esther's compassionate and youthful heart, of what she was to see that morning.

It was a bright day: the hot sun, shining out of a pale blue, cloudless sky, only served to point the gulf between the purity of nature and the gross contamination of man. Latterly, Dr. Worthington's special lenses had been hurting Esther's eyes, and she was not wearing them on this occasion; she was thus able to observe, closely and accurately, the squalid horror that was this township. The two of them arrived about noon, when the mobile soup-kitchen was making its first distribution of the day: the queue of negro children—half-naked, ill-fed, rickety, clutching every kind of utensil, from tin cup to metal cooking-pot, beneath faces turned towards the kitchen as if towards God—the queue stretched for fifty pitiful yards, winding through the crowded shacks of wood and corrugated iron and sacking, that were the only shelter the children and their parents were ever likely to know.

Mrs. Bannister, for form's sake, described the scene to Esther, and was photographed doing so: the girl could hardly maintain her pose of blindness, so degraded and yet so heartening was the scene around her, so moving the patient line of small black faces, and the wretched pots and cups, and the pennies clutched in the free hands. . . . Then Esther came nearer to the distribution point, and was photographed patting a child—a preoccupied and ravenous child intent only on its ration of soup. The onlookers, black men and women, chattered among themselves as they watched this. Then they fell silent, as they saw that Esther was crying.

Her tears were explicable: Mrs. Bannister had been 'talking' to her about their surroundings. But Esther's next action was not.

The small, ragged child whose head she had patted—a girl of not more than four—secured its helping of soup, in a china bowl that looked like an old-fashioned soap-dish, darted aside for a few paces, and began to wolf the meal. Esther seemed to be watching it, with her face working, and her tears now flowing freely. The child seemed unbelievably hungry. She was, in fact, too hungry altogether; for after a minute's swift, gulping activity, the little girl turned aside and vomited what she had eaten on to the sunbaked ground.

Esther watched for a long moment: then she walked over, took a handkerchief from her breast, and wiped the child's face, with so much tenderness and care in her hands and eyes that it was obvious to everyone watching that she could see exactly what she was doing.

Both the photographers had wandered off: Mrs. Bannister retrieved the fearful moment by stepping forward, putting her arm round Esther, and recalling her to her proper world again. But the ring of black faces reflected an undisguised amazement, at what could only be a miracle. Whispering broke out: absurdly, there was some clapping: an old man in the crowd came forward, hat in hand, and greeted her ceremoniously in Zulu as *Inkosazana*—Little Princess.

Mrs. Bannister smiled vaguely, and began to lead Esther towards the waiting car again. One of the Press photographers came up.

"What's the trouble?" he asked. "Is she O.K.?"

"It's the sun," answered Mrs. Bannister. "I'm afraid it's a bit too strong for her."

"Better take her indoors," said the man, sympathetically. "We're high up here, you know—six thousand feet. That, and the sun, can get you unless you're careful." He shut the car-door after them; then he became aware of the excitement among the negroes at his back, and he turned, while Mrs. Bannister's taxi began to gather way and make for the location entrance. "What the hell?" he asked curtly, of the man nearest to him. "What's all the uproar?"

After a moment, the man said, respectfully: "She can see, *Baas*."

"Nuts!" said the photographer. "She *can't* see—that's what it's all about. . . . Dumb bloody kaffirs!" he said, shouldering his way towards his own car. "Trust them to get the thing upside-down." And to his driver: "Let's get to hell out of this place! It always depresses me."

There could be no consequences to so ill-attested a mishap: in a sense, there had been no witnesses to it at all, and the occasion died as soon as it was born, on the malodorous breeze that hung and wavered above the township. Soon afterward, their party moved on to Cape Town, *en route* for Canada and the States, and the tour resumed its triumph—

and, for Esther, its fearful ordeal. She had no friend to talk to, no one in whom to confide: she bore it all alone, drilled into total submission, earning thanks and plaudits by a performance always fraudulent, watched from morning till nightfall not only by huge throngs of strangers, but by those near her who loved her so dearly. . . .

The hundreds of crowded miles, the thousands of clamant people, unwound before and after her, completing the blank spaces of a pattern foredoomed to success. There were no more slips, no more incidents save the expected, acceptable ones, the ones that fell within the world-tour routine, suiting the newsreels, delighting the Press. There was the small child at Cape Town that refused to surrender its bouquet: the young man in Quebec who tried to climb into her room— 'to offer her a donation', the papers quickly added: the old lady in Chicago who handed over to Esther her entire life-savings, crammed into a much-photographed stocking.

These were the formal oddments that people looked for, and they were not disappointed. But there was nothing more serious, nothing out of line, nothing crucial—however much Esther, forlorn and hopeless, might have prayed for disaster to overtake her. She did not dare to fail on purpose: that was a conviction ever present, looming above her every hour of every day. . . . Though there were many times—after the Johannesburg visit was one of them—when the whole thing seemed to have become too wicked for her, too dangerous, too disgusting, and she begged to be allowed to give it up, yet her prayers died always on the margin of her lips, unacknowledged, ignored, falling into defeated silence, like faint torture-cries lost behind walls of monstrous thickness, unplumbable depth.

Mrs. Bannister would not hear a word on the subject, and, meeting those level, competent, masterful eyes, Esther knew that she could never make a move of her own accord.

She remained, to the end, a prisoner isolated at the core of a huge swindle: alone, dishonoured, beyond hope of rescue or redemption. When Harry Grant had entered her room, and spoken to her in the knowledge that she could hear him, it had meant to Esther something more than the overturning of the heart in love. It was her first honest contact with the world she had mourned and coveted, for more than ten years.

CHAPTER FIFTEEN

IT was very late when Esther finished—so late that for the last hour Harry Grant had had his ear cocked for the sound of the outer door, the return of Mrs. Bannister. But they were left alone, in their uneasy, magical peace. . . . It was very late, and Esther was tired and overwrought; when Harry said to her, at the end: "Come away with me—now," he did not really think that she should agree. There was nowhere for them to go; most of the hotels would be full, and he did not like the idea of their wandering about for half the night in search of shelter, with Esther near the limit of exhaustion, and likely to be recognized by a hotel-clerk or a taxi-driver, with all the complications that might follow.

She sat now on the edge of her bed, staring at him with shadowed, enormous eyes: even in tiredness, she was lovely, but it was a loveliness so frail and vulnerable that he knew he must not tax it further. She had cried once during her story, when she had told him of the last plea she made for deliverance, to Mrs. Bannister; he had lent her a handkerchief, and quickly she had mastered her tears, and gone on with what she was telling him. But there must be no more tears that night, no more strain upon her.

When he said, again: "Come away, Esther," she had nodded.

"Of course, Harry. You must take me away from all this. You'll look after me well, I know. . . . But tomorrow, not tonight."

"But will you be all right, Esther?" He stood up, a

deep frown on his face, and looked down at her. "It's such a horrible story—the worst I ever heard. Will you be all right, here alone?"

She nodded again. "For tonight, yes. Nothing can happen. I'll say nothing to her."

"And tomorrow?"

Esther smiled enchantingly. "Tomorrow will all be different. Tomorrow is *our* day, Harry. I'll talk to her, and then we can be together."

"I'll come and fetch you," he said. "What time?"

"I'll call you. I've been longing to use the telephone. . . . Where will you be?"

Harry Grant hesitated. "At the paper, I guess. There's this story. . . . What shall I do about it, Esther? It will all have to come out."

"You write it," she said. "Write everything."

"There's no way round it."

"I know," she said. "Write it—write it for me. And then we can be happy."

"I love you, Esther."

"Always do that." She held out her arms, and he bent and kissed her gently. "And always do *that*."

"Go to bed, now," he said. "And take care of yourself. If you like, *I'll* talk to her in the morning."

"No," said Esther. "I want to do it. There are some things I have to say, good things as well as hard things. There was a time when she was everything to me. . . . You begin writing the story, and suddenly you'll hear my voice on the telephone."

He smiled. "There's a thing to look forward to." Then he kissed her again, repeating: "Take care of yourself, Esther," and made towards the door and the fire-ladder. He turned for a last look at her: she was still sitting on the bed, smiling at him, but drooping now on the very edge

of exhaustion. It came to him then that there would be
other times when he would love her, when she would be
strong or drowsy in his naked arms; but at that moment
he loved her very much, without further need for either
of them.

Harry Grant was never wholly clear how he spent the rest
of that night. It was past one o'clock when he got back to
his car, but he was as far from sleep as he had ever been:
the turmoil of his thoughts, the mingled love and pity, the
enormous challenge of the story he must write, all burned
inside his brain unceasingly.

By now, it was too late for him to return to the paper;
his story would have to keep until morning. But there was
no danger of its disappearing. . . . He went downtown
first, for a drink at an all-night bar off Boylston Street;
then he started driving, far along the coast-road towards
Scituate Beach, then inland in a great circle through wooded
country and lonely moors, then back to Boston with the
dawn coming up on his right hand, and a wild thirst nagging
him again.

It was not a night for drunkenness, and he did not get
drunk. But the thoughts within his skull were heady and
chaotic enough; and as the hours of that night went by, he
might well have been drunk, so wayward, downcast, and
exalted did he become by turns.

Esther's was the worst story he had ever heard; and to tell
it was the worst task he had ever been faced with. He knew
that she must suffer abominably in the telling, and in the dark
future also. But it was there to be told: Esther wanted it to
be told: he himself was to tell it; and it had to be told absolutely
right—as Ryan had said, so many hours ago—if the whole
vile tangle were to come out straight.

As he drove, the phrases started queueing up in his head:

H*

strong, authentic, matchless phrases, snatched out of the air, composed from shadow and aether, like Beethoven, like God. . . . Back at the all-night bar, he lost them again —but there were always other phrases, only waiting to be snatched and lured from the infinite: lucid strings of them, clearer, more concise, more exact and vivid all the time, making up a story that would go round the world in explicit triumph.

"Esther Costello—The Truth," he said to himself—or it might have been aloud, for the yawning barman frowned at him over the top of his newspaper. He swallowed a last drink, and went out into the cold deserted street, lit now by pale shadowless light from the east. Then he drove to the *Star-Telegram*, doused his head in cold water, washed and straightened up, and sat down at his typewriter in the empty city room. The very act of taking the cover off the machine, and reaching for a wad of paper, was like the prelude to some fantastic play, which he was to write and to watch at the same time.

He typed: 'COSTELLO. One. Grant', and drew a deep breath.

Immediately, lavishly, the magic words began to tumble from the air again, slipping within his brain, coursing down his arms, leaking into freedom and triumph from his fingers poised above the keys.

Towards nine o'clock that morning, when he was half-way through, the room around him started to fill up: the cleaners came and went, the copy-boys began a slow version of the activities which would later rise to a bustling inter-office crescendo; the men who had spent the night in the various police precincts scuffed their way in, bleary-eyed and resigned to human frailty: the morose characters condemned to cover openings and lectures assembled for their day's assignments. Harry Grant, sitting preoccupied at his desk, was widely greeted, mostly on a caustic note.

"Look who's here!"

"Buster, the boy reporter."

"Trying to catch the boss's eye?"

"If you just pay the rent, you'll have a home to go to."

"What's the novel going to be called?"

"Wait till the union hears about this."

"Get yourself a girl, Harry—then you won't be here so early."

He smiled automatically at each greeting, but none of it interrupted him or threw him out of his stride; he felt supremely confident—light-headed with the sleepless night, exalted by the outpouring of words. His hands were composer's hands, tapping out on the keyboard a flowing, cascading masterpiece. . . . By the time that Ryan, the news-editor, came in, Harry was nearly through. The pile of sheets lay on his desk, seeming to promise to him and to Esther a complete and blessed release, as soon as they were finished.

Ryan paused by his desk. "How did you make out, Harry?"

"Fine." Harry Grant gestured. "It's all here."

"You saw her? She talked?"

"Yes."

"Good boy. . . . How are you writing it?"

"News item—then the back history—then the why and where—then what we think about it."

Ryan grinned. "What do we think about it?"

Grant stared up at him. "We think it wasn't her fault," he said, levelly. "We think she was forced into it. We think she's O.K."

"Funny thing," said Ryan. "That's just what we were thinking. . . . Bring it in when it's ready."

Presently the last half-page was pulled from the type-writer, and Harry Grant started to read back what he had written, and to correct it. There was little for him to change: the story had come out smooth, accurate, persuasive, just as he had felt it, just as he had hoped. It was Esther's whole story—Esther the idol of millions, Esther the dupe and martyr, Esther whom no one could love one whit the less for what she had been made to do.

Then there was a stir at the main door opposite the elevator, and a man—a reporter called Sparrow—came in, walking briskly, almost running, making for the glass enclosure that was Ryan's office. Harry Grant, still intent on his last few paragraphs, looked at him briefly as he approached and drew level. Opposite his desk, not stopping, Sparrow called out something from the corner of his mouth. It was a single sentence: it sounded like: "Your girl-friend's dead." But it couldn't be that. Nor could it be important. Harry bent his head to the pages again.

The last sentence ran smoothly, as everything about the story had run smoothly, once he had begun to write from the true, un-tricked-out centre of his heart. He altered a few final words, scored out something about 'the judgment of the Almighty', which sounded false—and liable to usurp the functions of the *Star-Telegram*'s readers—and gathered the sheets together. It was long, detailed, definitive: it was the Esther Costello story, as nearly as any one human being could get it.

Then he became aware that someone was standing by his side, and someone else in front of him, straight across the carriage of his typewriter. He half-raised his head, still preoccupied. The man beside him was Sparrow, the reporter who had just come in; the man in front was Ryan.

Harry looked straight up, to meet Ryan's eyes. He smiled vaguely, smoothing a cold bristly chin, wishing he

could smooth his slightly fluttering brain at the same time.
He said:

"It's all finished."

Ryan said: "Hold it, Harry."

Sparrow said: "She just died."

Harry Grant turned his head, seeing Sparrow properly
for the first time. He knew the other man slightly—a young,
tough, unshockable reporter who covered a lot of ground
around Boston, and whose best connections were with the
police. Sparrow was looking at him speculatively, as if he
knew he had a good story and wanted to gauge its effect
upon Grant. But whether it went well or not, the *Star-
Telegram* would certainly print it. . .   Harry said foolishly.

"That was what you said when you passed my desk."

Sparrow nodded, unconcerned. "Sure, Harry," he said.
"I know what you did for her. . . .   It just came through."

Harry turned back to Ryan. Already he knew that he
must cope with this, and that it was about to crash down
upon his head with fearful weight. He could only remain
foolish, and simple, and hidden, for a very little while longer.
. . . By way of prolonging it, he pointed to the typewritten
sheets on the edge of the desk, and said:

"I finished the story."

Ryan looked at him with compassion. "Hold it, Harry,"
he repeated. "This is something else again. . . .   We just
got word——" He jerked his head at Sparrow. "Esther
was found dead this morning. About an hour back."

The time to cope was nearly at hand. "You're crazy!"
Harry burst out. "I was with her myself, a couple of hours
ago!"

Ryan's eyes sharpened. "*How* long ago?"

Christ, thought Harry: that's another angle to it. . . .
He swallowed, and said: "Longer than that. . . .   I was
driving around all night. . . . I left about one o'clock."

"Was she all right then?"

"Of course she was all right. . . ." He groped for a firmer hold on what was going on. "What's the story? What happened?"

"Police report." That was Sparrow, telling about his friends and their routine discoveries. "She was found dead in bed this morning. Overdose of sleeping tablets."

Harry swallowed again. "How?"

"Accident, maybe." There was an infinitely long line of accidents in Sparrow's voice. "Or suicide." There was another long line of suicides, mostly with guns or disinfectant. "What else could it be?" Sparrow was talking tiredly, unmoved by spectral deaths that boiled down to simple police reports. But he had one more thing to add. "She died some time between one and four."

Harry Grant stood up. There was a wild moment when he wished with all his might that he could confess to it, and so end his life with hers. But he said:

"She was O.K. when I left."

Sparrow nodded. To him, this was straight witness stuff, either suspect or not suspect: the police would give the verdict on that. Dead girls always had fellows who'd left them a few hours before. Occasionally they died of that too—but very rarely, very rarely. In that respect, they were mighty tough and recuperative. He said:

"She was blind. She must have reached for a bottle of something, and taken the wrong sort of pill."

"Is that the police angle?" asked Ryan.

"Yes."

"Jesus," said Harry. "I don't believe it!"

"You know something?" asked Sparrow immediately.

Harry shook his head. "No. But she wouldn't do that. She was too—too clever."

"You mean it was suicide?" There was another train of

thought in Sparrow's voice, a minor variation: the girl who killed herself after the man left. "We had a quarrel," the man always admitted, loosening his collar. "Nothing serious, just a lover's quarrel." But it was invariably enough to tip the girl over the edge. Either that, or she was going to have a baby almost immediately, on Tuesday next, and the man wouldn't come across with that old gold ring. "Was she having a baby?" he asked straightway.

"No," answered Harry after a pause. "She wasn't having a baby."

Ryan was staring at him. "Looks like an accident, Harry." His voice was almost pleading. "What else? She wouldn't commit suicide. And who in the world would kill her?"

"Mrs. Bannister," said Harry Grant.

Sparrow raised his thin eyebrows. "Now *there's* an angle. But why?"

Harry knew why: 'why' was lying in front of him, enshrined in the thick wedge of typewritten sheets he had been working on for the past three hours. But the knowledge was not to be shared yet. He passed his hand over his eyes.

"I'll work it out," he answered. "Right now, it's all mixed up. . . ." He turned back to Ryan. "There's your story," he said, pointing. "Do you want it?"

Ryan shook his head. "It'll keep. You better go and see her."

"Her?"

"Mrs. Bannister."

"I could do that," said Sparrow.

"No," answered Ryan. "Harry."

"But the story," said Harry, persevering. "Don't you want it?"

"It'll keep," repeated Ryan. "Maybe for ever. . . . **Go** and see her, Harry. And take it easy."

CHAPTER SIXTEEN

THERE were no crowds yet round the Commonwealth Avenue apartment, no pressmen in the elevator, no photographers with their thumb on the bell. Sparrow's police contact must be a very individual one. . . . Harry Grant, making his way to the top floor—using this time the formal approach, where a few hours before he had crept secretly up, and down, by the fire-escape—Harry Grant had few thoughts within his hollow brain. There was love, which he now knew must die. There was hatred, which would live for ever. And there was a fearful remorse that he had left Esther alone in the apartment, instead of taking her away that same night. He should have known that Mrs. Bannister, if ever she discovered what Esther planned, would never let her go; and she must have discovered it, as soon as she arrived.

He wondered how she had found out, but he did not have to wonder for long.

Mrs. Bannister herself opened the door. When the two of them were face to face, she stood looking at him for a long moment, not barring the way, not seeming to consider the possibility that he would want to come in. Finally she said, with the edge of a sneer in her voice:

"Back again so soon? You've certainly got a nerve!"

Taken by surprise, he said: "What do you mean, 'back again'?"

She nearly smiled at him. "You left your handkerchief here. Initials and all. . . . You as good as murdered her, Harry."

"What the hell are you talking about?"

Mrs. Bannister sprang to the attack, as clearly as if she had run up a flag. "Why did you creep in here last night? What did you do to her?" Her eyes were still meeting his, but they were perceptibly hardening, icing over. "You drove her to it. Or else you got her so worked up that she didn't know what she was doing. Either way, it's your fault —*your fault*!"

It was nothing like what he had expected—it could not have been farther from reality. He looked at Mrs. Bannister, utterly astonished, and saw her still standing in the doorway like a watching fury: a big woman, cold, commanding, in charge of this and of all other moments. It was as if, even though he entered the apartment, he would never get past her: she was the last opponent—like the death she masked —the last enemy who would always defeat him.

He felt confused, and his sleepless brain ticked and fluttered uncontrollably. He had come here to handle this with ice-cold logic, with quick, all-embracing observation—and already she had thrown him off balance, with a single look, a single counter-charge.

"I came up to see her last night," he said with difficulty. "I love her."

"Fine sort of love!" answered Mrs. Bannister scornfully. "Creeping in like a thief. . . . What did you do to her? *And how could you love a girl who was blind and deaf and dumb?*"

Oh Christ! he thought, she's not even giving *that* away. . . . Suddenly despairing, he brushed past Mrs. Bannister, and walked into the living-room. It was deserted, and all the doors leading out of it were shut. The whole apartment had a peace about it—a suspect peace, a bitter silence. A few yards down the barred-off passage, where the silence was deepest and most bitter, Esther lay. His thoughts grew fanciful, toying with a phrase from the morbid air. Death's bony arms, clipped round her, had supplanted his own.

Mrs. Bannister followed him inside. "I don't know what you want here," she said hardly. "It's all finished now. The police have just gone. They think it was an accident. I didn't tell them anything different. I didn't say you'd been here. I didn't show them the handkerchief. I don't want a scandal."

There were two things, Harry thought, not listening to Mrs. Bannister's tirading, nightmare voice, which was already assuming his futility and defeat. It could have been an accident, or it could have been murder. If Mrs. Bannister knew that he had been there, it was very likely to be the latter. But how did one make a start on that, when she held all the cards and was dictating the game?

"I did nothing," he said. He realized it was a mistake even to seem to be on the defensive, but he could not summon the wit to handle it in any better way. "You know that damned well!"

"I know nothing of the sort," answered Mrs. Bannister. She stood opposite him, growing tougher, harder, more triumphant every moment. "I know you crept in, and out again, and that Esther died—just about that time, or soon afterwards. Whatever happened between you, she took the wrong sort of sleeping-pills—the knock-out kind instead of the harmless ones—as soon as you left. Or did you force her to take them?" Her glance flickered like the exploring tongue of a snake. "Was that it? Did you have to keep her quiet, for some reason?"

"We talked," said Harry. "That was all."

"What do you mean, 'talked'? You know she was deaf and dumb."

They were staring at each other, in the ultimate contest

of wills. Total evil brushed him fleetingly, and then drew back, waiting to see what he would do.

"Esther could see and hear," he said.

"You must be crazy."

"We both know that she could."

"You're out of your mind."

"I talked to her."

"You dreamed it."

"When she told you that I knew, you killed her."

There was not a movement in Mrs. Bannister's face, save the curving of her grim lips as she spoke.

"You *are* out of your mind."

He summoned all his strength, all his failing enterprise, for a last assessment.

"You must have come back here, found my handkerchief, talked to Esther, realized that the story was going to break, and killed her."

There was still no movement in the bloodless, inhuman face. "I don't know why I'm listening to this—this raving," said Mrs. Bannister. "But *if* you want to know—*if* it's any good explaining—if you're not mad, or drunk, or covering up for yourself—when I came back here, Esther was already asleep. I didn't suspect she had taken those pills. Why should I? They were ones I kept for when she had really bad spells, migraine. She was only allowed one. . . . The handkerchief was lying on the bed. I left her as she was. She was dead this morning."

The silence between them lengthened intolerably. Each had used their weapons, and Mrs. Bannister's were carrying the day. Harry suddenly realized the reason for his approaching defeat; it was that Mrs. Bannister had had a margin of at least seven hours to figure out all these angles—and probably many others he hadn't even thought of yet. . . . In one fearful corner of his brain, he even knew that she might be telling a conceivable aspect of the truth. Esther could not have taken the wrong pills because of her blindness, but it could still have been an accident—she had been so overwrought, so confused. Or it could have been suicide —if, on reflection, Esther had found that she could not face the world with her story.

But whatever was the truth, he knew already that he would penetrate no farther, and must retreat now in shame and rout. Even his story was no good any more—he could prove nothing, effect nothing, change nothing. There was a dead girl called Esther Costello, whom all the world loved. What use to blacken her name, without evidence of any sort? There was Mrs. Bannister, whom all the world knew as a saint and ministering friend. What good to bring these insane charges, when he would run into a blank wall almost before he started?

Work it out, sap, he told himself, wearily, finally. Add it all up. She's dead, and the evidence is dead with her. There's no story any more. There's no nothing. The only thing out of tune is that Mrs. Bannister has no grief in her face—and *that* will be taken care of, by this afternoon at the latest. . . . Work it all out, and quit. Quit now. You don't even want to see Esther. She isn't there any more. Death's arms have her, like you said to yourself.

"She could see and hear and speak," said Harry, in careful farewell. "We both know that. You probably killed her. Or she killed herself. Or it was an accident—not because she was blind, but because she was all worked up. I don't know. *You* know. But if I ever do find out——"

Mrs. Bannister continued to stand there, rock-like, un-shakable. She shrugged slightly, to mark the wildness of his words. She gave the impression of bearing no malice. . . . He turned on his heel, unsteadily, and walked out of the apartment again, leaving to her the mortal battlefield and the single corpse.

To his exhausted, wrung-out brain, there was an odd silence in the city room when he returned to it. It was nearly twelve o'clock—not a busy time, never a dead one; but it seemed to Harry Grant that he was entering a morgue —a morgue where the inmates, chattering to one another, fell silent when he came in, and raised their chalky heads to look at him as he passed. . . . He made his face firm, concealing his grief, and then real'zed that he was concealing nothing at all. Grief must be for tomorrow— it had not yet arrived. Here there was just dullness, and the need to tie up the strings.

Ryan was waiting for him, facing him across the broad desk—strong, experienced, prepared to deal with anything that came. Thank God, thought Harry, he need decide nothing for himself. It was all in the hands of this dependable man.

"Well, Harry?" said Ryan.

"I didn't get anywhere," Harry answered.

Ryan nodded, as if he had guessed that already. Then he said:

"I read your story. Best you ever wrote."

"Mrs. Bannister killed her," said Harry. "I just know she did."

"Any proof? Did she talk?"

"No. Not the way we wanted, that is. She had all the answers ready."

Ryan nodded again, once more unsurprised. "Then the thing's dead," he said, slowly. "It's hell, but there it is. There's nothing left."

"Why?"

"Everything died with Esther We've nothing to go on, at all."

"We could still print it," said Harry. He knew that Ryan would not print it: indeed, he had known this while he was still in Mrs. Bannister's apartment, and he endorsed the decision; but perversely he wanted to put in a last word for his story—and for Esther Costello. "We could print it, just the same, and let the fireworks start."

Ryan shook his head. "No. It's no good. We've nothing to go on."

"There's still the money angle."

"How do you mean?"

"Even if we can't prove anything about Esther being able to see, or about how she died, there's still the money to be accounted for. All those collections and gifts—the whole racket. We could get Mrs. Bannister on that."

Ryan nodded. "Maybe. But what does that do to Esther?"

"She's beyond the scandal, beyond the reach of it."

"But her memory isn't."

"Who the hell cares about that?"

"A lot of people, Harry. Blind people. The people who look after them. The people who *really* collect money for them." Ryan glanced up swiftly. "And you yourself —you care."

Harry Grant swallowed. "It's still worth doing. Just to stop Mrs. Bannister. We wouldn't have much trouble proving it, either."

Ryan shook his head again. "There's no guarantee on that. You've got to remember, these Bannisters are smart. They'll cover up—they'll have cast-iron accounts for every-thing, *and* a lot of money in the bank, which they were just going to distribute. It wouldn't be an easy thing to pin on to them. And look at the choice it gives us! If we win, Esther's name will stink, all the way round the world, and millions of blind people, and their friends, will feel miserable

and frustrated and swindled. If we lose, we'll never sell another copy of this newspaper. . . ." He waited, watching Harry Grant's face. "The whole balance of things is weighted against us, Harry. We're bound to spoil more than we heal, much more."

"We'd stop *her*, anyway."

"We might—and destroy every good thing about Esther in the process. . . . It's no good, Harry," Ryan said again. "We've got to kill it."

There was a long pause.

"If only I hadn't left her alone," said Harry.

"I'm darned sorry," said Ryan. "About everything. . . . It was a wonderful story, too."

The typed sheets were on one side of Ryan's desk. On the other was the spike—bare now, ready for the day's rejects—the spike with NO printed on its base.

"Everything was wonderful," said Harry vaguely. He looked at Ryan. He wanted to talk for a few moments more. "Everything came right, last night. We—she was—we would have got married. It was as sure as that. I thought it would be all right to leave her."

"I'm darned sorry," repeated Ryan.

"But I left my handkerchief in the apartment. In Esther's room. Mrs. Bannister found it. She must have guessed what had happened."

Ryan shook his head again, this time in shared regret. But already his eyes were wandering—towards the telephone, the basket full of copy, the wire clips with the photographs. He was waiting to become the news-editor once more, with the current deadline twelve hours ahead.

"She must have guessed," said Harry. He had one other thing to do, and he could only do it while he was talking. "She knew it was the finish, for her," he went on, reaching out for the spike with NO on the base, "and she took **the**

only way out. . . . Now she's in the clear again." He held
the spike balanced in his hand for a moment, and then advanced it. "Sorry about the story," he said. "I really tried
all I could, with that one." He put the spike down again,
directly in front of Ryan, close alongside the typed pages.
"But all the best stories——"

He turned without finishing the sentence, and began to
walk out of the room. He found that his eyes were pricking.
Perhaps grief was near at hand, after all. . . . Ryan allowed
his glance to follow the other man for a long moment, com-
passionately, before he reached out his own two hands,
towards the story and the spike.

EPILOGUE

THE great Boston hall, the largest in the state, was crammed to the rafters; all tickets, indeed, had been sold out weeks before, and the rush when the doors opened had mirrored the traffic tie-up in all the nearby streets—a purposeful, close-packed, mainly silent crowd of people, converging on a single target. Many of them had been waiting outside for three and four hours: when the hall opened, and they had surged into their places, they settled down again with subdued, reverent patience for the meeting to start. It was not an ordinary crowd: there was over the whole vast concourse an air of dedication which gave it a special quality.

On the platform were seated, not only all the Guild trustees, but representatives of every religious and charitable body in the state. They waited, grave-faced, unsmiling, for Mrs. Bannister to appear; and down below in the packed hall the audience waited too—row upon row of them, and tier upon tier in the upper galleries of the hall. They talked in low tones; and just above the hum of voices, a string orchestra played gentle airs—not gay, not sepulchral, but poised between the two, on a sustained note of comfort and charity.

All round the hall, and down each aisle, was ranged a guard of honour of children—the City of Boston Tapalongs, in their green-and-white uniforms, and their white wands with the shamrock-shaped collecting bags on the ends. But there was one essential difference: tonight, every child wore a broad black sash, draped across the breast in the manner of an English diplomat; and the white wands had small black bows tied round their handles. Many of the smaller children were already crying. They, and the collecting bags, had been very busy, none the less.

It was the first memorial meeting in Boston for Esther Costello.

In the body of the hall, towards the back, near Harry Grant, two people were talking. They were a man and a woman, middle-aged, soberly dressed, whole-hearted in their devout attention.

"Wonderful crowd here tonight."

"She deserved it, poor kid."

"Mrs. Bannister will be pleased."

"*She* deserves it, too. She gave up her whole life to Esther. And then to have it finish like that."

"She'll carry on, I guess."

"There's still plenty of work to do. For the blind."

"You could say it was blindness *killed* Esther, in the end."

"Easy to make a mistake, when you can't see and there's no one by."

"Terrible thing for Mrs. Bannister."

"Perhaps she'll tell us about it—share it with us."

"It might be a help to her."

"Have you got the ten dollars ready?"

"Yes. We'll give it at the end."

There was a vast sigh over the whole hall, growing and dying like the mutter of a storm a hundred miles away.

"Here she is."

"Ah. . . ."

At the end of an hour, Mrs. Bannister still held her audience as if in chains. The single tall figure in the centre of the platform was the focus of an unwavering, hypnotic concentration: there was scarcely a movement in the hall, scarcely a cough, never a whisper. Everything about Mrs.

Bannister aided this spell. She was dressed from head to foot in black: below the pale face, a black cape like a monk's, with a cowl at the shoulders, reached to the floor. She had a priestly air; and her voice had the same quality— insistent, commanding, certain of attention and belief.

"I have lost the dearest friend of my life, the dearest child," she said. Her motionless figure never wavered, never surrendered to grief; but the grief was in her voice and eyes, flowing down to the audience like an enveloping mist. "What you have lost is something different. You have lost Esther Costello—a symbol of the whole handicapped world, the centre of a great charitable enterprise. Here in this town, her own town of Boston, she had a special place. And I like to think that she had a special place in your hearts as well. In fact, I know she had that place, because of what you have done to help the helpless, because of what you gave to Esther during the past months and years, to pass on to other blind people.

"Now she has gone—this girl whom we loved so much, this poor child who touched all our hearts because she was so afflicted, who died because of that affliction—this girl who lost everything."

By God, that was true! thought Harry Grant, half-enthralled, half-sickened by what he heard. Esther *had* lost everything: she had lost more than anyone in this whole audience, save himself, would ever know. She had lost speech, sight, and hearing: virginity, honour, and her own will. At the end, there had only been her life. . . . The charmed, moving, useless phrases began to slide into his brain, creeping from the air, rustling like spiders: the phrases which he would never now set down, and which must go to waste even as they formed tormentingly within his mind.

"Because Esther is dead," said Mrs. Bannister, gathering

the last threads, knitting the audience, and their generous grief, and the sombre evening together, feeling towards the certain climax, "we must make up our minds that nothing else must die. Because she is dead, we who are left behind must never stop carrying on her work. I gave up many years and much time to Esther—and I gave them gladly, willingly, because she was a wonderful child, and the work we were able to do together, by God's grace. was wonderful also. That work must go on. . . . You all know that this is a memorial meeting, the first of many such meetings all over the United States, all over the world. There are thousands of people in every country, waiting to hear about Esther, waiting to give their help towards what she stood for. I would like to see, as a result of these meetings, a temple for the blind and afflicted"—Mrs. Bannister seemed to correct herself—"a great chain of temples, girdling the earth, caring for those who cannot care for themselves, carrying Esther's message of hope and love to the farthest corners of the world.

"With God's help—and with yours—we will see those temples, built and inhabited and doing their blessed work." There was tremendous determination in her voice. "And if anything I have said tonight advances that idea, that vision, one single foot on its way, then I have not spoken in vain. . . . Good night, and God bless every one of you."

The applause caught up her last words, so that as she stood there, her hands lifted, her face losing its immobility and beginning to soften, she seemed to be drowning in its thunder. The noise was deafening—a solid cataract of sound breaking over her, in wave after wave of acclaim and worship.

Then, after a moment, raised arms began to appear among the audience, waving cheques and bills. The moving points of white and green sprouted and spread: soon the whole